The Crocodile;
Or, The War Between
Good and Evil

The Crocodile;
Or, The War Between
Good and Evil

by
Louis-Claude de Saint-Martin

Translated, annotated and introduced by
Brian Stableford

A Black Coat Press Book

Visit our website at www.blackcoatpress.com

ISBN 978-1-61227-568-0. First Printing. November 2016. Published by Black Coat Press, an imprint of Hollywood Comics.com, LLC, P.O. Box 17270, Encino, CA 91416. All rights reserved.
Printed in the United States of America.

Introduction

Le Crocodile, ou La Guerre du bien et du mal, arrivée sous le règne de Louis XV: poème epiquo-magique en 102 chants, here translated as *The Crocodile; or, The War Between Good and Evil* [omitting "which occurred in the reign of Louis XV, an Epico-Magical Poem in 102 Cantos"] was first published in Paris in "*An VII de la République Française*" [1798], advertised as an "*oeuvre posthume d'un amateur des choses cachées*" [posthumous work by a lover of hidden things]. It had actually been completed on 7 August 1792 by Louis-Claude de Saint-Martin (1742-1803), who was still very much alive, but who had had difficulty publishing it in the midst of political turmoil. The precise date is important because it was two days before the Paris Commune was established and three days before the suspension of the Legislative Assembly—which is to say, on the eve of the second Revolution in Paris. Saint-Martin never signed any of his books with his name, but the great majority were signed "*le philosophe inconnu*" [the unknown philosopher]; the present work was the only one to bear the pseudonym he attached to it, and it was his only work of fiction.

The published version is interrupted by a long essay on the relationship between words and ideas, which makes no contribution to the story and was obviously added immediately prior to publication. The essay had been written in response to a question set in an essay competition held in 1797 by the Institut National de France, the body with which the National Assembly supervising the reforms of the 1789 had replaced the Académie Française, and within the bosom of which Napoléon subsequently reinstated the Académie. (The competition was won by Joseph Degérand; Pierre Prévost and P.-F. Lancelin were the runners-up.) Given that, it is obvious that the canto containing the essay and the previous one, which introduces it, were not part of the original text completed in

5

1792, which must have been exactly 100 cantos long. Saint-Martin subsequently published the essay separately, so there was no need for him to insert it where it clearly did not belong in order to get it into print, and I assume that he would have removed it had *Le Crocodile* ever been reprinted. I have therefore deleted the essay and its introductory canto, and restored the original numeration of the cantos, so the text of this version is uninterrupted.

The author is nowadays known almost entirely because of his connection with "Martinism," which—somewhat confusingly—was not named after him but after one of the unorthodox thinkers under whose influence he developed his own philosophy: a man generally known as "Martinez de Pasqually," although he sometimes decorated that appellation with various other ornamentations and his birth name remains uncertain, as does the year of his birth, although he died in 1774. Saint-Martin met Martinez in the 1760s, when he had recently embarked, somewhat reluctantly, on a military career, which he swiftly abandoned when he fell under the older man's spell.

Martinez was the founder, in 1754, of the pompously named *Ordre des Chevaliers Maçons Élus Coëns de l'Univers*, an esoteric society modeled on the Freemasons and commonly known in English as the "Elect Cohens" [i.e., Priestly Elite]. Everything known about Martinez's theories is second-hand, mostly conveyed via his other celebrated disciple Jean-Baptiste Willermoz (1730-1824), the principal architect of "Martinism" as it became known when it briefly became one of the influential occult disciplines of its era, entangled with both Freemasonry and Rosicrucianism, with which Willermoz also involved himself. Martinism faded away after Willermoz's death before being revived and revamped by Gérard Encausse, alias "Papus," during the occult revival of the 1880s, which guaranteed a version of it a fugitive survival thereafter in the strange social fringe of occult lifestyle fantasy, where Saint-Martin's philosophical texts still serve as guide-books to a favored few.

Although Saint-Martin assisted Willermoz to formulate the original doctrine of "Martinism" he was not much involved in the esoteric societies in which Willermoz delighted, and although he had other associates and a handful of acolytes, he was essentially a writer, with little interest in ceremony and ritual. His own esoteric philosophy was extensively reformulated in the 1780s under the influence of the German mystic Jakob Böhme (1575-1624), whose works he translated into French, and Böhme's ideas probably figure larger in the ideative background of *Le Crocodile* than Martinez de Pasqually's, although the story is so peculiar and, in parts, so deliberately enigmatic, that it would be difficult to trace all its individual elements back to their sources. Given that the story was evidently not intended to be read solely by initiates, it would, in any case, be wrong to regard it as if it were a kind of puzzle from which "Martinist" ideas are supposed to be deduced in detail, rather than simply dangled as teasing lures.

That is not, in any case, the reason for my own interest in the story, and I certainly do not want to offer it as a key to any kind of esoteric scholarly fantasy or lifestyle fantasy, but as a literary fantasy in its own right, akin to such calculatedly bizarre near-contemporary works as Giacomo Casanova's *Icosameron* (1787; tr. as *Icosameron*), François-Félix Nogaret's *Le Miroir des événemens actuels* (1790; tr. as "The Mirror of Present Events")[1] and Restif de la Bretonne's *Les Posthumes* (written 1787-9 & 1796; published 1802; tr. as *Posthumous Correspondence*)[2]. Like the second and third, it is in part a swift reaction to the Revolution of 1789; like the first and third it employs fiction as a means of elaborating a highly unorthodox cosmogony, and like all three of them, it revels in a kind of teasing obscurantism that makes an extraordinarily elaborate use of symbolism in a challenging quasi-comedic

---

[1] Black Coat Press, ISBN 978-1-61227-486.7.
[2] Black Coat Press, 3 volumes, ISBNs 978-1-61227 -513-0, -514-7 & 515-4.

fashion, thus acquiring a marked affinity with twentieth-century surrealism and the theater of the absurd.

The central theatrical absurdity in *Le Crocodile* is, obviously, the eponymous crocodile, an instrument of the Adversary whose claim to have created and shaped the material universe need not be taken seriously—the author takes the trouble in one of his numerous personal intrusions to inform us that the monster is a liar—but whose apparent role within it, both as a container of a strange Hell and as an attempted saboteur of the Divine Plan, is no less striking for that. In the same way, the story's representation of a version of the divinity as an invisible man—a jeweler by profession—with a wife who supervises a Society of Independents, the members of which never meet but are always in session, is calculatedly ridiculous but nevertheless suggestive by implication. Add to that the plague of books, which reduces all human knowledge, especially science, to a soggy pulp; the sunken city of Atalante, where everything stopped dead at the moment of its submersion, but the last words of its inhabitants can still be read in something akin to cartoon speech-bubbles; and the circumstance that the ultimate hope of a beleaguered Paris in the face of diabolical catastrophe is an aging Jew armed with a little box, and the cocktail is, to say the least, original.

The height of the story's deliberate surrealism is reached in canto 41, which reproduces the address made by the spokesman for the Academy's investigative commission on the manifestation of the crocodile, while under the influence of the confused broth of books. The passage is to some extent a parody of the calculatedly esotericism of academic discourse, but it is also deliberately paradoxical in its argumentative refrain, which is a remarkable admixture of contradictory positions in which a crucial element of conviction is supposed to show through in spite of all the obfuscation. A compendium of images that includes numerous deliberately nonsensical juxtapositions is employed as a matrix for sincere assertions, in a fashion that could not have been contrived in any context but that of a recklessly fantastic item of fiction. As to whether the discourse is ultimately comprehensible, or worth comprehending, readers will doubtless form their own opinion, but there is no doubt that it is, after its own strange fashion, a *tour de force*.

The full title is deliberately misleading, as the story cannot possibly have been set in the reign of Louis XV as it is and was known in our history; it is, in essence, an apocalyptic fantasy of a kind that can only really be set in the future—or, given that it represents a Paris prey to Revolution and famine, perhaps a present day of immediate wish-fulfillment. In the interim between its writing and its belated publication, of course, things in Paris had gone from bad to worse, having played host to the Terror, and the author, having been stripped of his modest patrimony (he was an aristocrat, but not rich), had been banished from Paris. His later works are apocalyptic in a different way, representing the Revolution as a day of divine judgment far more severe than the one depicted in the story.

If the reality were to be translated into the symbolic language of the story, the crocodile actually won a resounding victory in 1792, and all four of the central cast of heroic characters eventually went to the guillotine, in spite of everything that the invisible jeweler and Madame Jof could do to help them. The story's contemporary readers would all have known that, and would doubtless have savored the horribly bitter irony to the full, if they were cable of such subtlety of mind. Saint-Martin undoubtedly was, and nowadays we all are—the tiny minority of us who make an attempt to nourish our intellect on the contemporary broth of books, at least.

Such is, of course, the usual fate of optimism—but that does not make the particular optimism of *Le Crocodile* or its brilliantly peculiar narrative strategy any less remarkable. It is one of the rare books of which one can say that no one ever wrote anything else like it—which is always a compliment, and arguably the highest of all, for connoisseurs of the bizarre.

This translation was made from the copy of the text reproduced on the Bibliothèque Nationale website *gallica*.

Brian Stableford

Canto 1
Frightening signs in the heavens. The security of
scholars. Alarms of the people.

....I sing
Of the Fear, Hunger, Thirst and Joy uprising
Experienced by our ancient and celebrated city
When an impure reptile of Egyptian celebrity
Came without quitting Memphis to the Seine.
In order to…....……with an immense disdain.

Muse, tell me how many marvelous facts
Removed from some mortal eyes the cataracts;
Tell me what the Academic Corpus thought;
Tel me how the African Legate was fought
And finally punished for all he unchained;
Tell me, O Muse, or rather, refrain;
For the facts are written in the temple of memory,
And I don't need you to recall the whole story.[3]

(Dear reader, since I'm doing without the Muse, it will
be necessary for you to do without verse, for one ought not to
make them unless one of those goddesses dictates them to us.
Now, those favors being rare for me, you won't often be able
to find my verses in this work, but if you happen to encounter
any, you can be sure that they're not contraband verses, such
as my colleagues sometimes furnish you.)

---

[3] As the author's flippant note suggests, the verse in the
"epico-magical poem" is pure doggerel; in order to preserve
the rhyme-scheme I have occasionally taken slight liberties
with the wordage, while sticking as close to the meaning as
the rhyme-starved English language permits.

For several months extraordinary signs had been seen in the sky; the Virgin's Spica had failed to respond to the Observatory's summons; the Moon had uttered moans, as if she had been hard at work; Berenice's hair had first appeared powdered with white and then, with a gust of wind, had become as black as crepe. All the stars seemed to be giving simultaneous signs of sadness. There was no longer the harmonious concert that the celestial spheres once enabled Scipio to hear in the abode of King Masinissa;[4] they only rendered sounds as lugubrious as the false drone of cathedral organs, or as discordant as the howls of various animals. Finally, some people even thought they could see in the region of the stars, something reminiscent of big crocodiles, writhing with horrible contortions. The scholars, it's true, didn't see anything prodigious in all that. With a stroke of the pen they explained all those phenomena, or denied them when they couldn't explain them, so they seemed quite tranquil. But the people, who did not have, as they did, the key to nature, were dying with fright at the sight of those marvels; they only perceived the most sinister presages in them. They lamented, wandered back and forth, and ran everywhere that their despair and fear drew them.

> Yes, the valiant inhabitants of the Roman city,
> For them, for their hearths, were worthy of pity
> When, menaced by the blows of a powerful foe,
> The chicken-run fasted, and a priest full of woe,
> Testing pullets before the pious people's eyes,
> Sadly declared that they were..............[5]

---

[4] Masinissa, the first kind of Numidia, fought a successful guerrilla campaign against Scipio Africanus during the Second Punic War in 208-207 B.C., but then switched sides and helped Scipio to invade Carthaginian territory, in exchange for Roman support for his precarious throne.

[5] Perhaps "On the way to demise"? (The missing rhyme in the original is not obvious, but the implication is definitely that the chickens are in dire straits.)

Canto 2
The Narrative of Cape Horn.

What added to the consternation was a most extraordinary story that a frigate brought back on its return from Guyana. The captain had gone ashore in that country and, while hunting in a remote place, had perceived a poor cabin. He went in. He saw nothing but the remains of a skeleton lying on the ground, and beside it, a box in which he found this astonishing narrative written entirely in English. During his return journey to France he amused himself translating it into our language, and this is the translation that is being hawked in all the streets of Paris:

"I, John Looker, lieutenant of H.M.S. *Hopeful*, of Admiral Anson's fleet,[6] certify all the facts contained in the present narrative, and engage those who read it to be persuaded that it is not within the limits of our corporeal life that all our knowledge is contained.

"On 25 March 1740 at half past eleven in the evening, ready to go on watch, as the fleet passed through the strait of Tierra del Fuego, seeking, in spite of the most horrible of tempests, to double Cape Horn, I saw in the midst of the agitated waves something like a large mass of vapors, which was motionless in spite of the fury of the winds. It was dark brown in color, and an obscure light that emerged from its center in undulations rendered the mass somewhat transparent. After a

---

[6] George Anson (1697-1762) was in command of a squadron of ships sent to attack Spanish possessions in South America at the beginning of the War of Jenkins' Ear. After several misfortunes he reached Cape Horn late in the season and had to round it is terrible weather; only three ships, out of the six that remained to him, succeeded in rounding the cape, and he was then forced to sail round the world in order to get home again. There was no ship named *Hopeful* in the squadron.

few minutes, the mass was suddenly transformed into an edifice of vast extent, but so low in elevation that a tall man could have reached the summit with his arms.

"Scarcely had that edifice formed than it acquired a rotational movement. That enabled me to see that the whole exterior surface was circular; soon I could also see some way into the interior, for, the rotational movement still continuing, after the first turn an opening appeared in the wall in the form of an arched doorway, which allowed me to see the faint light from within more clearly.

"After the second turn, I saw a second doorway open beside the first, entirely similar; after that, every turn causing a new doorway to open, I could easily count the number; and the number of the doorways rose to eleven hundred, each at an equal distance from the next.

"When those doors had all formed, and the enclosure was thus pierced uniformly throughout its extent, the rotational movement ceased, and, as the edifice remained fixed, it was possible for me to see its interior distribution.

"The whole consisted of one huge room devoid of ornament, without any other furniture than a brown stool at the foot of each of the pilasters between the eleven hundred doors; which is to say that there were eleven hundred brown stools.

"I soon had the opportunity to determine the usage for which they were designed. In fact, a moment after the room was thus disposed, I saw advancing from all the points of the horizon a quantity of animals unknown to me, each of which was simultaneously winged, quadruped and reptilian. Their number was equal to that of the stools, and they each came to present themselves before one of the eleven hundred doors.

"Each of them was mounted by a man with wings of some kind on his shoulders and his head hidden beneath one of them, like birds when they sleep. Apart from the head that I could not see, the men seemed to me to be of normal stature.

"Each animal deposited its rider at the door before which it had stopped, and while depositing him, one cried: 'The genius of the Falkland Isles'; another: 'The genius of the Antarctic pole'; a third, 'The genius of Kaffiria'; the others the genius of Benin, the genius of Cochinchina, the genius of Senegal, the genius of the Sea-Bed, the genius of New Zealand, the genius of Bas-Bretagne, the genius of California, the genius of Mount Kropak, the genius of Nottingham, the genius of Tenerife, and so on for the various parts of the world, But there were a few among them that I heard announced as the genius of the Moon, the genius of Sirius, the genius of the Sunspots, and the genius of Mercury.

"The last-named appeared to me to be more agile than the others, even though he was much stouter. What struck me too was that, as soon as each animal had deposited its rider and made its announcement, it dissolved into three parts, in accordance with the three regions to which they all seemed to belong, and disappeared from my sight. As soon as the riders had dismounted, they all went—without removing their heads from beneath their wings—to sit down on the brown stools to the left of the doors through which they entered, all being careful to hold both hands forwards and open; they were each dressed in a different manner, in accordance with the costumes of the various regions of the World.

Canto 3
Continuation of the narrative of Cape Horn.
The President's speech.

"When they were all in place, the one I had heard named as the genius of Mercury, the stoutest of them all, whom I saw agitating incessantly on his seat, was the first to remove his head from beneath his wing. He took a moment to pull himself together, as if he were emerging from a torpor, after which he began by parading his gaze over the entire assembly and focusing successively on the hands of all the genii; then he said, in a loud voice:

"'Messieurs, independently of being the genius of the region of Mercury, as you are of the various regions of this universe, I am also the viceroy of the god of universal matter, and in that capacity, it is my right to preside over this assembly, which has been convened on his orders. In that same capacity, as viceroy of the god of universal matter, I have, on behalf of my master, personally placed in your hands, albeit invisibly, a natural sign that is the indication of your powers and the responsibility that is confided to you. That indication will assure me that you are in good form.'

"In fact, scarcely had he pronounced those words than all their hands, on which I had not previously perceived anything, seemed to me to be filled with various signs analogous to the various sciences that occupy the academies.

"When the President had concluded his examination he said: 'Your hands have been rendered apt to fulfill your employment, so cease to maintain that inconvenient attitude; entire liberty is granted to you'—the hands of the genii then assumed a free attitude, although their heads were still beneath their wings—'but as my titles are superior to yours, and as I do not bear the same marks as you, it is necessary that you can also recognize the validity of my powers; this is the sign I give you.'

"All the heads emerged from beneath the wings at the same moment. I saw a bright red crown tinted with the color of sulfur appear on the President's head, but instead of the projections that normally surmount crowns, his was accompanied by all kinds of symbols like those attributed by scholars to the planets, the elements, mineral substances and various divinities of mythology; and all those ornaments appeared to be the same substance and color as the crown.

"When the genii saw the crown on the head of the individual who had spoken, they all got up simultaneously, bowed to him and sat down again.

"Then he continued his speech: 'My dear colleagues, the god of matter wanting to consult us, who are, although spirits, his subjects, has summoned us from all the parts of the celestial and terrestrial universe in order to discuss the means of reaching the important goal he is proposing, and we have been chosen directly by him from all the enlightened classes of our various regions for a particular purpose. We are his intimates and the depositaries of his confidence; we have held our heads under our wings for a time as a sign of the entire submission that we owe to his will. Now let us do everything in our power to fulfill his aims; it is a matter of nothing less than coming to the aid of the English vessels that are in these parts, and defending them against the dangers that threaten them.

"'When England took up arms to humiliate the proud house of Spain, which wanted to dispute the empire of the seas with her, she had a plan that extends beyond the present war and the expedition confided to Admiral Anson; she has the hope of one day attaining the house of France herself, from which that of Spain obtains its origin, and of exterminating entirely the French nation, the frivolous nation that dares to be her rival and is importunate by virtue of her prosperity and her proximity; she will not cease to harass her externally and interiorly. I announce to you that soon, at her instigation, the present King of France will summon to head his finances a minister incapable of repairing their disorder; they will be brought to a head by his poor administration.[7] In addition, that minister will subject the means of subsistence to such depredation that the people will yield to all the fury that hunger inspires in them, and the court will be on the brink of its doom.

"'However, that will be nothing compared with what awaits France in another epoch, details of which I do not have instructions to reveal to you. In any case, all that I know myself is that we are approaching the moment when the mold of time will be broken for the entire universe, while waiting for time itself to be broken; and it is with France that the fracture will commence.

"'Now, as no greater blow can be struck against us than breaking the mold of time in which we frolic, and as our faithful friends the English are more closely bound to time than any other people, as witness the splenetic fashion in which they pay time the price of what they have received therefrom, it is essential that we support them with all our might in their enterprise against the Spaniards, since their success might have so many important consequences to the disadvantage of France. Besides which, for our honor, we have to avenge ourselves personally against those two nations, one of which burns without hesitation those who serve us, while the other mocks so loudly those who believe in our existence.

"'The blood of the Indians that Spain has shed in floods assured her briefly of our help and assistance, but a man too celebrated in that nation has abandoned all those measures; he has become a kind of tutelary angel of the Spaniards, and he

---

[7] The next minister of finance to take that office after 1740 in France was Jean-Baptiste de Machault d'Arnouville, who found the state finances in a parlous state, but did what he could to repair them. On the other hand Étienne Charles de Loménie de Brienne, who was briefly finance minister in the run-up to the French Revolution, and his successor Jacques Necker, were both considered incompetent and unpopular, and were blamed by some people for playing a large part in creating the conditions that led to the Revolution.

18

has made it very difficult for our sovereign to find a genius of confidence to summon in their territory, and we cannot promise ourselves anything against Spain if we do not succeed in enabling the English fleet to round Cape Horn.

"'Know that it is Spain that, although long-dead, having had knowledge of this event by means of secrets we have been able to penetrate, is making the impetuous winds blow that desolate this region and oppose the progress of the fleet so constantly; she it is who has been able to procure so much ascendancy over the elements and render them so deadly to our plans that, without extraordinary means, we can never be confident of seeing them succeed.

"'But you are not unaware that the one whose subjects we are is also provided with a great power; you know that our knowledge and enlightenment can greatly assist that power, already so redoubtable, and that we have, above all, the power to take whatever form we judge to be the most advantageous to the success of our enterprise.

"'It is therefore a matter, at this urgent moment, of deliberating on the means that we shall employ to nullify the resistance that Spain and the winds are opposing to us. That is why the god of matter has ordered us to assemble here, in order that an expedient will result from the sum of our reflections, which might be useful to our plan. The session is open; impart your opinions to the assembly.'

Canto 4
Continuation of the narrative of Cape Horn.
Opinion of the genius of the Sea-Bed.

"'The genius of the Sea-Bed: I ask permission to speak first in order to propose a means I believe to be capable of fulfilling the objective that brings us together. You doubtless know, respectable colleagues, that among all the things that compose the universe, the extent of the seas is one of the most important of our sovereign's privileges, and it is a great good fortune for us that he reigns so powerfully over the seas because, by their means, we temper and contain the fire that never ceases to threaten us, and makes us find, in truth, the water of the seas a trifle salty, but hush...'

"Here the orator put his finger over his lips momentarily, and then continued: 'We ought therefore to cherish the English people eagerly for the ardor with which they seek to reign over that element in preference to all other peoples, because they become more immediately thereby the instrument of our sovereign's will, and, as it were, the minister of his empire.

"'That is why we ought to spare no effort in extracting Admiral Anson's fleet from the crisis in which it finds itself; but we can scarcely succeed in that better than by acting directly upon the sea itself, and trying to render it more docile, and the winds less harmful; for I fear that trying to change or appease the winds might be beyond our strength, in view of the redoubtable enemy that we are facing, according to the venerable President's speech; and if we cannot subdue those imperious winds, it's necessary to nullify all the effects they might produce. This is the expedient I imagine.

"'I heard Xerxes say, when he descended among us, that during his wars against the Greeks, he had an iron chain thrown into the sea of the Archipelago in order to enchain that element. He did not succeed in his project, because that act of sovereignty on his part had no other motive than pure childish anger, and he did not address himself to us.

"'But since that chain is at the bottom of the sea, I am convinced that, by virtue of the bite of coldly precipitated marine salt, it has acquired some new virtue that might render it appropriate to our designs. The sea-bed is my department, as you know; I offer to go this instant to the place where that chain is and to bring it here with all the promptitude of which I am capable. I have no doubt that throwing it over the waves that are agitating here with so much fury will calm them sufficiently to allow the English fleet to continue its route.'

Canto 5
Continuation of the narrative of Cape Horn.
Opinion of the genius of the Moon.

"'The genius of the Moon: I did not expect that, as a spirit, the previous speaker would make us such an absurd proposition.' A few rumors stirred the assembly, and violent murmurs on the part of the previous speaker, but calm was reestablished and the orator continued. 'Doubtless the iron chain in question would have acquired on the sea-bed the virtue that the previous speaker supposes, if the influence of my department had been able to penetrate to the deep location where the chain lies, because that influence would then have been able to operate upon the mordant part of the salt the cold precipitation that he mentioned, but he ought not to be unaware that although the Moon once acquired every day, by virtue of the burning impression of the sun, a sufficiently ardent thirst for her to need to slake that thirst every day by sucking up the volatile and sweet portion of the sea-water, that aspirant action no longer extends today to the surface of the seas, and the Moon no longer has anything to do with the tides.

"'For that is knowledge that a few mortal scholars have communicated to us, and we would never have known it otherwise, because, without the discoveries of those scholars, the world would still be as it was accustomed to be.

"'I could, it is true, excuse the ignorance of the precious speaker up to a point, since, his department being under the seas, it's permissible for him not to be up to date what is happening on their surface and in their interior; but what I cannot forgive him is forgetting the rights that are attached to our essence, and which are far superior to those that any species of material substance different from ours can acquire.

"'Yes, he ought to know that we shall never succeed better in the project that brings us together than by means of a few substances that emanate from our very being, and this is what I propose to you on that subject.

"'Several navigators have proved that by means of oil one can succeed in calming the waves in the most violent tempests. Doubtless the English fleet would employ that expedient if the long duration of its navigation had not exhausted even its substances of prime necessity; but it is up to us to substitute for it; and instead of the coarse material oil of which they are deprived, let us employ the power that is given to us of expressing from our own essence an oil that is even more abundant and efficacious. I believe that means to be so peremptory that the assembly will not hesitate to assent to it.'

Canto 6
Continuation of the narrative of Cape Horn.
Opinion of the genius of Ethiopia.

"'The genius of Ethiopia: If the expedient that the previous speaker has gloriously combated appeared to him, with reason, so absurd, I must say that the one he proposes to put in its place appears to me to be even more absurd.' Movement and murmurs, but also accompanied by a few nods of approval. 'Before putting forward such an expedient, the previous speaker should have reflected on the nature of the bodies we are wearing, and on the properties that are refused to them, as well as those that belong to them.

"'Let him know, then, that although we can express several varied substances from our bodies, oil is not numbered among them. No, our bodies can neither be transformed into oil nor produce it, because the seed of that substance is no longer in the roots of our being, and circulates around us without our being able to let it out through our skin. That is something of which we Ethiopians, above all, cannot be unaware, having always had shiny skin, like so many people of our countries.

"'If we still had that substance, we could march to conquests much more glorious and far more important that the ones that occupy us at present. But let us not look into the past; and with regard to the present moment, let us set aside that means, which it is, in fact, impossible for us to employ.

"'Nevertheless, I am far from abandoning our enterprise for that. I merely believe that, instead of oil, we ought to bring forth from our essence some aquatic transpiration in the form of a light rain, which we might be able to use successfully, for everyone knows that a little rain defeats a great wind.'

"And the orator sat down again, laughing covertly, and applauding himself for his ingenious expedient.

Canto 7
Continuation of the narrative of Cape Horn.
Opinion of the genius of Tenerife.

"'The genius of Tenerife: I shall not make use, in order to oppose the advice of the previous speaker, of the indecent expressions with which the two previous speakers have shocked my ears; reason will be the only weapon that I shall use. It is the only one appropriate to the dignity of this assembly, and I dare say that it will serve me victoriously.

"'The previous speaker ought not to be unaware that the element that is dominant within us is the igneous element; that that igneous element is even more foreign to water than it is to oil, since no two things are known to be more opposed than fire and water; and that that is why we cannot form any essential salt, because the volatile and the fixed are permanently separated for us. In fact, to propose to transform ourselves into water would be like demanding that a rabid animal, in order to cure itself, emit a spring, when it cannot even drink the water of the springs that are around it.

"'I should like to believe, therefore, that the previous speaker's error only escaped him by virtue of distraction; but it is an error nevertheless. Between ourselves, alas, we have to make an even more humiliating confession, which is that, far from being able to dominate the elements at our whim, we are under their imperious yoke; and in the various regions where we pass as their genii, we are really their slaves and their victims. They distil us all continually a with fire much more powerful than our own, and that is all the more disagreeable for us because they distil us without sublimating us, and we have no alternative but to be subject incessantly to the anguish of the operation, without succeeding in any departure or deliverance.

"'Air is the only element that, by virtue of its mobility, has some analogy with us; it is, therefore, in that direction that we must look; and we must neglect nothing in trying to distil it in our turn. Nevertheless, it is not upon the mass of the winds that it is necessary to direct our efforts; we can only employ cunning against the effect of those same winds, and it is not given to us to oppose them with overt strength.

"'Now, as the department that I inhabit soars above the winds of the earthly atmosphere, I have had the opportunity to observe them, and to know what it is necessary for us to do in order that they should no longer prejudice the English fleet. In tempests, they ordinarily move in great accumulated masses, in order to operate more forcefully upon the waves of the sea and ships, in the same fashion as upon edifices when they must exercise their ravages on land. So, in order to attenuate those masses in the present tempest, what I propose to you is this:

"'We should transform ourselves into vast open alembics, which terminate, in the inferior part, in long serpentines. By presenting ourselves, thus transformed, and intercepting a part of those masses of wind in our alembics, we would dissolve them by means of our own heat, and extract therefrom by evaporation the portion of air that is the principal ingredient of winds. The *caput mortuum* that remains would fall into the sea through our serpentines without doing any damage to the fleet.

"'That would be all the easier for us because the reign of air is in decline in the world; for a number of scholars, after having quite terrestrial life, have just informed us that the academies are diminishing it incessantly, and cutting back on the number of the constitutive principles of things. The air, therefore, already being threatened by imminent ruination, can hardly resist the power of our alembics, and we shall thus renew and continue that species of chemical distillation until we have exhausted its power.'

"'Admirable, admirable!' cried a Lapp genius, and was supported by a large number of voices.

"But the genius of Ethiopia, humiliated because his rain had been rejected, refrained from sharing that opinion, and he

26

and his partisans booed so loudly that it was soon impossible to hear.

"The genius of the Sea-Bed, who was no more content with the rebuff he had received from the genius of the Moon, and was still holding to his opinion regarding Xerxes' chain, did not want to adopt either the opinion of his rival or that of the genius of Tenerife, and he increased the racket further, as much as he could. Nothing was heard from all parts of the hall but confused cries of 'I demand to speak,' 'Vote for the rain,' 'Vote for the oil,' 'Adjournment,' 'Xerxes' chain,' 'The alembics,' and so on.

"The President shouted himself hoarse to no avail, crying at the top of his voice; 'Silence, Messieurs! Silence!' No one could hear him, and those making the greatest racket—such as the genius of Mount Hekla, and the genius of Saturn, who is also that of lead—in order not to be exposed any longer to his just representations, sought a means of sealing his lips in such a fashion that he could no longer proffer a single word. No one will be surprised that the genius of Saturn was employed in that task, since everyone knows that he is like the chancellor of the universe, and in that capacity, is charged with sealing everything in nature, all the more so as he is sealed himself, as is evident by his ring.

"Then everyone quit his place; the parties mingled, and presented nothing but a vortex similar to those with which René Descartes wanted to explain the origin of the world. Finally, after that horrible confusion had lasted for some time, the party of the genius of Tenerife appeared the stronger. On sitting down, the President recovered the use of speech; the matter was put to the vote and the alembics won by a mere two votes—which is to say, 551 to 549.

"The session was immediately lifted, the hall disappeared and all the genii, metamorphosing into alembics in the prescribed form, rose into the air in order to go and execute the decree that had just been carried.

27

Canto 8
Continuation of the narrative of Cape Horn.
The maneuvers of the genii.

"At that very instant, several of the vessels of the fleet received relief, and the one I was aboard was of that number. The alembic genii that were attached to it acquitted their function so well that the winds that had been tormenting it so violently a moment before became less furious, and it was no longer running any danger.

"It was the same for the flagship and a few lighters, and I could already hear cries of joy resounding through the whistling of the wind, and the words 'Triumph! Triumph! Spain is vanquished! Spain is doomed, and England will prevail over her enemies.' I even saw in the air a kind of winged frigate, flying in all the divisions of the fleet as an aide-de-camp might have done, and spreading the news, in order to encourage the mariners, and perhaps also to make sure that none of the alembic genii were neglecting their functions.

"Nothing, in fact, was more necessary, for if some of them were submissive and faithful to the decree, as I cannot doubt, by virtue of the number of partisans that the genius of Tenerife had attracted, I also had proof that that fidelity was not general. The genius of the Moon, the genius of the Sea-Bed and the genius of Ethiopia, furious at having seen their opinions treated with so much scorn, were far from having stifled that resentment, and even though, by dint of the decree, they had been obliged to transform themselves into alembics like all their colleagues, they were each engaging their clique to be fraudulent, to the extent that they could, in the execution that the same decree had ordered, and to spare no effort in opposing the decision that had been passed in spite of them.

"They were only too well served by all those who had declared themselves for their party. Some, instead of lining up to confront the winds, placed themselves in single file behind one another, in the fashion that there was only one effective alembic, while all the rest were useless.

"Others, it is true, held their front and their alignment, but at first they contained their heat and fire so much that they did not operate any dissolution on the masses of wind that entered into their alembics; in addition, they closed the external orifice of their serpentines so tightly that the winds that blew into them, no longer able to get out, flowed backwards, and only spread out in the air with greater fury.

"Others, on the contrary, prolonged their serpentines and broadened them to such an extent that, becoming vast cylinders, the winds traversed them without the slightest opposition, and came to fall, as before, upon the vessels that the decree was intended to preserve—infidelities that, at other times and in other circumstances than those in which I found myself, would have given me ample cause for reflection.

"A large fraction of the fleet experienced the unfortunate effects of that treason and vengeance; at every moment I saw some of our vessels assailed so cruelly that all their efforts were in vain. They put up all their sail and employed all the resources of the art, each firing so many shots of the distress cannon, that one might have thought that we were in a naval battle, but no one went to their aid and nothing could protect them from the malignity of the enemy that was pursuing them. I therefore saw some open up and break apart, so to speak, into all their parts, which floated thereafter here and there on the agitated surface of the sea. I saw others spin as if on a pivot, and end up sinking to the bottom.

"Throughout all those horrible catastrophes, I never ceased to observe and follow the progress and play of everything that was happening, and I can say that there is nothing comparable to the cunning and malevolence of those evil beings, the existence of which humans, buried in their matter, do not even suspect; and they appeared to me to be even more redoubtable when they want to do harm than useful and advantageous when they want to protect; the conclusion of our enterprise is the proof of that. In spite of the numerous party of the genius of Tenerife, it was only a third of the fleet that escaped the danger, and after having passed the famous Cape Horn, we found ourselves so small in number that it was veritably painful for us to see how many of our companions we had to mourn.

"Our admiral, however, had not seen anything of the secret mechanisms that had been active in that perilous passage, and nor had any of the other people in the squadron, so he gloried in his success; he attributed its merit to himself, as the majority of the triumphant do; he did not suspect, any more than them, the vile and despicable means to which he owed all his success.

"For myself, I understood clearly the voices of those who had favored us in the peril. They exhaled imprecations against the traitors who had abandoned them, whereas, if they had done their duty, the entire fleet would have been saved. I even thought I distinguished the voice of the individual who had been the President of the assembly, and heard him say that he would render an account to his master of those who had not faithfully fulfilled the intentions of the decree, and that he would be well able to punish them.

"Shortly thereafter, I saw all the alembic genii resume their human form, with their anterior costumes, except that they did not replace their heads under their wings. I even think that that the activity of the air in which they had just been fighting against the winds had influenced their wings, for they had grown prodigiously, and that enabled me to comprehend the power of the elements, and the rights they have over everything presented to their action.

"Scarcely had I commenced to reflect on a subject that seemed to me to be a mine of verities, however, than the President gave the order to his colleagues to return to their departments, recommending them to be ready to pursue their enterprises against the Spaniards and to commence those they were soon to direct against France. Immediately, I saw all the genii rise up into the air, fly away with the rapidity of eagles, and head toward different points of the atmosphere.

"The weak remnant of the squadron returned to the ordinary law of the winds, and continued on its route. I took advantage of that time of repose to write the story of everything I had just seen, but I did that work in secret without confiding in anyone, because no one appeared to have seen anything, and I feared being taken for a visionary, that no one would believe my story, and that I might be accused of having made a satire of my compatriot Milton, who built a Doric hall in Hell for Satan, in order for him to hold council with the devils.

"If the people into whose hands this manuscript might fall wonder how I was able to see and observe all that it contains while the service of the ship I was on doubtless demanded all my attention, and the vessel itself could not have failed to experience some movement and shocks occasioned by the tempest, I will reply to them that it was not the first time that scenes of that sort had been presented to my eyes; that since my childhood I had had occasion to make several proofs of it, which had accustomed me to it somewhat; that in addition, as anyone can observe, material labor is apart from phenomena that pass through our minds, and forms a distinct realm that has its particular regime; that my father, who was pious, because he had a very profound knowledge of nature, had the same gift as me, and had had the opportunity to enjoy it in secret, either on land or in the midst of the squadrons in which he served in the capacity of ship's captain; that he had had in consequence the good fortune sometimes to be able to give salutary advice to Queen Anne, and that it is to him and his secret sciences that she owes the glory that has made her reign illustrious.

"Furthermore, I do not propose to communicate any of this so long as I live, not only in order to make it known as late as possible to the French, who are my natural enemies, but also because I have a cousin who is a member of the Royal Society in London, and who, in his capacity as a scholar, would not fail to cover me with scorn if he knew that he had such a credulous relative.

Signed: Looker

31

"P.S. In spite of the evident help that I received in the passage of Cape Horn, H.M.S. *Hopeful*, in which I was sailing, was destined to be the victim of the hidden power that combated the enterprises of England against Spain. She was broken on rocks near the western coast of South America. During the shipwreck I heard a voice that said: 'I am in my department and I can avenge myself at my ease against the alembic party, which, during the passage of Cape Horn, prevented me from doing all the harm I would have wished.' I heard nothing more after those words.

"I spite of my disaster, having never lost confidence in the supreme power, nor my resignation to his will. I have had the good fortune of reaching the shore with three of my companions, and I have also had the good fortune to save my manuscript.

"Having arrived on land, my companions and I wandered in savage lands and in the woods, and reached the banks of the Orinoco, where I perceived a host of crocodiles, from the midst of which I heard these words emerge: 'I am also in my department, and I tell you that not only will Spain gain nothing from the wreck of the *Hopeful*, but that it will have no other effect than to make us more ardent against her for the time being, and even more so against France in the future. Yes, today, woe betide Spain, but in future, woe betide France, woe betide France, woe betide France, and above all, woe betide Paris, for one day, its inhabitants will be astonished.'"

Canto 9
The anxiety of the Parisians.

Such was the frightful narrative that was spread with profusion in Paris, and the last words of which, by virtue of their obscurity, were not at all reassuring. Everyone already thought himself engulfed in one of those extraordinary alembics that the story had depicted. Muffled rumors came to increase that alarm. There was talk everywhere of revolts in the suburban markets; then everyone began to open their eyes to the consequences that might result therefrom. For in the same way that, when the fertile dew of Abyssinia and the Thebaid do not pour their salutary waters into the Nile, Egypt entire, prey to painful famine, languishes in despair and sterility, when the countryside that surrounds our capital experience stagnation or famine in their subsistence, it is necessary that we feel the most disastrous effects.

The wise municipal administrators, it is true, attempted to ward off the misfortunes by all possible means, but things were disposed in such a manner that even abundance would not have stifled the rumor. Who did not know that the chief of finances, chosen a few days before, and not knowing how long he would keep his place, had a violent desire to ensure himself great wealth? Who did not know that he had among the number of his cruelest enemies a lady with a great name and great consequence, wicked, intrepid, indefatigable, always as clever as a man, and who, without showing herself, caused him to take all the false steps and iniquitous operations that she could imagine, but whom the minister thought perfect, as long as they could slake his thirst for gold? The fate of the poor did not enter into the balance for a moment.

And that great controller, whose senses were awry,
Became a dealer in food, in order to make us die.

For her part, the lady of consequence secretly excited the people against the controller and the municipal administration, supporting underhandedly all those who were disposed to put themselves at the head of the revolt, and secretly keeping the greatest resources in reserve, if ordinary means did not succeed.

Canto 10
The meeting of Rachel and Roson

On the first day, the troubles were limited to small gatherings. One of those gatherings, formed near the Rue Plâtrière, appeared to be more numerous than the others, in which a tall and handsome man, who seemed to be its soul and its leader, felt himself gently taken by the arm, and heard someone say: "Is that you, my dear Monsieur Roson?"

He turned round. "Well, yes, it's me, my dear Rachel," he replied. "Who brought you here? What are you doing here? Until tomorrow, Messieurs."

And, quitting the group, which broke up, he went to the Rue Montmartre with the young Jewess who had accosted him.

"What!" he said to her. "Dear Rachel in Paris? And your good father Eleazar,[8] is he here too? For how long? Why have you left Madrid? I'll never forget the service you rendered me—how happy I was in your home! Tell me, then, everything about yourself. It's at least ten years since I lost sight of you."

"The story of our adventures won't take long," Rachel replied. "It was known in Madrid, in the college from which you had been expelled for your misdeeds, that we had given you some money to escape and for your journey; we were placed under observation. An unfortunate event then happened to my father, and we were recognized as Jews. A friend advised us, prudently, to leave the country.

"We immediately set out for Paris, where we have been ever since. My father is living quietly on a tiny fortune, still occupied with his studies, as usual, and I, who have become a childless widow, stay with him in order to care with him and

---

[8] The Hebrew name Eleazar means something akin to "God's Help."

keep the house. In our moments of leisure he sometimes occupies himself in teaching me, and I never weary of listening to him, especially since the terrible announcements of the narrative of Cape Horn.

"We are lodging in the Rue de Cléry, near here. I came to this neighborhood in search of provisions; I saw the crowd gathering and drew nearer; I recognized you, and spoke to you—that, in brief, is our entire story. But you, what has become of you since you left us? What are you doing now? Are you tranquil? Are you happy? That poor Monsieur Roson! My father still loves you; he talks to me with pleasure of the times when you came to play at the house, but he often tells me that you were headstrong."

Canto 11
Roson's story.

"Headstrong!" exclaimed Roson. "He'll see that I'm not.
Tell him that I've acquired a large fortune, and a great position, and one doesn't get there by being headstrong—and
you'll see that the narrative of Cape Horn isn't as baneful to
me as you'd like to make me dread.

"On leaving Spain ten years ago, thanks to your help, I
took refuge in Portugal, where I served in the cavalry for four
years. I had a good enough captain, but I quarreled with him
and killed him. I ran away to a convent of Hieronymites in
Lisbon, where I was a lay brother for a few weeks. It was necessary to move on again, because I was obliged to knock the
cellar-keeper on the head when he refused to give me a drink
when I was thirsty.

"Fortunately, I learned that a Dutch ship had just moored
in the harbor, and was leaving the next day for Batavia. I presented myself as a sailor; I was taken on; we left. After a four-
month journey, a tempest ran us aground in the Persian gulf. It
was necessary to stay there for a century to caulk the vessel.
Homesickness gripped me; I joined a caravan that was leaving
for Damascus, but for fear that someone might come after me
I took the precaution, before leaving the vessel, to set a fuse
that blew it up half an hour later.

"New adventure. Arab thieves pillaged all the caravan's
effects, killing some of our company and putting the rest in
chains, dividing us into several groups to sell in different markets. The group I was in was taken to Damietta; there I was
bought by a local lord, a tall, arid fellow, a woman's dream, of
whom a rich gentleman had come in search from Paris by order of a great lady, to take him to France. He left, in fact, a
few days later, and as I spoke French, he took me with him.
On the journey I saved my master's life twice, once by pulling

him out of the water into which he had fallen and the other time by defending him against ten thieves.

"For my recompense, when we reached Paris I was set free and given some money, but it wasn't sufficient for me to live on, so I was amusing myself robbing passers-by in the evening when, last month, I was offered the most brilliant prospects if I would put myself at the head of a party. That word excited me; I accepted—and you've just seen me in the midst of my people. All the arrangements are made, and tomorrow you'll hear talk of me. Adieu, Rachel, let's not stay together for too long—I'm being watched, people are listening, and it's late. Tell your father that I'll come to see him as soon as I'm free, but he shouldn't worry. Adieu."

And he disappeared into the Allée du Saumon, leaving Rachel stunned by what she had just heard, and having nothing more pressing to do than go tell Eleazar.

Canto 12
Encounter with the volunteer Ourdeck.

"Poor fellow!" she said to herself, as she went. "My father was right to say that he'll come to a bad end. Poor Roson! So it's him that's going to accomplish that terrible narrative of Cape Horn. The work of those terrible crocodiles is in preparation, then!"

As she pronounced the final words, two men chatting together while walking precipitately went past her; one of them, named Ourdeck, struck by her compassionate expression and the kindness of her physiognomy, stared at her briefly, and said to her: "Madame, there is no crocodile, or narrative of Cape Horn, that need be feared in a country where there are souls as good as yours appears to be."

She thanked him for his politeness, and without paying any further attention to him, she went back home promptly.

As for him, he continued on his way, turning round from time to time and looking at Rachel with a great deal of interest.

"That woman has the appearance of a very honest person," he said to his companion. Then, pausing, he added: "It's singular that these ideas of marvelous and secret causes fill the heads of so many people. I've seen nothing but that in all the countries where I've traveled, in China, Tibet, Tartary and throughout Asia, when I was there as secretary to the ambassador of a northern power, and one can be sure that the travelers Marco Polo and John Mandeville didn't invent all the tales of giants, enchanters and monsters with which they filled the accounts of their voyages.

"The northern lands of Europe are inundated by similar opinions; there are no superstitions into which all those different people aren't plunged—and unfortunately, there are no crimes they don't commit at the behest of those superstitions. I hoped, after having quit the business, that by settling in

France, and especially among Parisians, who have the reputations of being so enlightened, that I wouldn't see such credulity reigning here, and I didn't think that the narrative of Cape Horn and all these rumors of the crocodile could turn so many heads here.

"Anyway, it's the same here as in all the other regions of the world that I've observed: always predictions, and never any accomplishments, other than disorder and the brigandage of the malevolent.

"For myself, I'm convinced that there's no other way of dissipating all this trickery than to oppose with a great deal of firmness and courage all the enterprises of malefactors, and that's what I'm determined to do, not only because of my philosophical principles, but also as a citizen, since I'm a naturalized Frenchman. I'm still of an age and strength sufficient to be able to render services to my new fatherland on this perilous occasion; I feel full of hope that the good cause will prevail; it seems to me that all dangers flee before the man whose heart is in the right place and who only seeks justice."

At the same time he plunged with his companion into a crowd, in order to obtain more detailed information about what was happening.

He heard it said that different companies were beginning to form in the various districts of Paris, and spreading a universal alarm; that all the inhabitants, including the mildest, thought that the end of the world was nigh, and that in spite of the savant doctrine that nothing perishes, and that new worlds must be forming incessantly from the debris and decomposition of others, the clever individuals who professed these consoling principles were probably insufficiently convinced themselves to rest their hopes entirely on the recomposition of another world, and would surly prefer not to be forced to let go of this one. Thus, anxiety was taking possession of all minds at the same time.

Fear, agitating its funereal plumes,
Shows Paris as nothing but a mass of tombs

The ignorant and the learned, rich and poor
Are becoming as thin as polish on a floor.
Frightened, shivering at destiny's threat
No hope remaining but mortality's net.

Canto 13
The vigilance of the Lieutenant de Police.
Ourdeck meets Madame Jof.

The protective surveillance of the Lieutenant de Police only made a mediocre impression on minds. They saw Sedir, the honest and faithful magistrate charged with the security of Paris, giving orders to all the troops at his disposal almost without paying any attention to it. They forgot that his vigilance had often prevented or dissipated riots; that although he was made, by the mildness of his character and the candor of his soul, to be in a different employment than the position he occupied, and to associate with men other than spies, he had conserved that position out of attachment to good and the capital, and filled it with a dignity and justice that made him honored throughout society.

In the midst of the universal depression, Ourdeck does not allow his courage to waken. By his speeches, he reanimates that of several of his fellow citizens; he seeks to dissuade them from all the extraordinary and superstitious rumors that seemed to be turning all heads upside down; he engages them to hold hard against malevolence, to unite like the army of volunteers who watch over the security of the city, and pay generously with their person for the salvation of the fatherland, assuring them that it is the surest means of warding off enchantments and enchanters; that above all, it is at birth that it is necessary to stop and dissipate all fermentation, and that it is necessary to cut evil at the root if one does not want it to make great progress.

Straight away, he goes with those whose courage he has revived to the places where he presumes the danger is; and it is necessary to agree that he performs prodigies of valor.

Alas, though, the disturbing predictions that were being spread were unfortunately only too true, and were already beginning to take effect. In spite of the firmness that he showed everywhere, a hidden power seemed to be parrying all his thrusts; he still did not open his mind for that to the veritable cause of his defeats, but he was beginning to believe nevertheless in the incomprehensible power that protected all those hordes of brigands, for he had no doubt, given the way he and his men comported themselves, that he did not have all the advantages.

As he returned home, deep in thought, a woman in tears came to meet him and said to him: "You afflict me a great deal, Monsieur, and you're one of the causes of my tears."

"Who, me, Madame? How can that be? I've never had the honor of seeing you before."

"I'm well aware," she told him, "that you don't know me, and that's what causes me so much difficulty. My name is Madame Jof, and I'm the wife of a skillful jeweler. I'm keenly interested in you, for I've known you since you've been in the world, and I've come to give you some advice, as evidence of the attachment I have for you. You've traveled in many lands; you have a great deal of knowledge; you know many languages; you have virtues and you love justice; but you rely too much on the strength of your arm and the kindness of your heart; that's the cause of the scant success you've had.

"Why would you need to direct your martial arms with intelligence and sagacity if your enemies didn't also have a sagacity of their own to direct against you? But if you don't centralize your human virtues, how can you obtain the advantage over the factions that might perhaps have centralized theirs in the direction opposed to the truth? Raise yourself up, then, to the principle of all the virtues, since you have to combat the principle of all the vices.

"The better you know the powerful aid of that principle of all wisdom, the more you will see that it would not be so prompt to develop its keen activity if it did not have to reduce the principle of all dead activities. Arms of flesh do not know what is good or what is evil; they would not move themselves, either for a good cause or a bad one, if there were not hidden but contrary powers that alternately make them move.

"Yes, in what is happening before your eyes in Paris, at this moment, everything proves to you that there are particular mechanisms that are still unknown to you. You probably cannot comprehend the meaning of my words at present, but you will understand them one day. Although you have traveled a great deal, you will only understand them after having made a further voyage, which you are not expecting."

Canto 14
Madame Jof's story.

As she spoke those words, the so-called woman who had named herself Madame Jof dissipated in the air like vapor, and disappeared in a manner so sudden and extraordinary before the eyes of the volunteer Ourdeck that she left him in an astonishment that the reader will easily be able to imagine. But as it will not be so easy for you to imagine what this Madame Jof was, it is necessary that my pen transmits what a little-known tradition has conserved in her regard.

The woman in question was born in the year 1743 in the depths of winter in the capital of Norway, on the sixtieth degree of latitude. She was the fruit of an extremely difficult labor, and her birth was signaled by extraordinary events. For eight days, counting the one on which she had come into the world, the sun remained over the horizon every day for as long as it remains there at the summer solstice. All the ice melted; the rivers became liquid; the meadows were covered with verdure, the gardens with flowers and the trees with fruits. But what was most remarkable of all was that thistles, brambles and poisonous or unhealthy plants did not grow at all.

It is even said that the famous gulf of the Maelstrom was closed, and that vessels could approach it and sail across it safely. It is added that evil magicians, with whom the North is swarming, were troubled in their operations to the point that they were obliged to abandon them, and that ordinary malefactors were so tormented in their conscience that for twenty leagues around, no mention was heard of any crime.

A historian profound in all sorts of knowledge, a member of the academy of Saint Petersburg and a friend of the child's father, with whom he was staying for a short while, found himself suddenly seized by a prophetic spirit. He approached the infant's cradle, and after having looked at the little girl attentively, he announced that she would be great in enlightenment and virtue, but that the world would not know her; that she would nevertheless be at the head of a society that would extent to all the continents of the world, which would bear the name of the Society of Independents, without having any kind of resemblance to any known society.

He stared at the little girl again, and made a second pronouncement, tenderly, in her regard, that was unknown to anyone at the time and is doubtless only known today to a small number, which was that she would teach men not to die for 1473 years. A short time afterwards, he took his leave of his friend and returned to his homeland, where people were not a little surprised on hearing him recount the marvels he had just witnessed.

The young Norwegian girl gave evidence at a very early age the singular destiny that he had predicted for her. She could walk on her own and without strings a long time before ordinary children can even stand on their own feet; she was often seen to retire to one side, as if the frivolity of the world were already burdensome to her. As soon as the first rays of reflection were manifest in her thought, she said things so far above her age that all those who heard her speak were utterly astonished.

If a few learned people were introduced to her presence, and they discussed a few matters related to the sciences and the most profound knowledge, she not only demonstrated that she understood everything they had said but also made them understand that of they wished, she could say much more about them.

"For it's in the order of the sciences," she often observed to them, "that the retroactive power ought to reign particularly; and if you retrograde yourselves, you'll see what marvels you'll discover and what enlightenment you'll be able to procure for your listeners. Could a flute-player charm our ears with the sound of his instrument if he didn't take the precaution in advance, and incessantly, to aspire air?"

Having reached the age of seven, she disappeared from the paternal house at the moment when the sun rose, and since then, no one has ever known what route she had taken or where she stayed. All that has been learned from tradition is that she often took different names and qualities; that she had the extraordinary faculty of making herself known simultaneously in different countries, as well as to people very distant from one another, with no relationship between them; and in sum, that it was because of that power that she had lived everywhere, that it was impossible to know where she lived , and that she was regarded as a veritable cosmopolitan, in the rigorous sense of that oft-misunderstood word, which is presently only used to give the idea of a wandering individual.

As she lived everywhere she also had her Society of Independents everywhere—who, to tell the truth, ought rather to have been called the Society of Solitaries, since every person has that society in themselves. In view of the unfortunate circumstances that were menacing Paris, Madame Jof assembled her society there from time to time, in order to instruct it in the veritable causes of the great events that were in preparation there, and to engage it to take advantage of all the useful means of which the members of the society were custodians.

As that society differed from all known societies, and was not even a society, it is necessary not to take the word "assemble" in the sense that it is commonly understood. Thus, although I am representing Madame Jof here as assembling the various members of the Society of Independents, it is nonetheless true that they did not assemble at all, that the pretended assembly was held by each member in isolation, wherever they might be, and without being subject to any location or ceremony, not limited by any enclosure; that each of its members had the privilege of being able to see all the other members simultaneously, wherever they were, and to be similarly perceived by all the others; that, in sum, they had, for the very best of reasons, the privilege of all being in the presence of Madame Jof, as Madame Jof had the privilege of being simultaneously present for all of them whenever she wished, no matter how far apart and how various the locations where they lived might be.

It is in consequence of those privileges that, as the various members of the Society of Independents communicated with one another in the troubled state into which the capital as plunged, Madame Jof often found herself among them; and this is a summary of what she said to them in those various assemblies—which, as we have said, were not assemblies.

Canto 15
Madame Jof's speech to the Society of Independents.

"I don't doubt, my dear colleagues, that you're very far from vulgar opinions, some of which only attribute a false cause to the extraordinary rumors that are spreading, and regard them as the fruit of lies, but which inspire a universal fear in others. You have adopted and freely acquiesced to the healthy and instructive impressions that the truth never ceases to impose on all human beings. That is how you have become its friends, and as such, you can no longer fall into such gross errors. You are not unaware that the rumors have a cause that is only too real, which I shall not pause to explain to you, because it is too well known; but I want to fix your gazes on the true reasons that have given that cause the right to go into motion today.

"Paris is not deprived of the substance that is said to be of primary necessity, and is only punished by dearth and hunger because it has not listened sufficiently to the hunger for subsistence of another order, which is even more necessary. I have not stopped wanting to nourish it with the bread of my doctrine, which is as indispensable to humans for the health of the mind as the fruits of the earth are for the health of the body, but a torrent of deceptions has inundated human intelligence in general, and that of Parisians in particular; because their city, which contains scholars and doctors of every kind, possesses very few who turn their minds to the search for veritable knowledge, and even fewer who march toward that veritable knowledge with a veritable intelligence. Most of them only devote themselves to dissecting the bark of nature, to measuring, weighing and enumerating all the molecules, and attempting, insensately, the definite and complete conquest of everything that enters into the composition of the universe, as if that were possible for them, in the manner that they adopt.

"Those scholars, so celebrated and so noisy, do not even know that the universe, or time, is the reduced image of the indivisible and universal eternity; that they can contemplate it and admire it via the spectacle of its properties and its marvels, which succeed one another every day, in order that the world can be a representation of its principle, but that they can never take possession of the secret of its existence, because the secret, or the key to the existence of a being, can only show itself when the existence of the being ceases; thus it would only be the death of the universe that could offer them, by a great act, the development of its base, and the link that suspends the partial world from the universal eternity; and that, in consequence, they can only know it when it no longer exists.

"They do not know that the reason why they think that the universe will not pass is perhaps because they hold themselves to a degree in which it is always past, or continuously perishing, by virtue of the isolation of the qualities that compose it. It is in the same way, in fact, that the cadavers in a cemetery have no idea of their death, and are bound to say that they will not pass, since they have passed, and under the rule of destruction, by virtue of the dissolution of their elements. It is not by placing oneself underneath a region that one can judge the laws that direct it, and the fate that awaits it; it is by placing oneself above it. It is only the living that can judge the dead, and judgments will surely be different in placing oneself in those two classes.

"Because of that, they do not know how much more insensate those are who want to take possession of the secret of the existence of the universal principle itself. Since the secret of a being can only be revealed with the cessation of the existence of that same being, the secret of the supreme principle could only be known at the moment when that principle ended, and if that principle could end, it would no longer be the supreme principle—which one would have to say of any principle one wanted to substitute for it.

"For the atheists themselves, who assert the nonexistence of the supreme principle, abuse the name of atheist of which they want to boast. An atheist is, in truth, a being for whom there is no God, or, if you wish, who is without God. One does not contest the fact that they are sufficiently separate from him for them to be, in fact, without him, and that God is as if devoid of existence for them, but the fact that they are without God does not prove that there is none, just as the fact that a blind man is devoid of the Sun does not prove that there is no Sun for other humans.

"There are others who, led by profound knowledge by indirect paths, do not know where that knowledge ought to lead them, nor at what price it ought to be bought; and after having entered it imprudently, they aliment their pride therewith, or cupidities even more criminal, which cannot fail to become infinitely deadly to them.

"Chief among those cupidities is the one that leads them to want to penetrate the future by other ways than those that the truth itself opens to humans when they are careful not to oppose barriers to it by their unregulated desires. Drawn by that culpable curiosity, they want to anticipate the divine act that they ought to await, and which delights in self-creation.

"They do not know that if, in truth, it is only the vastest enlightenment that can balance for human beings the consequence of the incalculable darkness with which they are normally surrounded, that same enlightenment can only ever strike their eyes when they have found a kind of natural homogeneity with it; and that as their entire atmosphere is infested with the pollution of the very air they breathe throughout their lives, they can only return to that sublime degree insofar as they do their best to preserve themselves from the approach of all the poisonous and corrosive substances that envenom their own essence and obstruct all their faculties.

"You know, my dear brethren, that it is the lack of those sanitary precautions that has introduced into the world a thousand errors for every truth, deluges of crime for every impulse of virtue, and torrents of superstitions for a few veritably luminous sparks. For wisdom had said to the imprudent a long time ago that it would put their illusions to election in order to

51

teach humans that the greatest punishment that can experience is that their false designs lead to their accomplishment.

"It is also for that reason that so many writers, friends of truth, have only presented it tremulously, hiding it under symbols and allegories, so much so that they fear to profane it and expose it to the prostitution of the wicked. That is why, finally, if one stops at the sometimes singular frames of their writings, not even scrutinizing the root of what is exposed—which is nothing other than the unfortunate state of degraded humankind—one cannot judge accurately; for they complain loudly of being thus obliged to constrain themselves and keep quiet.

"A third class, perhaps glad to complain of the previous two, is that of people devoted to the maintenance and preservation of those same luminous and pure sparks, and charged by that estate with favoring their development, who, instead of fulfilling their employment fruitfully, have allowed them to go out, and have ensured that nations no longer perceive the faintest vestiges of the lights that ought to serve as their beacons.

"I cannot think of that class of people without my entrails being penetrated by dolor, so frightful to the consequences of their negligence seem to me, both for them, and for the peoples that expect support from them, and the healing of their ills.

"You are not unaware that the time has come when the truth wants to reclaim its rights over the Earth. Yes, it will soon unmask the deceptive philosophy with which the false sages and the false scholars have so long abused people; it will soon overturn all those altars of iniquity to which people have been led by the vain curiosity of wanting to penetrate the future without having the sole key that can open the way for them; finally, it will soon raise tempests in the veritable domains of human beings, which are their thought and intelligence: tempests of which the disorder and privations that they experience today in material subsistence are only indicative images, signs given to their intelligence and reflection, in order that, after having purged the atmosphere of the thick and unhealthy vapors that obscure it, truth can show itself in all its splendor.

"Those are the reasons for which it has permitted a hidden cause to receive the power to act in these great events; that is why that hidden cause has already commenced to spread so many rumor and alarms among the people; for the truth never fails to announce to nations the important catastrophes that confront them, in order that they have time to stop the effect, by their prudence and their return to regular ways; that is also why the hidden cause that truth employs, has been preparing its work for a long time, as the narrative of Cape Horn confirms for us today; and I must agree that since I quit my paternal house to accomplish the work that called me to Earth, I have not known any epoch more important than this one.

"So all of you, my brethren, who are instructed in these profound secrets, have no more to do than redouble your zeal and efforts in order to come to the aid of good people, who will have visible employments to fulfill in the great events of which Paris is to be the theater. For you know that other people are charged with the ostensible work, in order that the plans of wisdom are not lost for the vulgar, and for those who need to be struck via the senses.

"You even know in advance what the consequences will be of everything that is in preparation, since by virtue of the aid of the true light that is within you, you know everything that must happen between 1743 and 1473 years hence, which is the epoch of the rehabilitation of humankind in its privileges, as that of its birth. You can see, as I say, the good or evil mechanisms that are already in motion, and will move even further in the necessary time. You see them uncovered, because that is the privilege of beings of your class. Those who are of an inferior class only see the same things as an image; but it is still your own glance that is the motive force of what they see in image, either awake or in their sleep; for it is the eye of the faithful friends of truth that forms and engenders the recurrent dreams of other people."

Such is the summary of the story of Madame Jof, of what happened in the Society of Independents, and of the profound doctrine to which its various members applied themselves.

Canto 16
The powers of the Society of Independents.
The story of a professor of rhetoric.

But in accordance with the astonishing rule, that it is the glance of the friends of truth that forms and engenders the recurrent dreams of other people, that Society of Independents only assembled—or, to put it better, only put its powerful faculties into action—in order that other people might perceive them and feel their effects, either by means of dreams or in some other way. So that so-called assembly, of which I have just given a sketch, had no sooner gone into action than several people felt the effects of its power and manifested it in various results, in the stories that they told their friends and acquaintances.

Among others, a professor of rhetoric related that in a region high above the Earth, he had seen in a dream and assembly of several individuals, who had seemed very respectable by virtue of their age and the dignity of their bearing.

"I saw luminous filaments emerging from their eyes and mouths," he said, "which extended to all the continents of our world, and which formed in the minds of other people, as so many moving pictures, agitating and speaking, by means of which they found themselves in a state to anticipate, to see and know what they could not anticipate, see or know in their ordinary situation.

"The pictures that those luminous rays have formed in my mind have presented me with such catastrophic presages for the city of Paris that I am still beside myself, and cannot think about it without shivering; and those presages seem to me already to be realized, by virtue of the famine and trouble in which we find ourselves.

"Among those presages there is one that, without frightening me as much, has nevertheless caused me great surprise, because I perceive nothing around me that can aid me in finding its meaning and explanation.

"A luminous filament emerging from the mouth of one of those individuals has formed an image in my mind sinister for the libraries; I seemed to see a serious wound there, by which they are menaced, and which will not be glorious for scholars. However, the luminous ray is not extinct, and even seems to have increased in brightness. Will the sciences fall back into barbarity, or take on a more brilliant character? That is what my dream has not told me, and all that I can say is that nothing is a singular as the kinds of dreams that have been afflicting me for some time."

Canto 17
The story of a Colonel of Dragoons.

There was also a Colonel of Dragoons who came, completely out of breath, to tell his family about all the terrors from which he could not defend himself, including the evils which seemed to him to be bound to fall imminently on Paris.

"A little while ago," he said, "I went with an architect to see a house that one of my friends is having built. That friend has frequented magicians all his life, in whom he has not ceased to believe, whatever I have done to dissuade him. Suddenly, a muffled noise was heard in one of the cellars. After several noises similar to drum-rolls, there was a terrible explosion that cracked the vault and caused it to collapse into the cellar. From the midst of that chaos a hideous head rose, holding a loudhailer to its mouth, with was suspended alone in mid-air, and was warped in so many ways that I have never seen anything similar.

"That head turned successively toward the four points of the horizon; and to each of those four regions it pronounced, by means of its loudhailer, with a sound that the ear could barely tolerate, these sad words: 'Our reign is nearly over; but far from waiting for the hour to come, we can take our revenge in advance, and pour over Paris all the evils of the body and the mind, by spreading famine and ignorance there. It is not enough that we being disorder to subsistence; it is also necessary to bring it into the heads of the people, especially the heads of the learned scholars who are regarded as the world's enlightenment—and that will be the least difficult for us, because they have already prepared the way perfectly themselves.'

"As the hideous head pronounced those malevolent words toward each region, it launched from its mouth, through the loudhailer, a trail of thick vapor that traveled a long way through the air, and filled the four parts of the atmosphere to such an extent that, but a single ray of sunlight being able to filter through, which dissipated everything, the darkness would have blinded me. I've come to make you party to my surprise. Perhaps you will be tempted to laugh at me, but you know that I do not have an estate or a character to be boundlessly credulous."

The reply was made to him that they were far from subjecting him to ridicule; that, on the contrary, they shared his surprise, and that it was impossible not to believe that extraordinary and very unfortunate events were in preparation, since a part of those threats had already been accomplished.

And, in fact, the rumor was already running around Paris; from the greatest to the least, everyone had lost their heads; there were even some who claimed to have seen some of the thick vapor blown out by the hideous head enter into those of several learned men, those of the majority of the people, and especially the heads of the distributors of subsistence—which explained why it was so scarce and of such poor quality.

Canto 18
The hopes of a few inhabitants.
An Academician's story.

It is true that among these baleful stories there were also a few less disastrous. A few good people were seen gathering together, and telling one another the consoling things that had been presented to their thought by the Independents, who were unknown to them.

Some said that they had seen conquerors triumphing gloriously over all the enemies of the public, and brilliant standards floating in the air, announcing all the signs of victory.

Other said that they had seen a radiant sun detached from the firmament coming to settle above Paris and spread a universal light there.

A few others said that they had seen a great crocodile slain by a little animal whose name they did not know, and abundance immediately reborn in Paris, to the point of making the slightest traces of famine disappear; and all of them agreed in saying that they had seen all the Parisians shedding tears of joy on finding themselves thus delivered from their woes, and rendering solemn thanks to the supreme and omnipotent hand that, in its commiseration, had wanted to put an end to their misery and heap them with benefits.

There was even one scholar, highly distinguished by his knowledge of mathematics and physics, but very incredulous, who, at the moment when he least expected it, found himself as if transported into the astonishing assembly of the Independents; and there, without suffering any proof, without being subjected to any ceremony or formula, he was even able, for a moment, to consider the depiction of the disasters that were menacing Paris, and that of the consoling events that were to follow those disasters.

He was able to contemplate therein the profundities of ways hidden from the people of this world, the new order into which the sciences and nature were about to enter, and the real bases of the veritable physics, which demonstrated to him the insufficiency and puerility of the famous academic theories with which he had cradled himself thus far.

He was so struck by it that when the instant of that brief enjoyment had passed, he no longer recognized himself as the same man; torrents of tears flowed from his eyes, burning repentance tore his heart, ardent prayer expressed everything he felt, and in his shame for his anterior blindness, as well as the transports of his present conviction, he wanted to share his new situation with everyone, especially his colleagues.

But after the first attempts he made, judging correctly that he was preaching in the desert, he enclosed his secrets in his bosom again, and contented himself with offering to men of verity who lived in ignorance and silence the interesting spectacle of a scholar who recognized a God and prayed to him.

Nevertheless, all the secret and marvelous things that were communicated to a few individuals, the superior mechanisms of the Society of Independents, and the extraordinary Madame Jof, were utterly lost on the vulgar, who only knew the needs of the senses, and only grasped what they touched. Thus, the enemy power had free rein to accomplish its destructive designs, by frightening and arousing the people to the sight of the evils and dangers by which they were surrounded.

On the other hand, the vigilant and generous Sedir, that rare man, susceptible of everything that tended to virtue, was as skilled in the métier of arms as in the useful magistracy that he fulfilled, as if he had inherited that legacy from his ancestors, and even having a great attraction to sublime and religious verities, although he had barely perceived them, did not neglect any of the means that were at his disposal to remedy the small hitches that the good cause had already experienced. He fortified the posts, and went everywhere that he supposed his presence might be useful, without fearing any danger; and he sent his emissaries in all directions in order to discover and eliminate the authors of the revolt.

Canto 19
Conversation of the emissary Stilet and Eleazar,
a Spanish Jew.

One of those emissaries, named Stilet, had perceived Rachel at the moment when she had just quite Roson. He had seen her raise her hands toward the heavens, moaning, and he had heard her final words: "He'll come to a bad end. Poor Roson!" He had followed her, at hazard, and had made a note of her abode.

Weary of having sought Roson in vain, he decided to go see Rachel at daybreak, pretending to have been sent for Roson.

"I'm addressing myself to you, Madame," he said, right away, "in order to discover where I might find Monsieur Roson. I've been asked by one of his friends to give him an important message, on which nothing less than the salvation of his life depends. The law is searching for him; he's said to be the leader of a party; I've come to offer him a means of escape and to reach safety. I'm assured that you know him and are interested in him; if so, enable me to render him the greatest service."

"It's true, Monsieur," Rachel replied, "that I knew Monsieur Roson in Madrid, and that I wish him well, but in the ten years since my family and I left Spain, as Jews, I have lost sight of him. I met him yesterday for the first time since then; she gave me a sketch of his adventures; he seemed to me to be in a hurry, and very busy with a great project of fortune. As I parted from him without him having given me his address, I can't tell you where to find him. But come in, Monsieur; my father will surely be glad to see someone who is interested in poor Monsieur Roson. We knew him when he was very young; he lived in our neighborhood in Madrid, and came to our house almost every day."

Stilet goes in, salutes Eleazar and tells him the object of his visit. Eleazar listens, and cannot hold back his tears, so touched with gratitude is he for that good intention. "But the unfortunate is making himself the leader of a party," he said, "going to mingle with the rabble that is putting all Paris in uproar. Alas, how many times did I say to his mother, in accordance with the proverbs of our good King Solomon: 'Raise your son well and he will console you and become the delight of your heart. The rod is the correction given to wisdom, but the child who is abandoned to his whims will cover his mother with confusion.'

"She didn't listen to me; she spoiled her son. Now see the fruit of the seed she sowed. But the proverb also says that if corrupt men destroy the city, the sage will appease the fury."

Profound words, although Eleazar cannot explain their meaning in its full extent.

"But Monsieur," he said to Stilet, "since you wish our friend well, and you seem familiar with all the troubles that are rife, tell us what is happening, in order that we can aid you in your charitable enterprises."

That tone of humanity in the mouth of a Jew astonished Stilet slightly; he could not make out the character of the man with whom he was dealing. Just as he was about to reply, however, a frightful noise became audible in the street. Everyone was shouting and running away as best they could. Eleazar, Rachel and Stilet ran to the window.

"It's the revolt," said Eleazar. "It's going to pass before the house." To Stilet, he said: "Alas, Monsieur, all your concern is becoming futile. Roson will doubtless be armed, at the head of the rebels; may there be mercy for him."

In fact, scarcely had he spoken than the column appeared, having the effect on the eye of one of those torrents that, squeezed into a narrow passage, emerged in seething foam, piling up. Roson appeared at the head, saber in hand, with the expression of the god Mars, or at least the son of Periboea when he fought for Achilles' armor.[9]

"There he is," said Eleazar. "Roson! Roson! What are you doing, wretch?" And he held out his arms to him, to engage him to renounce his enterprise. But all his efforts were in vain; the noise prevented Roson from hearing anything, and his impetuosity prevented him from seeing anything. Eleazar sat down and shed tears, taking from his pocket, at intervals, a little golden box in the form of an egg.

---

[9] The reference is to the Telamonian Ajax, who squabbled with Odysseus over Achilles' armor in the *Iliad*; his mother was Periboea.

Canto 20
Stilet and Rachel see the revolt draw away.

Rachel, no less sensible, but a little more curious, remained at the window and said to Stilet: "Tell me what these various troops behind him are, and of whom they are composed."

"Madame," Stilet replied, "I can tell you while waiting for the street to be sufficiently clear to make my escape." And, indeed, he told her the state and profession of those forming the various hordes as they went past the house. He pointed out to her infantrymen, rag-pickers, tinsmiths, pavers, merchants, poets, dancing-masters, locksmiths, wig-makers, cab-drivers, chimney-sweeps and many others. He named all the leaders that were at the head of each of those groups."

She put in whimpers at the different reflections that the spectacle inspired in her. What would she have said, alas, if the demonstrator had been able to tell her about the hidden enemies distributed in the ranks, and he had shown them to her mounted on swarms of little crocodiles, which were following the mass, and seemingly giving it all its impulsion, But he did not have sufficiently open eyes himself with regard to that menacing phenomenon.

When that review of sorts had concluded, he said to Rachel: "Adieu, Madame; the passage is free now. I shall go to render a prompt account of my commission. If I were not so pressed by this affair, I would not leave without knowing what will come of all that."

"Monsieur," Rachel said to him, "save Roson, save Roson if you can! The danger he is running makes us anxious, as if he were still worthy of our attachment. But the crowd is very large, don't you fear exposing yourself too soon?"

"Let him go, Daughter," said Eleazar. "Far from being sent for Roson, he's a police spy, a man who follows all métiers, including that of thief, and has come here with evil designs. I've just learned that by secret means of which he is unaware, but which you know are not foreign to me."

Thunderstruck, Stilet studied Eleazar momentarily; then, without saying a word, he opened the door and escaped. He immediately went to render and account of his steps to Sedir, especially the singular adventure that had just happened to him with Eleazar.

Canto 21
Precautions taken by Sedir against the revolt.

Sedir gave evidence of a keen curiosity to make the acquaintance of that Israelite, and ordered someone to go and search for him immediately.

The zeal for the good cause with which Sedir was animated had acquired a new degree of ardor, by virtue of the accounts he had already heard from his other emissaries, and the new dangers by which the capital was menaced.

"So," he said to those who composed his council, "I must occupy myself seriously with confronting the storm; it appears to be more considerable than I had thought at first. I know that the narrative of Cape Horn has disturbed all heads, and that all of the inhabitants of Paris believe that they have a crocodile on their heels; I know that a few learned men are drawing parallels between the extreme voracity of that animal and the cruel famine that is devouring us; I know that others, more incredulous but ill-intentioned, are taking advantage of that terror to attract all disorders upon us; I know that Roson is the leader of the revolt; I know that the rendezvous is in the Rue du Grand Hurleur; that the majority of tradesmen are up in arms; that the marketplace will be the principal battleground; that a woman of consequence is stimulating the revolt, paying its leader; and that far worse is threatened if it is pushed to the end. I have even been told that a foreigner arrived a little while ago, a tall, arid man of whom she is very fond.

"But I hope to disrupt all their projects, by stopping, from now on, all the efforts they make to accomplish them by violence; and I flatter myself that Roson will not succeed in his criminal enterprise. I have sent numerous reinforcements, which will arrive at the marketplace before him. Those reinforcements are commanded by an excellent officer, and he has under his orders a few volunteers about whom I have been told so many good things that I am relying as much on their sagacity as their courage. I shall go to various places to see what is happening, and make sure personally, if it is possible, that not a single drop of blood is spilled."

Canto 22
Eleazar goes to see Sedir.
The powder of double thought.

Scarcely had he finished speaking than Eleazar was announced. Sedir was extremely surprised by that, for since the moment when he had given the order to search for him he had scarcely had time to leave his house.

In fact, Eleazar arrived with his daughter Rachel, who, being fond of him, had not wanted to be separated from him in this time of troubles. No one but him, having a known connection with the leader of the revolt, the intrepid Roson, would have dared to present himself to the Lieutenant de Police, but Eleazar, sure of his innocence, had also received other bases on which his security rested. Since his youth, he had been in intimate communication with an Arab scholar of the Ommiad race, which had taken refuge in Europe after the usurpation of the Abassids. The first or sixth ancestor of that Arab had known Las Casas,[10] and had obtained very useful secrets from him that had been passed down from hand to hand, until they had reached those of Eleazar.

They consisted, in particular, of a salt or powder extracted from the root, stem and leaves of a flower known in vulgar parlance as *pensée double*.[11] It was necessary to bind those

---

[10] Sebastian de Las Casas was the last *Grand Souverain* [Grandmaster] of the order of the Elect Cohens prior to its formal dissolution in 1781. The reference obviously cannot be to him, but the Dominican friar and historian Bartholomé de las Casas (1484-1566) is unlikely to have had any secrets to hand on, so the reference is probably to some real or imaginary ancestor of the Las Casas the author knew.

[11] Pensée [thought], when applied to a flower, is the equivalent of the English pansy, although it is used more generally to apply to numerous flowers of the violet family. None is com-

three things together, to allow their gross juices to evaporate until desiccation, and then grind them in a mortar expressly prepared for that purpose.

The saline powder that resulted was contained in a little golden box in the shape of an egg, which Eleazar always carried in his pocket. When he wanted to know something, it was sufficient for him to sniff that saline powder seven times; then, by collecting himself momentarily, the spirit of the powder penetrated his brain, and he knew immediately what he ought to do, what the characters was of the people surrounding him, and even what the hidden intentions were of those in his presence or in some relationship with him.

The powder also had other properties, and he had different ways of employing it, in accordance with the use he wanted to make of it. He had cultivated that gift carefully throughout his life, and like all seeds that are cultivated, it had reached a perfect degree of maturity, while those that are neglected deteriorate and degenerate to the point that no one believes that they ever existed.

From the rumors that were running around, and the narrative of Cape Horn, in which there was a question of a crocodile, he had learned by virtue of his own science how Paris was about to suffer from that animal, and he had been driven to combine with his powder of thought the ashes of a roasted ichneumon in order to have both an offensive and a defensive force to employ, according to circumstances, for although he was not a member of the Society of Independents, he was one of its agents, and for that reason he had all the knowledge and all the gifts that can make a mortal useful and commendable down here.

It was, therefore, by those hidden means that he had been preserved from the spy Stilet when he came into his house to offer his insidious help to Rachel. He had been informed, by the same means, that the Lieutenant de Police wanted to see

monly known as "pensée double," which is an improvisation by Saint-Martin.

him, and thus, shortly before the magistrate gave the order to go in search of him, he had set out immediately, knowing full well that the honest and virtuous Sedir had no evil intentions in his regard.

Canto 23
Conversation of Eleazar and Sedir.
Eleazar's doctrine.

Before going into the apartment, Eleazar told Rachel to wait in a neighboring room. Then, hastening to Sedir, he said to him: "You did not expect me so soon, Monsieur, and your presence would doubtless be useful elsewhere, but it is also useful for you to stay here for a few minutes, and I hope that you won't regret it."

Sedir contemplated him silently for a moment, and then said to him: "I've been told, Monsieur, that you know Monsieur Roson well, and it's to obtain clarifications on his account that I desired to see you. I've also been told something rather surprising in your regard, about which, given the circumstances in which we find ourselves, I had a desire to talk to you." He told the people who were in the apartment to leave, and to go openly to the important places, and wait there until he could arrive himself. Then, turning back to Eleazar, he said: "Sit down; we're alone; you can speak freely."

"Monsieur," Eleazar replied, "according to our proverbs, he who sows injustice will reap evil, and will be broken by the rod of his wrath. I would have liked to spare the unfortunate Roson from the dire consequences to which he is exposing himself, but I have only ever had links of amity with him, without any right of authority. I have only been in contact with him in Spain, where, from a very early age, he came to my house to play with my children; even then, I could easily foresee what his arrogant and audacious character promised. I grieved over that, without it being in my power to apply any remedy. If you grind the imprudent man in a mortar, you do not take away his imprudence, Solomon says."

"At fifteen, he did something that forced him to leave the country; I thought I ought to be useful to him in his escape. Since that time, until this very moment, his life has been a sequence of crimes and disorders that he is crowning with brigandage. I abandon him to the law. I have nothing more to say about him. You have doubtless been told everything that my daughter said about him to one of your agents, and you can be sure that she has not imposed upon him.

"As for myself, Monsieur, about whom you desire more ample information, know first of all what the motives were that led me to quit Spain and come to establish myself in Paris: it was not the hope of making a fortune. From the moment that the first glimmers of reason began to penetrate me, I perceived that fortune was like a statue deprived of all the senses, similar in all respects to the idols of stone, wood or metal that our prophet Baruch has described so well, which are not only incapable of seeing the victims that are immolated for them, respiring the incense burned for them or hearing the canticles sung in their honor, but are not even capable of defending themselves or sensing the disdain or the insults of which everyone has the mastery to heap upon them. I thought I ought not to offer my homage to that impotent goddess, who seemed to me to be as likely to favor those who had done nothing for her as to neglect those who had sacrificed all their time to her, and I devoted all my concern toward the cultivation of my reason, the sole occupation that seemed to assure me a durable wellbeing.

"Among the duties that study has imposed upon me, that of being useful to my fellows was always one of the most important, and it is that duty to which an adventure afflicting for me rendered me the victim in Spain, and forced me to take refuge in your capital.

"In Madrid I has a Christian friend who belonged to the family of Las Casas, to whom I have, albeit indirectly, the greatest obligations. After a few prosperities in commerce, he was suddenly ruined from top to bottom by a fraudulent bankruptcy. I went to his house immediately to share his troubles and offer him the few resources of which my mediocre fortune permitted me to dispose, but, those resources being too slender to restore parity to his affairs, I yielded to the amity I had for him and allowed myself to be drawn into the matter to the extent of making use of a few particular means that assisted me in soon discovering the fraud of his exploiters, and even the secret place where they had deposited the wealth thy had stolen.

"By those same means, I procured him the facility of recovering all his treasures and returning them to his home, without those who had stolen them suspecting that they had been despoiled of them in their turn.

"I was doubtless wrong to make use of those means for such a purpose, since they ought only to be applied to the administration of things that have no relation to the riches of this world, so I was punished for it. My friend, instructed in a timid and umbrageous faith, suspected sortilege in what I had just done for him, and his pious zeal prevailed over his gratitude, as my officious zeal had prevailed over my duty; he denounced me to his church as both a sorcerer and a Jew. The inquisitors were immediately informed; I was condemned to the fire before even being arrested, but at the moment when they were setting out in pursuit of me, I was warned by the same particular means of the fate that threatened me, and I sought refuge in your homeland without delay."

"What an abysm of horrors!" exclaimed Sedir. "And these men, who profess a religion of peace and charity, believe they are serving God by ingratitude and such cruel and precipitate judgments! I need more time to judge the facts and examine the particular means that you have mentioned to me, and which, I confess, you have given me a great desire to know."

"I don't hold it against them," Eleazar replied. "I've learned from my own weaknesses to excuse those of my fellows. Even less do I hold against them the religion they profess. As it is believed to be above the enlightenment and feeble powers of humans, I believe it to be even further above their ignorance and depravity, considering it in the purity and lucidity of its eternal source, apart from everything that fanaticism and bad faith have introduced into it, and all the abominations that monsters have carried out in its name.

73

"That language, Monsieur, might astonish you in my mouth, but since you brought the subject up yourself, and since I have begun to let you glimpse my sentiments, I shall have no fear of completing a confession at which I cannot blush, and which I can do no better than to address to you, insofar as I sense myself transported by the same secret movement and particular means that have rightly piqued your curiosity."

"Speak with confidence, Monsieur," Sedir said to him, "and bring the interest you have inspired in me to a head."

"I confess, Monsieur," Eleazar went on, "that for anyone but you, what I have exposed to you would have to be repeated ten times over, if they wanted to grasp its meaning and spirit, but in addition to the fact that I know to whom I am speaking, the time that is pressing upon you would not permit me that prudent precaution. It will be up to you to substitute or it by means of your reflection.

"I shall therefore tell you, briefly, and only once, that for a long time, nourished by human study, I thought I had glimpsed within it bright and luminous gleams with regard to its relationship with all of nature and all the marvels she contains, which would be overt if one did not lose the key that is given with life.

"In fact, sensible objects occupy us and attach us to such an extent because they are the reduced and visible assemblage of all the virtues and invisible properties enclosed between the degree of the series of things at which they commence to be and the degree to which they have the power to be manifest. Yes, those objects are nothing other than all the properties anterior to them, sensibilized; just as a flower is the visible union of all the properties that exist invisibly, all the way from the root. All objects contain a portion of that scale, in accordance with their measure and species; and nature, only existing in her entirety by that same law, is nothing but a greater portion of that scale of the property of beings.

"That is why sensible objects fix our attention to such an extent that they inspire so much interest in us, and spur our curiosity so keenly; so, it is not so much what we see in them that attracts us, as what we do not see, which is the veritable goal of our research; and that is why, when the most eloquent naturalists strive to charm us by means of the elegance with which they describe what is visible and palpable in those sensible objects, they are not fulfilling the employment that they seem to have taken up with regard to nature. They are not telling us anything about what sensed nature tells them herself, in preference to other people, or about the series of anterior properties and the hidden progression of which the object is, both in general and in particular, only the ostensible and indicative terminus. They deceive our expectation, and do not satisfy our ardent and pressing need, which bears us not so much toward what we can see in sensible objects as to what we cannot see therein.

"Nor have they satisfied their own expectation, or the same need that surely presses them as often as other mortals, and no matter how much they seduce themselves, and astonish us by the perfection and color of their depictions, it is nevertheless true that internally, and for their satisfaction, their minds, like ours, expect from all the natural objects that surround us some instruction more substantial than those depictions.

"But why is that need felt in our being? It is because we contain, by virtue of a privilege, over all sensible objects and nature herself, all the antecedent properties that exist between the supreme point of the universal line and us; that is what constitutes the key to nature that is given to us with life; that is why we have the power to embrace all the degrees in the series, and to interrogate everything sensible that is manifest in those various degrees; whereas the sensible objects, and nature herself, only enclose a part of the great scale.

"That is why those who, before having analyzed human being, supporting themselves on nature both to attack verity and defend her, march imprudently, only enabling those who follow them to take false steps. How can one speak, for or against, about what is inside a palace, if one does not have the key that will open the door? Yes, that key, which, in all discussions of this sort, ought to have the leading role—which does not hold its rank either in sensible objects or in traditional books, and, in consequence, must walk alone, and keep all secondary witnesses silent until it judges it appropriate to interrogate them—is the sublime dignity of our being, which summons us to soar above the universality of things.

"But how can we make use of our pre-eminence, if the properties that belong to us are not developed within us; and how will they develop in us if we separate them at the summit from the universal line to which they are linked by our essence, which alone can sense and demonstrate their existence to us, which is simultaneously the necessary source and the exclusive root from which they draw their activity?

"That is what has made me believe that it is both and obligation and a right for us to work to extend our existence, our enlightenment and our wellbeing, reanimating and vivifying the original relationship that we had with that supreme source, and which is as if buried and concentrated within us by causes that we cannot know, but which are also impossible for us to deny.

"In addition, I thought that the most astonishing of all the knowledge that we could acquire was that of the inexhaustible love of that source for its productions, which causes it to fly before us every day, into all the precipices in which we find ourselves, and which engages it to modify and insinuate itself everywhere into our wounds, as does the industrious tenderness of a mother, whose anxious thoughts bear continually upon her child's wounds, and repair in spirit all the derangements that it might experience, and as the material remedies do for our everyday injuries and maladies.

"Already being convinced by my observations, of all the important and fundamental verities that exist in all humans before existing in any book, I thought in consequence they ought to be studied by us and in us, before we hurl ourselves into the maze of traditions. For one cannot calculate all the evils that have been poured to the Earth and into the minds of humans by the maladroit or the wicked, who have only been able to make progress by way of those traditions. So I sense with joy that the time will come, and is not far away, when purely traditional doctrines will lose their credit.

"There are those whom ignorance and incompetence serve as a reflection that makes them take pride in the philosophy that is their incapacity, on blindness and base credulity, on hostility to those who see any other divinity then them, and animosity toward the sects that believe in a measured fashion, and possess the truth while they are thrown to the other extremity by the errors for which they are reproached. When that mirror with too many facets no longer subsists, philosophy will no longer be halted by the obstacle that repulses it; simple people will be able to raise their eyes to the throne of verity without concentrating them on intermediates; sects will have the leisure to perceive what they lack, and even Mahomet, having no more antagonists, will recognize his nudity; for it is written that they will all be informed by God. Such is the plan of Providence. Woe betide those who oppose or retard the effect of its designs!

"Penetrated as I am, therefore, with fundamental verities that are in human being before being in any book, I savored, I confess, an inexpressible joy in then finding a perfect conformity between a part of those verities and the faith of our forefathers in our sacred writings, which have since become for me what all true traditions ought to be—which is to say, the terminus of a fact whose existence is demonstrated to me by my own nature, and of which I would have had no doubt, even if our sacred books had not spoken to me about it.

"So I was not surprised to see Solomon announcing, as if he knew the disposition of the globe of the Earth, the virtues of the elements, the origin, the middle and the end of time, the courses of the heavens, the order of the stars, the nature of animals, the strength of winds, the varieties of plants, the properties of roots, the thoughts of human beings and all hidden things, because I am convinced that all human beings can likewise know all those profundities, if they do not draw away

77

from the portal of nature, which, at every step, only seeks to reveal to us the principal superior source of everything that the key to the door of nature holds.

"I have also found striking relationships between the other part of those verities and Christian traditions, about which I am very suspicious of the stubborn belief of my nation, and in which I believe with a profound blindness. Not daring to face them head on, however, and not being yet as enlightened as I want to be, I kept my faith in my heart, and I am waiting for a favorable opportunity to make a public confession of it."

"You are undoubtedly speaking to a man less enlightened than you," Sedir replied, "but sufficiently convinced for me to be able to congratulate you on having reached the degree that you have, and I pray that the one who is listening to both of us will accomplish his designs in you. But for the present, can you not also tell me, briefly, what is the particular means that has engaged you to speak to me so confidently?"

"It is the same one," Eleazar replied, "by which I escaped the fury of the Inquisition; the same one by which I recognized the spy you sent to my home in the disguise of benevolence; the same one that let me know that you desired to see me, that I ought to come to you without anxiety or disquiet, and that you were not asking for me for any malevolent reason; in sum, it is the same one that tells me now that one day, you will render to your fatherland even greater services than you have rendered thus far.

"It is the same voice that has brought me to make the confession about the beliefs of my nation, and which will doubtless let me know when it is time to take other steps.

"It is the effect of a particular gift that was made to me in my youth by an Arab scholar, whose value I learned subsequently by reading in *Ecclesiasticus* that a man has no better counselor than a heart firm in the rectitude of a good science, and that such a man sometimes sees the truth better than seven sentinels posted in an elevated place to contemplate everything that happens. I also thought, in the times we find ourselves, of making a few additions to that present, as the Arab recommended me to do, in accordance with the circumstances and my enlightenment."

He told Sedir a part of his secrets, while showing him the box and the ingredients it contained, but without telling him from which plant and animal the ingredients were extracted. Then he added: "Monsieur, I have followed faithfully the instructions the Arab scholar gave me; I believe what *Ecclesiasticus* says, and cannot express what I have derived therefrom. Yes, Monsieur, if all humans wished it, their abode would become an asylum of peace and light, instead of the disorder and darkness that surround them."

"Like you, Monsieur," Sedir told him, "I have thought that humans were summoned by the sublimity of their intelligence also to have a sublime relationship with nature; I judged as much by everyday research and even by the discoveries made from time to time in the domain of the sciences. I have also thought that the dignity of their origin might elevate them far enough to have for their guide in that vast career the hand of the same principle to which they owe their birth; finally, I have thought that I perceived indication and evidence of that in your scriptures and ours.

"However, being too scantly instructed in the fundamental principles of the nature of human being, as well as the links between those principles and traditional evidence, I am far from having extracted from all those notions the same advantages as you. Since destiny has judged it appropriate to treat you, in that genre, with a distinguished predilection, can you not employ your gifs in favor of this afflicted city and enlighten me as to the progress of the powerful enemies that threaten it? The relief of a great people is worthy of stimulating the zeal of good souls, and can only be divine work."

Canto 24
Eleazar reveals the enemies of the State to Sedir.

Eleazar employed his two procedures, and collected himself momentarily. Then he said to Sedir: "Monsieur, mention has been made to you of a tall, arid man recently arrived from Egypt; he is the most redoubtable of your enemies. He is the agent of a woman whose is dominated by the vile passions of jealousy, vengeance and self-interest, but he alone contains more vices than ten men put together. What renders him so redoubtable is that he is the instrument of hidden enemies who are a thousand times more redoubtable than him; and although the narrative of Cape Horn has brought only fear and no enlightenment into the minds of the vulgarly credulous, I cannot leave you in ignorance of the fact that all the extraordinary things with which it is full, as well as all these ideas concerning a crocodile, which were running around Paris before it had even appeared, contain verities, unfortunately all too certain; and that exceedingly dangerous man will spare no effort to make us feel their mortal effects.

"It is not without foundation that the narrative contains so many imprecations against Spain and France; the invisible enemies of which it speaks want to avenge themselves against Spain for the fact that it gave birth to me, and they want to avenge themselves against France because it has granted me asylum, because every man devoted to the same career as me awakens their anxiety and their malice. The tall arid man is one of their instruments.

"What makes him so fearful is that by means of a little false enlightenment and a few powers even more pernicious, he fascinates the eyes of his disciples and closes the entrance to veritable enlightenment. I do not know all his plans as yet in detail, because my instinct only reveals things to me as they develop, but I can already see clearly enough into his present

80

enterprises to assure you that their consequences will be terrible.

"He is sustaining the revolt, as best he can, by the means that are known to him; he is blowing the spirit of vertigo into the minds of the conspirators, and is preparing to support them in all the disasters with which their party is menaced by loyal troops; but I am far from despairing of public affairs and believing that he will prevail over justice. Even if the sworn enemies of the cause of good have a few successes against it—and I have reasons for speaking to you thus—it is necessary that you are not alarmed by them, for those successes will only be temporary. He cannot bring an enterprise to a successful conclusion, because he is unaware of his own relationship with the breadth of nature; and when he attempts to try the key, which is indeed to be found everywhere, he will always turn it in the wrong direction.

"Since I have shown you the slight glimpse that I am presently able to have of everything that composes and directs his infernal machinations, and in which a crocodile will, in fact, play a large role, it is necessary that I also give you a few glimpses of what will be powerfully opposed to him...

(Dear reader, I am truly afflicted not to be able to depict for you nakedly the latter glimpses that I have just advertised to you, but if you are just, you will not hold it against my Muse, who had not given me permission to do so.)

Sedir was so struck by the details that Eleazar told him; he sensed so forcefully how useful the worthy Israelite might be to the public good, that he threw his arms around him and embraced him.

"Monsieur," he said, "we can no longer separate; you have become necessary to the salvation of this city; I have no hesitation is regarding you in advance as its liberator, and I beg you to have no other dwelling henceforth than my house. I don't even want you to return home; I don't want you to take the risk; there's too much danger and disorder in the city. I'll

81

send someone to fetch your family, under a strong escort, and everything that composes your household. You'll be at home here; you can live in accordance with the usages of your religion; you'll have complete liberty."

"I'm profoundly touched by your generosity, Monsieur," Eleazar replied, "but I believe that in the interests of the matter for which you want to employ me, it will be prudent for me not to accept. A displacement, and a common habitation with you, and too close a connection on your part from that moment on with a man of my nation, would open eyes to the object that occupies us, which requires, by its nature, that we avoid anything that might call attention to it for as long as circumstances do not constrain us to do so. Permit me, then, to remain in my home; I shall be no less at your orders at any moment that you might need my help, and a time will perhaps come when we can admit our liaison publicly.

"As for the danger that you fear on my behalf in the streets, be tranquil; I hope, may it please God, that nothing will happen to me, as nothing happened on the way here. If had had any anxiety, I would not have allowed my daughter Rachel to accompany me; she is the consolation of my days, and like you, Monsieur, extends all her inclinations toward verity. Yes, Monsieur, when one has the joy of fearing God, and fearing nothing but him, one is protected from all perils."

Scarcely had he finished speaking than a kind of luminous atmosphere formed around him, of which the usage and the properties were at his disposal, and which, if he wished, would have rendered him isolated in the midst of the greatest multitude. That phenomenon struck Sedir strangely, and made Eleazar even more precious to him.

(Dear reader, this might be an opportunity to make a fine comparison, such as is found to be consecrated in the fabric of epics, in order to express to you the surprise of the curious Sedir and the magnificent envelope with which Eleazar was surrounded. But if I were to draw one from fable, and speak to you about the petrifications operated by the head of Medusa, or the naked beauty that deceived Ixion so completely, I would depreciate my subject. In any case, if I wanted to make those comparisons, you wouldn't believe them, so it's better to leave them out.)

Struck with astonishment, Sedir tried in vain to redouble his pleas to keep Eleazar with him; he went to rejoin his daughter Rachel, whom the virtuous Sedir wanted to see, and whom he saluted with a respect and an interest that cannot be described. She responded affectionately to those attentions on his part, but she was even more occupied with the pleasure of finding Eleazar so calm after the anxieties she had conceived for him with regard to his interview.

After a few polite remarks, they took their leave of the honest Sedir and returned peacefully to their lodgings, where, independently of caring for the household, she assisted her father as best she could in all the visible or hidden enterprises that he made continually for the good cause.

Canto 25
Sedir hears distressing news from his emissaries.

Sedir was getting ready to go out himself, in order to see for himself where the combatants were, when two of his men arrived, out of breath, and hurtled into his apartment. They announced that all was lost; that, emboldened by the fidelity with which Sedir's orders were being followed, which forbade the shedding of a single drop of blood, the army of the rebels had dissipated the army of the good Frenchmen; that even the commandant had been disarmed by Roson; that the volunteers were unable to resist his efforts and had been obliged to surrender the most important position, that of the wheat-market, which would decide the fate of the entire capital; that Roson had taken possession of it and had granted its pillage to his own men; and that he no longer had any option but to flee, or see himself buried under the ruins of the city.

The brave and generous Sedir, still full of the words he had heard from Eleazar's mouth, replied to the men with an inimitable coolness: "Even if the danger were greater, I would not make decide upon the course that you are proposing to me, and I shall never despair of seeing the good cause triumph sooner or later. Since the danger is increasing, it is necessary for us also to increase our means of resistance, and we have not a moment to lose in summoning troops of the line; we have, in addition, loyal supporters who will not abandon us, and on whom my firmest confidence rests."

Immediately, without further explanation, he went to see the governor of Paris and the commandant of the valiant troops who had shown their courage at Denin, Guastalle and Fontenoy.[12] In a few words, he explained the state of affairs, of which renown had already informed them. He engaged

---

[12] The battles in question were fought in 1712, 1734 and 1745 respectively.

them nonetheless to spare the lives of their fellow citizens, and made this short speech:

> Companions, summoned to useful acts,
> Who have faced so many dangerous facts,
> The moment has come to show France
> What coolness can do allied to valiance;
> Spread in the combat alarm, not hate
> Nor any blood; the glory of the state
> Forbids you to forget that all the reckless
> Are no less your brothers for being in excess.

He was promised what he asked. In an instant, the general had the drum beaten; the troops of the line were assembled, the officers at their head, and marching at the double toward the principal place; on the way their number was increased by numerous volunteers, who, ashamed of their defeat and reanimated by the presence of the regular troops, were ardent to recapture from the enemy the post that they had been forced to abandon.

Sedir would have joined their ranks himself if his duty had not summoned him to show himself elsewhere, and not to act like a simple soldier. Everywhere that he presented himself, however, he brought the calm that only belongs to duty, and perhaps, without knowing it, he also brought some of those fortunate influences to which Eleazar had opened his eyes, and to which his heart and mind naturally rendered the instruments.

Canto 26
The audacious courage of Roson.
His weapon. His flight.

Roson was no sooner warned of the danger that was threatening him than, summoning up all his genius and courage, he assembled his lieutenants and gave them prompt and precise orders to assume defensive positions. His martial attitude animated his troops. By retracing the memory of their recent victory, he increased their intrepidity, and he had no need, in order to encourage his army, to throw his baton of command, like the great Condé, into the midst of the enemy battalions.

But what brought Roson's ardor and valor to a peak was a sword that the woman of consequence sent him at the very moment that the regular troops appeared. The woman of consequence, knowing that her party was under threat, had had recourse to the tall arid man from Egypt, and she had asked him to develop his talents in her favor. The arid man, while waiting for the time to do better, had made the provision of a marvelous sword to the woman of consequence, who had immediately sent it to Roson.

The guard of that sword was its most remarkable part, and had the advantage even over the famous buckler of Thetis, for it was more than defensive, being garnished by several animate and mobile sculptures, the mere sight of which suddenly engendered vertigo in all those who looked at it, and caused them to fall down. If any of the number was sufficiently robust not to be bowled over, and dared to fix his gaze on the enchanted sculptures, he was involuntarily and irresistibly attracted by their magical power, and came of his own accord to meet the blade of the redoubtable sword.

Furnished with that redoubtable weapon, Roson confronted the regular troops with a pride greater than that of all the lions of the Zara desert. Instantly, the irresistible power of his sword felled the first rank of his adversaries, but at the very moment when the other ranks were also about to succumb, by some unexpected prodigy, the terrible weapon was seen to escape Roson's hand of its own accord and fall at his feet.

Worthy Ourdeck, my Muse ought to render you justice here. Yes, she agrees that it was to you that the prodigy was due; she agrees that it was because the instructions of Madame Jof had penetrated you deeply that Roson's sword did not give you any vertigo, and that you were able to fix your gaze on the magic sculptures without spearing yourself on its blade; she agrees that you merited, by your confidence in her good advice, having proof of its accuracy; and she says that for your recompense, your mind is beginning to be no longer so opposed to things that you do not know.

Suddenly, the ranks of regular troops that had been knocked down got up again, quivering with rage. They took possession of the fatal sword with all the fury that the hatred of being defeated inspires. Following the orders that the commanders of the divisions had received to spare the blood of the enemy, however, they did not make use of the sword against them, and were content to break it into a thousand pieces; and the entire army coordinated its movements in order to hem the rebels in more tightly.

Disarmed, Roson seized the saber of the first soldier standing near him, although that saber did not have any of the properties of the sword he had just lost. His natural courage, however, similarly aided by fury and the shame of what had just happened to him, enabled him to put up a defense that can only be compared to that of Leonidas at Thermopylae. He struck redoubtable blows in all directions and although, thanks to the uncanny power of some protective power, he did not kill anyone, each of his thrusts was a victory.

Finally, however, pressed by numbers and exhausted by fatigue, he was obliged to abandon the post that he had defended so well. He fled toward the Rue Saint-Honoré and from there to the faubourg; but even in his flight he deployed such great intelligence and so much valor that to find anything similar it would be necessary for us to go back to antiquity again, and recall the retreat of ten thousand Greeks and the glory of the famous Xenophon.

Canto 27
The rebels retreat to the Plaine des Sablons.
They are charged by regular troops.

All the rebels fled with their chief, Roson. Their flight was all that the regular troops required, but the warriors nevertheless pursued them closely, and gave them no relief until they had chased them out of Paris.

The enemy was then seen to emerge in columns from the city and the faubourgs like as many torrents and come to throw themselves in a crowd toward the place where there was most room. Boilermakers, dancing-masters, cooks, chimney-sweeps, cab-drivers and poets were all mingled pell-mell in that horrible confusion. They fled in that fashion all the way to the Plaine des Sablons, the place to which the brave Sedir directed his steps like the others: a place significant by virtue of its name, and doubtless chosen by destiny to accomplish its plans.[13]

There, courage was reborn in those in revolt. Roson stopped, and saw with delight the ardor that was rising in all breasts. Then, straight away, regaining control of their ranks, he led them, with the rapidity of eagles, against the regular troops. The latter, seeing the audacity of the mutineers, had a great deal of difficulty remaining within the bounds that had been prescribed; they fell on them with the impetuosity that was natural to them. They struck with the pommel and the flat of their blades, and with the butts of rifles, and, giving the enemy not the slightest relief, hemmed them in and knocked them down on top of one another, causing entire ranks to fall.

---

[13] La Plaine des Sablons is nowadays a residential district in the suburb of Neuilly, but in the late eighteenth century it was an open area outside the city, where horse races, markets, military maneuvers and reviews were sometimes held. "Sablon" is fine sand once used routinely for scouring.

In an instant, the ground was strewn with fallen rebels. Their party was undoubtedly about to be exterminated in its entirety, and the war was almost over; but the arid man and the woman of consequence still existed, and destiny had caused those terrible ministers to be born for the woe and punishment of the capital; so, in spite of the glorious success that soon seemed bound to crown the efforts of the regular troops, we shall see the battle change its face so much that it is impossible to imagine a more striking and more unexpected evidence of the uncertainty and instability of things.

Canto 28
An unprecedented prodigy.
The Academicians examine the prodigy.

It is here, Muse, that it is necessary to resume all your rights and develop all your talents. It is no longer a matter of depicting mobs, combats and battalions lying in the dust; it is necessary to reveal to the eyes of posterity events so extraordinary that never, without your help, would the human mind be able to conceive the idea of them.

At the moment when the clash of armies is most violent, when death, or at least the shame of defeat, threatens all ranks, an unknown force suddenly lifts the battlefield into the air, with all the champions that are on it. For a few moments, their cries of fright and surprise are heard, but those cries cease as soon as they are heard, either because the champions have all died of fright or because they have been precipitated into some gulf, as some of them presume.

A kind of grey column is seen to emerge from the ground, of immense girth, still moving, as if by the effort of an earthquake, and yet not allowing the slightest part of the matter composing it to fall away. Independently of its unimaginable breadth, the column rises up to such a height that it is lost to sight.

Noisy vapors emerge in a rush from that marvelous gulf, in such a fashion that the noise, the shocks and the eruption are as many scourges, which might have been frightening separately, but in combination are capable of petrifying everything.

Sedir, who has had time to approach the scene of the event, is struck by surprise at the singularity of the spectacle, which he cannot comprehend at all. After having considered that column for a few moments, he races back to Paris, in order to prepare new means of defense there, if it is a new enemy that is announcing itself, and, at the same time, to consult

91

Eleazar, whom he summons immediately, believing that he could not address himself to anyone better to explain the surprising enigma.

In the general alarm that the phenomenon has cast into all minds, the curious, who do not have the same resources as the fortunate Sedir, believe that here is nothing better to do than address themselves to scholars to obtain clarification of such an extraordinary event; some of them therefore come back pensive, and present themselves at the Academy. One of them, charged with acting as spokesman, says:

> Illustrious Academy, ornament of France,
> Sisters of Apollo, allies of cognizance
> Who acted so cleverly with Jove
> That he hardly dared afterwards to cough
> Explain this frightful prodigy so well
> That we won't believe it's come from Hell.

"From Hell!" replies the President. "If that were the case, it would no longer be within our competence, but don't worry; we'll appoint a commission, and you'll soon know what it is that has worried you.

In fact, shortly thereafter, a detachment of Academicians is seen to set forth with all their sextants, octants, astrolabes, achromatic binoculars, etc. They arrive at the edge of the Plaine des Sablons, but the ground has been agitated by the great shocks of the unknown force that made so much noise, so they remain at a distance and bring their instruments to bear. Here are the results of their observations:

Height of column: six thousand toises, or eight thousand five hundred toises, or three thousand two hundred and fifty toises three feet; or twenty-five thousand toises five and a half feet.

Color of the column: Gray or green, or the color of the belly of a male toad, or the bottom of a bottle, or Paris mud.

Substance of column: Quicksilver, or slate, or quartzous granite, or the portion of molten glass that is still liquid at the center of the Earth, according to our most savant naturalists.

Canto 29
The decision of the members of the Academy's commission. Their astonishment.

The members of the commission, who each had a particular result, wanted nevertheless to make a uniform report to the Academy; thus, they were obliged to pass on to opinions, and it was decided by a majority vote that the column would be forty-five thousand nine hundred and fifty-two toises three and a half inches in height and three thousand three hundred and thirty two toises in diameter, and that it would be composed of volcanic lava still incandescent.

They were about to return to the Academy to make their report when they heard a voice emerging from the column, mingled with a few bursts of laughter, and which said: "The clever men! Oh, what clever men!"

The nonplussed members of the commission turned round. The voice continued: "The clever men! Oh, what clever men!" and then fell silent.

"It's an echo," said one of the members of the commission. "Some joker in the crowd must have uttered it to amuse himself, and the echo of the column repeated it, by virtue of the laws of Tautology."

They were about to continue on their way. They stopped again, as if petrified, on hearing the voice say to them:

No, don't mistake my voice for an echo.
It isn't, I know, the first quid pro quo
In which you've exposed your vast science
But with me, you need to seek reliance.
Moderate yourselves, and try to embed
A new prodigy within your head
And don't just judge me by my pallid hue
For I am, when I wish, as trenchant as new.

The surprise, alarm, shame and anxiety that passed through the souls and over the faces of the all the spectators, Academicians and others, was indescribable. They all fell to the ground, face down, and the voice continued:

I'm no volcano, lava or any kind of fossil;
I'm a living crocodile, and quite colossal.
My permanent abode is the plains of Memphis,
Without quitting them, I've come to Paris.
I wanted to see how it would react to mystery;
I too like to play my role in history;
I ought to take part in your dissents
And go on campaign with your regiments.
Let your souls, however, not take fright
At having seen me swallow two armies outright
You'll learn in time what's become of those;

(At this point the Parisians remembered the last words of the narrative that threatened them with being astonished, but before that unexpected engulfment, they would not have been able to understand their meaning.)

Until then, what I want to propose
Is to give you a little science lesson:
The secret of the universe, my confession.

The spectators, who had already raised their heads slightly at the word "crocodile" and mention of the animal's miraculous voyage, lifted them entirely at the words "science lesson," and everyone listened as the voice continued.

Canto 30
The crocodile's science lesson.
The origin of things.

"The universe that you see didn't exist as yet, and yet there was already a great and beautiful crocodile, which was me, and of which I'm no more than a feeble image. It wandered freely in space; nothing hindered its movements; nothing stopped it in its tracks.

(Dear reader, I feel compelled to warn you that what it says there is either a lie or a great mystery, if one assumes that it is using figurative language; and that the creative power that it depicts in the rest of its discourse is suspect, to say the least; that the creative power in question belongs to a source unknown to it; that it seems, moreover, not so much to be seeking to educate as to parody ancient and modern theories regarding great subjects; that if it isn't very choosy about the means to satisfy its malice, you ought not to be sure of anything it presents to you; and finally, that if you are instructed in the profound sciences of verity, rather than in the vain sciences of the schools, it will be easy for you to substitute for what the professor does not say, to rectify the false things it says, and to sense when its blows strike the target.)

"It wasn't content with that existence; it wanted, by means of a superior chemistry, to take account of the ingredients that were contained in that space, and it paused to examine them. But instead of attaining the ingredients it wanted to analyze, it obtained one of an entirely different species, and a genre that it didn't expect. For as soon as it has stopped, it ceased to conserve the elongated and free figure that its body formed. Its two extremities curled back in a circle and joined together naturally by virtue of the atmospheric current against which it had positioned itself sideways.

"Soon, the effluvia that emerged from its body inside that circumference accumulated, became concentrated, warmed up and were transformed into vapors. But as those effluvia escaped its body and became coarser, it became heavier itself, because they were also mephitic in nature, and until then they had aided it to move through space. That was the means by which present nature became visible, and that is the original principle of the mold of time, which threatens to break one day, and which I have so much interest in conserving.

"In fact, by virtue of their accumulation, the vapors acquired different degrees of density and solidity, and thus formed the different entities that constitute the universe.

"It was from the less dense effluvia nearest to their former subtlety that the stars and the empyrean heavens emerged; the second degree formed the planets; there were a few vague effluvia that formed comets; and the body itself, reduced to its solid part by the emanations that had emerged from it, formed the mass of the Earth. A few bitter humors remained, however, which could not become earth or rise to the class of limpid effluvia, and formed the basin of the seas. Others rose up like clouds, and those formed the rain. Others were fixed to the surface like arrested transpirations, and they are the snow and ice of mountains.

"A portion of incandescent air was caught in the middle of that circumference, and left a void that no substance has been able to fill; that is what has made philosophers say, as if by inspiration, that the nucleus of the Earth was empty and hot.

"They also spoke in accordance with the principles when they said that everything commenced by being glass, although they might have said it without design, for although they had probably mistaken, for the primitive state, what was only destruction and residue, they nevertheless proved thereby the two orders of things, or the first order and the second order, which I shall explain to you.

"In fact, does not chemistry tell you, Messieurs, that in order to make glass, it is first necessary to assemble vitrifiable materials; that it is then necessary to combine them with alkaline substances; and that those alkaline substances are not native substances, since you obtain them from other bodies that you dissolve? Now, if all those givens are necessary to make glass, you can clearly see that there were things anterior to the formation of the world, according to the theory of your famous philosophers; thus, I'm perfectly in accord with them on the existence of the anterior ingredients, although we differ completely on the nature of those ingredients.

"Your famous Buffon is also nearly in accord with me when he thinks that the satellites of the planets are concomitant masses formed at the expense of the matter of their principal planet, as the planets themselves appear to be formed at the expense of the mass of the Sun; for he does not mean by that what I have just told you, to wit, that all of nature is only formed by the effluvia emerged from the body of the primitive crocodile; only I shall add a corrective to his system, which is that the entities that constitute it were not formed thus at the expense of the others, and that each of them is the product of a particular effluvium that is proper to it.

"At the risk of being accused of plagiarism myself, I will add that the theory is not new, and that he could, had he wished, have extracted it from other philosophers; for the theory, modified by my corrections, has been rendered public in German, in Amsterdam in the year 1682;[14] and I am all the more honest in making such a declaration because the man who laid bare that discovery at that time has said a great many bad things about me.

---

[14] The reference is to *Mundus Subterraneus* by Athanasius Kircher, an edition of which was published in Amsterdam in 1682, although it had first been published in Latin in 1665; it is a work of attempted geology, including cosmogonic speculations.

Canto 31
Continuation of the crocodile's science lesson.
The system of the world.

"The system of the universe, formed in the manner that I have just explained to you, resides in its measures and its laws, because the light effluvia, no longer having anything gross to lose, could not rise up any higher, and, the solid mass no longer being subject to subtle evaporations, the earth could not descend any further. But as the body of the great crocodile, which was me, had taken the figure of a circumference, as by virtue of that it embraced and compressed everything, and the portion of air that was at the center opposed that compression, as Newton and Kepler have depicted in their laws of attraction and repulsion, the result was that bodies descend as they spin, and spin as they descend.

"As a natural consequence, it imprinted the same movement to all the effluvia of various degrees that emerged from it; that is why all the stars circulate; and such is the principle of the universal rotation."

The orator paused there for a moment, and then added, as if regretfully: "An unknown voice obliges me to tell you that it is the movement of universal rotation that is the cause of all of nature being as if asleep, as if in somnambulism, unaware of anything she is doing, and you can regard all the corporeal entities that compose her, as the cockerels with which you sometimes amuse yourselves by putting their heads under their wings and making them turn, and with which you can then do as you wish, without them perceiving it."

Since the beginning of that discourse, all the listeners had wanted to flee, partly in disdain and mostly in fear, but a subterranean force retained them regardless; they felt beneath their feet something like the effect of a vacuum pump, which, by dint of drawing off the air, stuck their feet to the ground and prevented them from moving away.

99

When they heard that singular explanation of the system of the world, there was a considerable rumor in the assembly, especially among the Academicians, who had long been accustomed to seeing things differently; but the same force that made them stay where they were also made them shut up; the vacuum pump extended its action, via their arteries and their sinews, all the way to their mouths, and by dint of pumping the air away from inside, it closed their lips so firmly that they could not open them, nor proffer a single word, like the auditors condemned to silence in schools where certain professors insist on repeating their lesson from their pulpit.

The orator therefore continued at its ease.

Canto 32
Continuation of the crocodile's science lesson.
The formation of individual entities.
The pyramid.

"Independently of those fundamental bases of nature, there were other classes of entities produced by particular effluvia that emerged from the body of the great crocodile. Those effluvia took on different characters and appeared in different forms; and as some of them had a portion of life, or a globule of subtle air, that air made those forms move in all directions and wander over the earth. That is what composes the animal kingdom.

"Other effluvia remained attached to the surface of a few fleshy parts of the body of the great crocodile; that is what forms the trees and all the vegetation. Others were trapped inside or caught between the hide and the flesh, and that is what forms the metals.

"Your learned men do not know what they owe to the current of subtle air, which cannot be contained in iron, because that metal is, as you can see, too fusible to endure. That is why that air, in consequence, always tends northwards, where, by virtue of its action, the principal effluvia, which are ascendant like fire, have formed the elevation of the pole, and have caused there to be more land in the northern hemisphere than the southern hemisphere. For the same reason, that is also the veritable cause of the direction of the compass toward the northern pole, because air and fire are closely analogous; but it is not for me to reveal their secrets.

"All these particular corporizations,[15] as well as those forming the fundamental bases of nature, became as many

---

[15] Although it did exist previously, most of the early uses in English of the word "corporize" and its derivatives cited in the

101

senses for the great crocodile, which was me; previously, I had had no need of them since I perceived and approached everything without any intermediary. So I remember clearly that as those senses were formed for me, I lost as many ideas in exchange; which appears to be absolutely the contrary of what your learned men tell you today, since, according to them, the means of retrenching ideas is to retrench the senses; but in my opinion, all that is just a quibble over words; I have not claimed to be saying anything except that all those productions that formed around me were no more than corporized figures of what I could previously perceive and know in reality; and your learned men would surely not claim anything except that you now need your organs to extract from those corporized figures the scant reality that they might have conserved: everything, in sum, that the ancient harmony, and the primitive circulation still entertains, to the extent that is possible.

"When that new order of things was thus established, I found myself almost sovereign within my petty empire. However, it was not long before I wanted to play another role there, about which I have no need to talk to you, because you repeat it yourselves every day; but a powerful genius, doubtless attached to the region of ideas that I no longer enjoyed, perceived my design, and, fearing that the derangements I had occasioned in that primitive harmony might go even further, commenced by breaking the circular form that I had taken during my change of state, and which had to supply all my strength henceforth, since—take note of this, I beg you—it bolted my tail to a nut underneath one of the highest pyramids of Egypt, which it had built expressly for that purpose with a few pieces of granite, which my own effluvia had formed.

"From the nut to which it bolted my tail, four branches departed, which each extended over one of the faces of the pyramid and consolidated its base; and if one were to dig underneath those pyramids one would see why, in spite of the

---

English dictionary came from commentaries on the work of Jakob Böhme.

shocks they experience every day, they have nevertheless conserved their exact direction toward the four cardinal points of the world.

"In fastening me thus, the genius that had destroyed my circular form left me the liberty to travel, with the rest of my body, to all the continents of the globe, and in all directions, imposing nevertheless the harsh condition that the entire human race, as well as that of all the good genii, would combat me in my enterprises, and would not allow me to attempt any without opposing me with all their might.

"At that price, I have the power to traverse all the entrails of the globe, to elongate myself at will all the way to the extremities of the globe, and even beyond, and to tighten myself to a measure of fifteen or twenty feet, like an ordinary crocodile; in sum, although my tail is always fixed underneath the pyramid, I can turn like a sling and embrace, in my various circuits, all the countries and climes of the world. So, I have used the rights left to me in such a fashion that, in spite of the conditions imposed on me, I have succeeded in reaching with one of my hands all the way to the sun, whose spots you would never have been able to understand without the key I've just given you. I've also succeeded, by the means at my disposal, in making a sufficiently celebrated name for myself, not only in Egypt but in several other parts of the world.

"That faculty of movement, which I've conserved, in spite of the power that keeps me fixed beneath the great pyramid, and the opposition I experience on the part of the good genii, is the reason why no one has ever been able, either in the time of Herodotus, the time of Strabo or the time of Monsieur Maillet,[16] to measure the exact dimensions of that great mass, which I try to keep perpetually in motion, and it's the same cause that has occasioned so much diversity in the deci-

---

[16] The reference is to Benoît de Maillet's *Telliamed*, first published posthumously, in a severely bowdlerized version, in 1748, for fear that its ideas concerning geology and the evolution of life on Earth might be considered heretical.

sions of the Academicians who tried to submit me to their examination a little while ago.

Canto 33
Continuation of the crocodile's science lesson.
The deputation of the sciences.

"That isn't the only difficulty they've had to experience in their scientific career, for I've used my rights on the sciences as well as all the other objects I can attain. So, when I commenced to establish my reign, I received a deputation from all the embodied sciences, each of which asked me to be able to exercise their talents in my empire. I gladly granted them that permission, but only after imposing on one indispensable condition that I thought necessary to the maintenance of my glory and my power.

"I therefore said to mathematical science that I would permit it to count, weigh and measure throughout the extent of my sovereignty, but on condition that it would deposit permanently in my archives the standard of weights and measures, and that it would compose one as best it could.

"I said to physics that it could speak about the forms of things and occupy itself with the mode or manner in which they exist and operate, on condition that it deposited in my archives the why of their existence, because I would lose too much if that knowledge were broadcast. By that means I hold physics entirely under my laws, because it's impossible to know the mode of entities perfectly without knowing the reason for their existence, and the why is the key to the how, not the how the key to the why.

"I said to chemistry: you heard what I just said to physics. If it's impossible to know the how of entities without knowing the why, I can let you manipulate as you like all the chemical substances, but by reserving the key of how, since I reserve that of why, you can only decompose and recompose anything in appearance.

"I said to astronomy that it could amuse itself making an almanac of all the celestial bodies, and even trace the exterior laws of their movement, but with regard to the pivot around which they circulate, and the rights that I have over them, I expressly forbade it to speak about it, and that secret had to remain in my archives.

"I said to botany that I would allow it to reel off its systems of the classification of plants by their shapes, by their sex organs, by their fruits, by their calices, by their leaves or by their families, but that I forbade it the only veritable classification, which is that of their constitutive elements, and that key would be deposited in my archives.

"I said to medicine that I would abandon the care of human health to it, but that it had to leave in my archives the vitally important secret of purging the medicinal substances themselves with which it tried to purge the sick, and it would have to substitute for that as best it could.

"I said to music that I gave it the vastest scope to paint whatever it wanted, but I imposed two conditions on that: the first was that the diapason would remain in my archives; the second, that the range of the voice and its instruments would be limited to the planetary scale, like nations—except that I only imposed the second condition for a time, until Herschel had discovered a new planet, which would be the bass register of a new scale, and the tonic of a new octave.

"I said to grammar that I had no permission to give it, nor limits to prescribe for it, because the true secret that concerns it could not be consigned to my archives, and that it was the prerogative of a sovereign other than me; that the archives to that sovereign were always open, which would enable grammar to be universally practiced, although universally misunderstood.

"I said to painting that it would be free to represent all objects, whether physical or mental, that were offered to its pencils, but that it would be obliged to leave in my archives the secret of vivid colors, and, in consequence, that of making living images that would present a veritable light to the eyes.

"I said to poetry that it would have the right to express as it chose everything there was of the most sublime, but that it would be reduced to making portraits of ideas and imagination, for the models must remain in my archives, unless it had the skill and good fortune to draw upon the archives of grammar.

"Finally, I said to history that I consented to it assembling the deeds of humans, but that I reserved to myself the knowledge the secret articles of the universal social contract and the hidden motives of everything that passes between the nations; that is how I hold the peoples in my hand, and historians can only depict the apparent play of those marionettes, without being able to say anything about the strings that are attached to them and move them.

"I then imposed one obligatory condition for all the sciences in general, which is that there would not be, in the mechanism of any of them, any discovery of which the knowledge was not communicated to me, and that they would not have any disciple who was not specifically devoted to my glory and my service.

"At those words, all the sciences went away confused, complaining in whispers about the restrictions to which I had submitted them—but in spite of all the efforts they have made to obtain more ample franchises within my empire. I keep such a close watch on them that they are far from having attained the goal to which they aspire, and the tax I have imposed upon them has rendered me more than I expected.

"It's true that there are a few particular sciences that were not in the deputation, and to which I had nothing to prescribe, since they had not judged it appropriate to ask me for anything. But if they believed that they were able to do without me, I had all the more reason to be suspicious of them. They have often tried to oppose me in my designs. Fortunately, my surveillance has thus far maintained all my rights, and I hope to maintain it long into the future."

The members of the audience were still fixed and mute, by virtue of the power of the pump. The audience was also augmented continually by a curious crowd brought by impatience to know what was happening and what had become of

107

the Academic commission. As those curious individuals approached the atmosphere of the pump, they were caught like the others and forced to remain in place, without saying a word.

(Dear reader, try to penetrate the immense verity that it has just offered to you here, perhaps against its will, and you will be compensated for your trouble.)

The voice did not interrupt itself for that, and continued its instruction.

Canto 34
Continuation of the crocodile's science lesson.
The condition of the human species.

"Now I come to the story of humanity, and you ought to know by now that my present reign isn't only limited to the domain of nature and that of the sciences, but that it also includes that of the human species. I confess, however, that the origin of human beings embarrasses me slightly, and I haven't yet been able to divine where they come from—but it's sufficient for me to dispose of them, as they've let me recover that right.

"The first trial I made of my power in their regard, as soon as they had set foot in my empire, was also to put their head under their wing—a figure of speech you'll understand. But in putting their head under their wing, I left them the usage of their feet, hands and tongue, and as I'd reserved that of the brain for myself, they have to be very clever if they want to speak, act or move other than in accordance with my will; so I employ them routinely in the execution of my plans, and hold them in a veritable somnambulism. By that means I've governed their empires for a long time, as I dispose of the laws of the universe.

"I agree, however, that it's the fault of human beings if things are like that, for they have the means of contesting my superiority, although I'm not the one who will tell them that. I shall prudently limit myself to talking to you about their history since the deluge.

Canto 35
Continuation of the crocodile's science lesson.
The history of the human species.

"I perceived before commencing the tour of the world that humans were trying to open their eyes a little and to emerge from the state in which I'd put them; then I took in my four paws and in my mouth all they could contain of the dried mud of the Nile, which is a true natrum, and which forms all the soil of Egypt. By virtue of its expansive and solvent quality, it has the property of having the same effect on the mind and imagination of human beings. So, before setting forth, I began by inspiring the Egyptians with such a respect for animals—among which I was numbered—that during the famines that people experienced thereafter, the inhabitants preferred to eat one another rather than eat the sacred animals, as Diodorus informs you. It wasn't difficult for me, after that, to establish throughout Africa and in many other places the worship of fetishes of every kind, living or dead, because I was able to speak everywhere and about everything, as you shall see.

"My first excursion was to China. I knew that a great genius had communicated magnificent knowledge to the people of that country, and I intended to go and recover a few portions if I could, in order to extend my empire over the Earth. On the way I traversed, sometimes overground and sometimes beneath the surface, all of Arabia, Persia, Syriaca,[17] Tartary and Tibet, all by extending myself at will, but without being able to detach myself from my pyramid. And it was by similar undulating movements that I formed throughout the globe

---

[17] "Syriaca" (Serique in French) is cited by ancient Greek geographers in connection with the Silk Road, although they disagreed as to where it ought to figure on their somewhat hypothetical maps of the world.

valleys, mountain chains and river beds. That's also why one never sees a straight line on the surface of the terrestrial body.

"I found the Chinese in full possession of a great deal of enlightenment, and one superb truth above all, for which, two thousand years afterwards, you've seen Pythagoras try to immolate a hundred oxen; they had even taken it to a higher level than him.

> They could boldly immolate a hundred thousand
> But, fertile in miracles, my Egyptian land
> Was able to blur their minds, and not by half,
> So today it's a lot if they immolate a calf.

It was to one of the most famous followers of Fo that I addressed myself, and after having worked on him a little, I promised to attach his name and glory to the greatest events that would fill the universe until the end of the world if he would only confide a few of his secrets to me and teach some of mine in his country. Flattered by the hope that I made him envisage, and struck by the proofs with which I supported my promises, the bargain was soon made. Then, furnished with the important enlightenment of Fo,[18] which I lacked but which I adulterated somewhat, I immediately left to make use of my provisions on Earth, to purchase by that means all that humans were able to sell me in return, and perhaps to by them from one another in the same way as time permitted,

"I then extended one of my feet as far as Japan. I offered the same provisions to the Dairi, who, thanks to my Egyptian earth, found them better than those of Fo, on which he had nourished himself thus far; and, in return for a few petty secrets that I obtained from him in his turn, I made him emperor of the Sun, and it's since that time that his successors never emerge from their palaces when there is a Moon, for fear of slumming.

---

[18] Fo is the Chinese term for the Buddha.

"After a slight excursion to the North, where Odin consented to let one of his eyes be plucked out on condition that I made him the greatest diviner in the land, I continued my route around the world, at first only skirting its confines, in order to make circumvolutions everywhere; and I took care to gain by that means all the leaders of the advanced posts. But there must be very redoubtable capes in nature, for the promontory of tempests that made Camoëns illustrious[19] is nothing by comparison with certain points of the world that I encountered, and if the poet's fiction seems so imposing, might it be because, like me, he knew the reality?

"When my exterior course was concluded, I approached the interior of Asia. There I made a treaty with the famous Semiramis, by which, in return for giving a few of my adjutants places in her temple of Belus, she was to enjoy all the illustriousness that signaled her reign. I had books invented by the family of Canaan, which did not take long to propagate them among its neighbors. I established a taste for argument and debate among the Brahmins and the Talapoins; I rendered the Lama venerable to the supreme degree among the Tartars; I promised a future superabundance of gold to the great Mogul, and I immediately delivered superb genealogical titles to the Indians—all in exchange for the doctrine of Fo, which I obscured in all those countries.

"When I had thus put all of Asia in combustion, I returned to Egypt in order to renew my provision of the native earth, but above all to put in motion the celebrated Sesostris, who had a great deal to do with the secret treaty I had made with China; I gave him unequivocal signs, so he never ceased to immolate to his warrior humor all the people I had delivered to his blade, and it's because I involved myself a little in his exploits that they appear rather extraordinary, so that scholars

---

[19] The reference is to the Cape of Good Hope (originally the Cape of Storms), whose tempestuous tendencies were incarnated by Luis de Camoëns in his epic *Os Lusiadas* (1572) as the giant Adamastor.

have regarded Sesostris himself as a fabulous individual. For myself, I know better than them what concerns me, and I declare that it's to the warrior spirit that he sowed in the various theaters of his conquests, reinforced by the new doctrine of Fo, that I owe the powers I have enjoyed since, of universal upheaval.

"In fact, I soon passed ôn to Greece, where, during a royal feast given by the beautiful Helen, I put a drop of the blood of the valiant Paris into her cup, impregnated with that double spirit, and that was the origin of the Trojan War. Don't be astonished that the beautiful Helen came to a tragic end as well as the unfortunate Polyxena; they were also an article of my treaty with Sesostris.

In consequence of my engagements, I returned to Assyria in order to fix there a fundamental era of human history, in the overturning of the realm of Sardanapalus, but I was in a hurry to extend one of my paws as far as Rome, in order to found a warrior nation there that, in accordance with my engagements and the need I had to stir, would one day invade Greece and a part of Asia. I had a little work to do to enable to Roman people to pass from the simplicity of King Arunce,[20] who only had two dogs for his regiment of guards, to the pomp of Nero and Domitian, but thanks to my Nile mud, I caused them to experience so many evolutions that I made its character flexible, put its head under its wing, and did anything I wanted with it.

"Meanwhile, the race of genii and humans gave me a little trouble during the commencements of the Republic; nor did they spare me in Greece, where the gifts most redoubtable for me came to rest in Pythagoras, but I took precautions to make sure that everything that emerged therefrom was slightly disfigured. Thus, Pythagoras had had wisdom in his mind and heart, but his disciple Socrates had much more in the heart

---

[20] Arunce is named in several eighteenth century French texts as a son of Tarquin the Superb, although he would never have reigned, since Tarquin was overthrown.

than in the mind, and, things always decreasing, his disciple, the famous Plato, had more wisdom in the mind than in the heart; Aristotle, Plato's disciple, had more in the memory than in the heart or the mind; and finally, his royal disciple Alexander, only had it in his stomach and on the tip of his sword ; and that was what I was waiting for before sending him to Assyria to dissipate the rich successions of Cyrus somewhat.

"During those preparations whose effect, although distant, could not fail, I made a brief visit to Egypt in order to treat the army of Cambyses, lost in the desert, as I've just treated two of yours—and that's the reason why historians have never been able to discover what happened to it.

On the way, I passed under the peninsula of Euboea, where I caused an earthquake violent enough to engulf the city of Atalante;[21] and that was only a little rehearsal for those I meditated in other epochs, especially the one that happened in your century in the province of Chennai, in which I crushed a number of cities while playing boule with mountains, so remarkably were my movements.

"I was in a hurry to get back to Rome in order to foment quarrels with Carthage, Spain, Greece, Asia Minor and Judea. You're too well-educated for me to need to spell out all those facts. I can't complain about my successes. Thanks to the likes of the Tarquins, Appius, Marius, Sulla, Cinna, Pompey, Caesar, Tiberius and Caligula, I agitated that nation enough inside and out to make it pay a little for the evil it did to others. In one of my journeys I passed underground near Naples, where, thanks to the rapidity of my movement, I set fire to several

---

[21] The island of Atalanti or Atalantonisi [Atalante in French] was fortified in 431 B.C. at the beginning of the Peloponnesian War, but the fortifications were partly destroyed in an earthquake in 426 B.C., when some of the land in the Euboean Sea was sunk. Some speculative historians have suggested that the event prompted Plato, born in 425 B.C., to invent the myth of Atlantis—a myth that Saint-Martin subsequently grafts on to the historical event in a remarkable fashion.

combustible materials, the explosion of which burst through Mount Vesuvius and engulfed Pompeii, Herculaneum, Stabia and other towns.

"I could only agitate Rome in the furious genre; it didn't have sufficient intelligence for me to make use of all my means. So, disgusted with it, I returned to the Northern regions, where the one-eyed Odin rendered me great service in exciting the entire north to revolt against the same Romans that I had rendered rulers of the world. Goths, Vandals, Scythians, Huns, Lombards and Herules obeyed his impulsion and mine, even more than the warrior impulse. I detached them from time to time against the colossus, from which, with every attack, they always carried off a foot or a wing. Otherwise, they would never have maintained their independence from that imperious people. Nevertheless, I had eventually to agitate them in their turn against one another, as you've seen in history, because Odin only had one eye, and all those who said they were faithful to him disputed as to which of them was going to appropriate it.

"While I agitated the Occident thus, the Orient became too tranquil by virtue of the genii that had brought peace there; it was necessary for me to hasten there in order to reawaken it from its torpor. I immediately went to Arabia. There, thanks to the negligence of those..."—he paused—"...I found in Mahomet a man after my own heart, analogous to my designs; I engaged him to preach with saber thrusts, having formed the project to oppose him to..."—he paused again—"...and, in consequence, to..."—he paused for a third time—"...for Mahomet had three eyes, because, in order to give him more determination, I had given him the one that Odin was lacking.

"That was what enabled him and his successors to extend their conquests so rapidly and so far into Asia and Europe, and were even about to subjugate all the northern nations that I had unleashed against Rome. I don't know where Martel had sharpened the sword that he opposed to them; otherwise, all of Europe would be wearing the turban.

"I took my revenge in the crusades that I was very glad to see appear, but which I couldn't have invented. I obtained enough profit from them for the Occident to be molested; so, in exchange for the complaisance of Eleanor of Guyenne[22] for Saladin, that cost Europe, in a single article, about three million men.

"In the meantime, Genghis Khan immolated scarcely fewer for me in Asia, because I rapidly transported to him the charm that I had put on Mahomet, who had not prospered sufficiently in the Occident. It was also me who, with a portion of that charm, established an apple of discord between Naples and Hungary, and then between Naples and Aragon—a discord in which my commissioner John of Procida distinguished himself in preparing the massacre of all the French in Sicily.

"Soon afterwards I made a treaty with Cecco d'Ascoli, in which I made him party to the greater part of the various secrets I had collected in my travels; he promised me in return to exercise with the greatest care and the greatest assiduity the powers that I had given him over the stars. It's true that he ended up being burned alive, but it wasn't without having fulfilled his promises.

"So it's by virtue of his influence that afterwards, the Orientals served me again by taking possession of Byzantium, the island of Rhodes and coming all the way to Vienna to menace the last images of Caesar, and finally abolishing the first empire of the Romans.

"By means of the same influence and in the same century I had the Portuguese discover a passage via the Cape of Good Hope; I had Columbus go to America, and I extended the power of Spain greatly. I enchanted Europe with printing, which I had learned long before in my dealings with the Chinese, but of which I had promised to make no use before a certain epoch; and that present I gave humans rendered me more than that of gunpowder, which I had given them in the previous century, because it was by that means that they has-

---

[22] An alternative title of Eleanor of Aquitaine.

tened to make known all they knew and laid beat al their secrets. Now, I love to learn the secrets of humans since I lost those I possessed by virtue of my nature.

"It was not without reason that I chose the fifteenth century to offer the world all those marvels. Nor is it without reason that I have chosen the reign of Louis XV to come in person to show myself on the banks of the Seine, and it is all because of the mold of time that I want to conserve. But in whatever epoch I distribute my presents, I take care only to lend them at interest, so the Arabs have not been able to escape Thomas-Kouli-Kan;[23] the Portuguese have been to seek the spices that heat their blood; the Spaniards found death in their pleasures in America after having sought gold in the blood of its inhabitants, and to them I have given the Inquisition, which is a kind of abridgement and elixir of all my industry. Finally Mahomet himself, in spite of his three eyes, was ready to lose his sight.

"I would be going against my interests if I explained further what the usury is that I exact ultimately from all those I favor; I have told you enough in confiding to you what I obtain from printing. With regard to gunpowder, and all the destructive inventions of which humans make use, they have a goal at least as useful for me, but which cannot be known on this earth. For they have not found the entire key who have said that murders and battles are a consequences of the great ardor of the thirst that devours me and which I can only slake with blood, having no other liquid at my disposal. It is sufficient for you to know how much all those powerful and redoubtable means have rendered to me in the last two or three centuries. The Thirty Years War, the various burnings of heretics, the Ligue, the Fronde, the two Wars of Succession are, for me, incontestable evidence.

"I have been amply assisted in my successes of a different genre under the long reign of the French kings. Europe, by

---

[23] "Thomas-Kouli-Kan," as he was known in France, was Shah of Persia from 1736-47; he is also known as Nadir Shah.

that means, has been on fire for a long time with battlefields, by virtue of cannon fire; and in studies and schools, by virtue of the savant futilities of learned assemblies, where I always have a place reserved; and the profit I have made from the discovery of the Indies and America is such that presently, it only requires a match to be struck to set the globe ablaze.

"Thus, politics, over the whole world, has become, by my ministry, akin to a game of chess, which is always commencing but can never finish, because the powers that form the various pieces can certainly take one another, but they cannot take me, because I am the king, and they do not know how to checkmate me; so the good genii, my adversaries, are in total disarray today.

"Under the present reign, the cannon has had a little less employment, but books have had a prodigious one, inasmuch as, when matters seemed exhausted, I had the means, thanks to the new doctrine of Fo and the influence of Cecco d'Ascoli, to remedy it. That is what enabled me to invent so many associations.

"It is wrong to accuse the members that compose them generally of knavery; the majority of members are not the masters of their movements; it is an active vapor that I blow at times, in order to make them carry out extraordinary actions. In any case, there are societies that only belong to me secondarily, which commenced by being under the law of the good genii. There are some that I still direct, but which the good genii threaten every day to remove from my empire. There are some we govern by division, the good genii and I—but in all of them, I neglect nothing to accredit myself in the minds of human beings, at the expense of the power that never ceases to oppose me, and in that I never fail to find a few sufficiently docile humans.

"It is to repay them for their confidence in me and their docility that I have delivered them to the power of the various mutilated sciences that I have allowed to be established in my empire. That is why I have caused the philosophers of this century to profess all the doctrines that teach humans that everything is nothing; that bodies think and that thought does not; and that they have no need for recourse to a moral sense in order to explain human being, but that it is only necessary to teach people to form ideas.

"I have not alerted them to the contradiction of those doctrines, which are profitable to me, for they would soon see that if there was no morality in the motivation and play of their ideas, it would be pointless to search for them and improve them, since their physical nature must take charge of the enterprise, as it is responsible for improving all your senses; but I have convinced them at the same time that human beings, moral or not, have not deteriorated since their origin, and that, in consequence, they have no need of any kind of renewal—which, in a single sentence, offers the measure of their logic, and gives me an immense advantage over the most redoubtable of my adversaries.

"I am preparing them new recompense for the time when I will have found great reinforcements among them, for I can only act with what they give me; I shall therefore give them secrets so astonishing, regarding magnetism and somnambulism, that they will be able at length to put themselves in my place, so that I can devote myself more freely to other occupations.

"I shall bewilder them so completely that they will represent the particles of substances that they will have obtained by their manipulations as specimens of nature, when they are only specimens of her demolition and fracture; for, when I fall silent, you are not unaware that one of your most famous actors has given them this lesson in advance, by carrying under his arm a stone that he displayed stupidly as a specimen of a house he had for sale.

"One day, I will make them say that water is not an element because they can reduce it to vapors, as if a piece of ice were not a solid and palpable body because it can be reduced to water, and as if they had ever enjoyed a pure element, to dare to pronounce on its nature.

"I shall make them say, on the contrary, that sulfur is a simple substance, because they have not been able to take account of what constitutes it; and that will be one of the cleverest tricks that I can play on them, for if I can persuade them that sulfur is simple, it will be necessary for them to believe that I am simple too, given that sulfur and I are as much one as the other.

"I shall make them find a new secret for the reproduction of the human species. Unfortunately, the fair sex will not welcome it, because will not be their responsibility.

"I shall put enough variety into their minds that there will be some of them who believe in nothing, but who will nevertheless go to consult sorcerers and card-readers.

"I shall inspire in a great navigator[24] the idea of being initiated into the ceremonies of the inhabitants of Hawaii, and that will lead him to be eaten by cannibals, for I can take men a long way with ceremonies.

"I shall confirm the geometers in the opinion that they have held for a long time, that roots are powers put in fraction, as if the powers of nature could be fractioned, and subjected to another law than being compressed, and roots could be anything but powers in compression.

"I shall give birth in a few heads to the idea of establishing throughout France fine scientific schools, and generalizing the fashion of a universal instruction, greatly favorable to my designs; but beware the hand that might hurl some stone at the head of a Goliath, and above all beware a lack of finances that might perhaps bring down the establishment! Oh, without those inconveniences, what fruits would I not obtain from the animate Encyclopedia that, pullulating incessantly, has successively extended my reign over the entire Earth!

"But the moment is nigh when I shall be amply compensated. Reason is about to be born; soon it will flourish; it is to me that it will be owed; it is me that will have revived philosophy, by purging it of every ingredient that is not mine. For

---

[24] James Cook.

the eminent service that I will have rendered them, the nations will raise altars to me, and say loudly: "Long live the crocodile! Honor and homage to the crocodile!"

Canto 36
The audacious projects of the crocodile overturned.

Either because the crocodile had partisans in the audience or the magic of its words operated naturally, some of the spectators were indeed heard repeating those final words: "Long live the crocodile! Honor and homage to the crocodile!" A few members of the audience were even seen to bow down, as if to worship it, and a colossal altar suddenly formed in front of it.

At the same time, a head even more colossal formed at the summit of the crocodile, or that mobile column on which all eyes were fixed, and from which such strange speech emerged. That head was beautiful in appearance, and had sufficiently regular external proportions. It bore, written on its forehead: *Universal Sciences*, but it was only the phantom of them, because, whatever the crocodile had boasted, in saying that it held in its archives the principle of the life of the sciences, it is evident that the vivifying principle in question is lacking, by virtue of the cares and continual torments to which humans subject themselves in trying to substitute for it everywhere.

It was nevertheless by that phantom of universal sciences that the crocodile hoped to obtain the most honorable homages! Scarcely had that head posed upon it, however, than it lost its beauty and the symmetry of its proportions; and it soon realized itself that all its hope had vanished, for there was immediately presented in mid-air, facing it, a little girl about seven years of age, whom some people have since thought to be Madame Jof herself, in another form. At any rate, the young child had a golden drinking-straw in her mouth, with which she blew upon the head seven times.

At each blast, the head seemed to diminish in volume; and each time, too, to colossal altar diminished in height, until finally, the seventh time the child blew, nothing any longer

remained of the head, and the altar was so reduced to ground
level that there was no longer any means of discerning it.

> At the seventh blow, the crocodile
> Replaced in its sheath the mobile pile
> The hole it had made closed up so well
> That where it had been eyes could not tell.
> Each listener then was no longer in thrall
> And no sooner were they free of it all
> Than they ran to Paris to tell the story
> With which the orator had painted its glory.

Canto 37
The stupor of the Parisians. An Academic Decree.

How can the stupor of the Parisians at so many marvels be depicted? They would, however, have delivered themselves to more admiration if fear had not continued to labor their courage, and hunger to rack their stomachs.

But the zeal of academic glory prevailed in the minds of the commission members over all those woes, and they hastened to make their report to the assembly. Each of its members started on hearing a doctrine and explanations so different from those of they had previously been given. After a quarter of an hour of silence, in which embarrassment and confusion occupied all minds, they passed on to debate, through the intermediary of the President, who collected opinions.

Go forth and rummage through library shelves
In Guebre, Greek and Teuton traditions delve,
To seek a natural explanation for everything,
A fact that seems at first to be surprising.
For in such a matter, with so much light
It would be shameful to remain in fright;
And to save the honor of our good name
It's necessary that we stake our claim.

Canto 38
The plague of books.

They all separated and hastened to consult public and private libraries. Never had the spirit of research animated them with such ardor, because no occasion so urgent had ever presented itself.

> But, strange marvel, prodigiously confused,
> By which the human mind was so bemused
> That here the truth seemed so very vague,
> And it was necessary to add an eleventh plague
> To those of Egypt that Moses brought down
> With the sternness of his voice and frown.

In fact, a plague suddenly fell upon all books—and what a plague! It was not rats that gnawed them; it was not the fire of heaven that consumed them; it was not darkness that hid them from view; it was not the waters of the Red Sea that inundated them; it was a certain softening humidity that brought debility into their entire substance, and transmuted into a kind of soft paste, gray in color, paper, parchment, cardboard, binding and everything that composed them: phenomena that had been announced by a few nebulous stars that had been seen wandering a few days before in several libraries.

> In sum, contemplating such a mutation,
> One could not help seeing a confirmation
> Of the fact that some malevolent imp
> Wanted, for fun, to make authority limp.

What encouraged that conviction further was that at the same time, in all the places that scholars happened to be, a quantity of women resembling maids and nurses suddenly appeared, all of whom had spoons in their hands, without anyone knowing where they came from or how they had got in. Immediately, dipping their spoons into the gray pulp, they raised it to the mouths of all the scholars.

The later, doubtless struck by the same magic power, forgot the objective that had brought them, appetite taking the place of the desire for knowledge, and, seeing the soft gray broth that the nurses were offering to them, they only stopped swallowing it when they had had it up to the ears, and when the nurses had withdrawn.

Canto 39
The result of the plague of books.

It was then that the project of the genius that had inflicted such an enormous plague on books could be judged. The mixture that had been made during their decomposition was also accomplished in the ideas of those who had nourished themselves upon them. What emerged from that was such a confusion of thought and language that by comparison, the Tower of Babel was a sun of clarity, because they all spoke at once, and each of them talked about all the sciences at the same time.

Sad speculators, unfortunate humankind!
What will become of the work of your mind?

It would have been bad enough if the scourge had been limited to the capital, but it was general throughout the country—what am I saying?—through all of France except for one single study, which we shall know when the time comes. The scourge extended not only to books that already existed but to those that did not yet exist, since it had acted on all the materials that might serve to transmit our thoughts to posterity, and our scholars no longer had at their disposal a single piece of paper on which they could even write a list of things to do.

Canto 40
A brief invocation of my Muse.

Muse, savant Muse, what pictures could you not draw for us if you wanted to employ your pencils here! You would depict for us the general upheaval of France: the irreparable loss of all genealogies; the annihilation of all political treaties, all civil contracts, all the written testimony of the fidelity of lovers, the annals of our forefathers' history, the depositories of religious verities and everything that ignorance and bad faith have substituted for them; in sum, all minds abandoned to frightful darkness, to an uncertainty worse than nothingness, and all because they no longer had paper.

But you have so many events to recount to us that you cannot amuse yourself drawing all those pictures at length for us, like a painter who can dispose of all his time.

At least dip your brushes momentarily in the brightest of your colors, then, in order to paint for us the scenes that seem to you most striking.

So, one of the commissioners sent by the Academy was seen arriving in haste. Either because the fibers of his brain were more electric that those of his colleagues, or because he had eaten more of the gray paste into which all books had been converted, a fury of words, citations and interpretations took possession of him, and, presenting himself before the Academy, he began his speech...

(Dear reader, I ought to warn you that in the midst of that confusion, a few instructive flashes escaped him from time to time, a few profound and instructive truths, which are scarcely accustomed to being manifested by the mouths of Academicians. I even know from a reliable source that every time these flashes and verities escaped him, he experienced a kind of secret violence, as if some superior power were pressing him, and forcing him involuntarily to render homage to the light;

and you ought not to be surprised by the effects of that power, if you are convinced that lies are not what dominates humans down here exclusively, and if you recall exactly how far the rights of the virtuous Eleazar extend, and the surveillance of the Society of Independents. You have, therefore, been warned on that point; now listen to the speech that our orator pronounced.)

Canto 41
The Report of the Scientific Commission to the Academy.

"Messieurs, the wig of the emperor Commodus, if one can rely on the description that Lampridius has given us of it, was the most marvelous in the world, so the poet Ossian always had it in mind when he sang of the blond hair of the handsome Caledonians, because the differential of the tangent of an arc is equal to the differential of that arc divided by the square of its cosine; for even though you sent us to the Plaine des Sablons to obtain information about a phenomenon that the people will doubtless call a prodigy, the paragoge proslambanomenos would nevertheless have ranked it beneath Hypate-Hypaton, as we assign the *Petit Albert*."[25]

The President: "Orator, return to your seat."

"Yes, Messieurs, let us leave the ignorant vulgar to give the name of prodigy to things they cannot understand; they are not, like us, naturalized in the sciences; they have not been alimented as we have, since the cradle, on the infantile nourishment of books, and God only loves those who live with wisdom, as Solomon said. Those profane individuals live too far away from out sanctuaries to have access to the truth; for us, who spend our days in its court, there is nothing whose explanation ought to embarrass us.

"Without having recourse to the savant collections of the Abbé Muratori or Père Mont-Faucon,[26] have we not for a wit-

---

[25] Proslambanomenos and Hypate-Hypaton both refer to the lowest notes in musical scales. The *Petit Albert* is a mid-eighteenth century book of supposed cabalistic magic that was enormously popular in the decades preceding the 1789 Revolution.

[26] The Italian historian Ludovino Antonio Muratori (1672-1750) and the French palaeographer Bernard de Montfaucon

ness the entire Teutonic Order, as well as Restaut's grammar? Do we not even know that the logarithm of minus one has an infinity of values, all imaginary, since, except for one, no values can exist that are real?

"Thus, mathematics is a science that does not penetrate as far as our radical and integral essence. It seems that the man who learns it and knows it is a lesser being than us and other than us. How could not be otherwise, since not knowing the square root of two, we cannot be perfectly sure of any the other roots that do not rise as far as that number; given that it is through it that they must pass, and thus we do not know where they are coming from, or where they are going, or where they will arrive? And we have nothing else in that genre but approximations, because we are only tabulating on axioms and suppositions, whose value is not even known to those who present them. Pilpai is not the only one who has spent his time in fictions.

"We have no need, however, to deny the facts, in the present circumstance, as, between us, that has sometimes happened to us when we did not know what to extract from them. Yes, let us agree that the two armies have been swallowed; let us agree that a monstrous column has risen, and swallowed all the champions; let us agree that an extraordinary voice made itself heard; let us even agree, if we must, that the animal in question is a veritable crocodile. Can humans, on Earth, believe that they are fulfilling their employment here, if they let an instant go by without prophesying?

"What will result from this against our glory and our knowledge? We have been told that we only speak about the cover of the book of nature, and never its spirit; that in painting the colors, dimension and forms of plants and animals with so much care, in calculating the movements of heavenly bodies with a scrupulous precision, but not knowing one iota about the destination of all those things, we are like someone

---

(1655-1741). The next reference is to the grammarian Pierre Restaut (1696-1764).

who claims to have given the moral and physical portrait of a man when he has given a description of his clothing. It is thus that Trimalchio, in presenting at the court of Mandamus the famous printer Christophe Plantin, born at Mont-Louis near Tours, greatly surprised the seven sages of Greece.[27] Now, if Leibniz has been persecuted by Galileo for having been the first to perceive the weight of the air, Nero was not so badly wrong to hold a grudge against Abbé de Pétrone."

The President: "Orator, you are committing anachronisms; sit down."

"We have been able to surpass the occult philosophy of Cornelius Agrippa, to teach people how things are; we have given them, without that, explanations of all the phenomena of nature, and we have simplified the sciences to such an extent that 'The daylight is no purer than the depths of my heart.'[28]

"But Messieurs, in teaching people how all things are, we have not forbidden ourselves the ability to add new enlightenment to that we have spread, and nothing prevents us from agreeing that things might still have another manner of being, as well as the one that we have given them.

"Our colleague Fréret has said, in fact, that all divine and religious ideas only come from phantoms of our imagination,[29] because he only looked at the tree from above and outside, and from there he did indeed find nothing but thousands of mobile

---

[27] The printer Christophe Plantin (1520-1589) became an influential Renaissance humanist; Trimalchio is a character in the *Satyricon* generally credited to Nero's courtier Petronius Arbiter (the "Abbé de Pétrone" to whom subsequent reference is made).

[28] The quotation is from Racine's *Phèdre*, spoken by Hippolyte, with a measure of irony.

[29] In fact, the work in which Nicolas Fréret (1688-1749) was credited with having said that, published in 1766, long after his death, is apocryphal. Saint-Martin surely knew that, and perhaps intended to suggest as much by the sequence of anachronisms that ends the paragraph.

leaves, incessantly agitated by all the winds; but if he had looked from the bottom of the tree and within, he would only have found, whatever we might say, a single sap and a single stem, a single seed and a single root, which the winds cannot even reach, and without which the tree would have neither leaves nor fruits; and let us even agree that the man who thinks he knows something does not even know how one knows; but *industriae nil impossible*. So the Agwans who overthrew the throne of Persia inflamed the genius of Catilina to such an extent that, seeing the statue of Narses near Charing Cross, and profoundly meditating the strategies of Polyaenus, he engaged the monk Alcuin to reconcile Pilbrac with Charlemagne.

"It is thus that in the exact science, after having recognized the three degrees of power that compose the cube, we have nonetheless imagined subsequent powers, which are, it is true, only multiples of the preceding degrees, but which nevertheless offer thought a different manner of being and a new mine for intelligence; besides which, is it not a certain verity that an effect can be attributed to several various causes?

"But what am I saying? How can we believe in a verity? We don't believe in the human soul, and the human soul is the sole mirror of truth down here. Thus we have no need to go back to the fragments of Sanchuniathon or the Ezourvedam,[30] and it's sufficient for us to observe that our soul embraces universality; that thus, in order or it to die, it would be necessary for plus to take the place of minus, while in the real and not the conventional order of things, it is only the minus that can take the place of the plus. So I was near to saying that there is nothing more august than our soul, if I had not re-

---

[30] The Ezourvedam, a supposed Vedic document, was forged by Jesuits; Voltaire did not know that when he used it as a source for information on ancient religions, but Saint-Martin might have guessed. He surely knew that Sanchuniathon, the supposed author of fragments of the Phoenician language relating to ancient religion was an invention.

marked that Voltaire, Crébillon, Racine and several of their colleagues have abused the right of the epithet by employing the word 'august' in subjects that were not worthy of it, and which were not only anterior to the reign and to the glory of the emperor of that name, but even the poet Ennius, who had applied that title to the augurs.

"For example, if we have attributed earthquakes sometimes to air compressed in the subterrains, sometimes to the effort of waters, and sometimes to the electric force of the atmosphere, does that prevent us being also able to attribute them to some foreign body, animal or not, sliding through the interstices of the Earth? We do not know all the animals as yet; we do not even know why the class of phalene or nocturnal moths is the most numerous, and we do not know ourselves, because the human soul, without being able to cease being immortal, has nevertheless become a phalene moth, and the everyday anxiety that devours it probes its degradation more than all the babbling of philosophers can prove the contrary. So does one see with much grief that the thornapple or sorcerer's herb is natural to the two Indies and that it is naturalized in our climes.[31] See the work of Monsieur de l'Ancre, counselor to the parliament of Bordeaux, on the inconstancy of the evil angels and demons."[32]

The President: "Stick to your subject, Orator, stick to your subject."

"As for the property of being able to extend itself all the way from Egypt to Paris, according to the voice we heard, we

---

[31] The reference is to *Datura stramonium*, or Jimson weed, native to Mexico but naturalized in Europe after its importation by the conquistadors, a powerful hallucinogen

[32] The witch-hunter Pierre de Lancre (1553-1631) attempted to justify his depredations in *Tableau de l'inconstance des mauvais anges et démons* [Depiction of the Inconstancy of Fallen Angels and Demons] (1612), which popularized the notion of the "witches' sabbat," entirely a product of his own imagination.

cannot pronounce for or against with certainty. Have we not before our eyes the prodigious ductility of gold? Have we not in the vegetal realm a marvelous substance of that genre, elastic gum? Have we not seen in the celebrated Metastasius, that when Don Quixote encountered the ostriches and the caged lion...

"I have still not embraced it today.

"I shall return to my subject. *Croix de Dieu:*[33] b, a, ba, b, e. be, b, i. bi, b, o, bo, b, u, bu: ba, be, bi, bo, bu. Undoubtedly, before that elastic gum was known to us, we would have mocked anyone who had dared to depict it for us as it is. How do we know that it would not be equally shameful to deny that the same property might have a force incommensurable for us in some class of the animal kingdom?

"We shall see, in times to come, that in chemistry, the formiates, the bombiates, the prussiates are of the number of the thirty-five genres of salts composed according to the number of acids; but we are in a little too much of a hurry to compose all substances with saline or crystallized molecules, for those substances, or aggregates, are only residues; nature only wants the fluid, and crystals and salts are not the substances of things; they are, in the absolute, merely the cadaverous carcass of them.

"We also know that the realms of living nature are linked to one another. Not only the realms of nature but also all the parts of those realms seems to be connected, and only distinguished from one another by imperceptible logarithms. But Condillac and Claude Bonnet,[34] less sage than the *Heptaméron*

---

[33] "*Je sais ma Croix de par dieu*" was a phrase used in French to denote knowing the elements of a subject, because of the ornamentation of an old textbook used for the purpose of teaching the alphabet to children, so it corresponds approximately to the English use of "I know my ABC."

[34] Étienne Bonnot de Condillac (1714-1780) was the leading supporter in France of the Philosophy of John Locke, of which Saint-Martin strongly disapproved. "Claude Bonnet" is a mis-

and the famous Baron Verulam, wanted so much to link things and confuse them, that to believe them, we would have no more need of discernment, since there would no longer be any difference; and in the Golden Ass of Apuleius that carried Clémence Isaure to Chesapeake Bay, one sees that if the substances of the vegetal realm often present us with the properties of the mineral realm, as we are convinced by our operations on plants, the animal realm could well participate in the properties of the vegetal realm. No, Linnaeus, Tournefort, Jussieu, Magnol, Sauvage, you do not hold the key to the real system of botany.

"It is no longer necessary to seek in Herodotus for that of the Egyptian hieroglyphs; nor do savant naturalists know why the petals of flowers do not bear the color green, which is only the color of expectation and not the color of triumph. That is why we ought to agree, with the sage organs of the truth, that we have abandoned that which is a source of fresh water, and that we have hollowed out cisterns that do not hold water; for in order to advance in a scientific career, as someone of my acquaintance said, it would not be the head that it is necessary to break, as so many people do; it would be the heart. That person would also like everyone to write books, but at the same time, he would like no one to read any. For in the final analysis, Messieurs, was Shakespeare not right to say that books are nothing but the sawdust of books?

"I find nothing in physics, therefore, to oppose to the notion that the crocodile we have seen was able to extend itself from Egypt to Paris; I don't even know whether we might not be able to demonstrate it by calculation. I've recently seen a piece of elastic gum in the home of a curious person, in the shape of a horse three or four inches long. By pulling the horse's neck he succeeded in elongating it, without breaking

taken reference to Charles Bonnet (1720-1793), author of *Essai analytique sur les facultés de l'âme* [Analytical Essay on the Faculties of the Mind] (1760), of which Saint-Martin also disagreed violently. "Baron Verulam" is Francis Bacon, it, to a length of a foot. Now, we know that the length of a crocodile is enormous, compared to that three-inch horse. *Ist es nicht zu bezweifeln dass unser wreck hiedurch cinen höhern grad der vollkommenheit erhalten hat*, as Pompey said about the battle of Salamis—for Klopstock and Herbelot's *Bibliothèque orientale* hold a place among the marvels of the Dauphiné."[35]

The President: "Orator! Orator!"

"If, therefore, we don't deny that this crocodile can extend its elastic property to an incommensurable length, compared to that to which the gum horse was extended, we immediately find a rule of three, by which the gum horse, in its natural state, is to the crocodile, in its natural state, as the gum horse in its extraordinary state is to X, which is the veritable prolongation of the crocodile, from Egypt to Paris.

"That does not prevent human science being as null and vain as the void. As the prophet Isaiah said, truth does not put its joy in doctors. So we can regard ourselves, in the matter of sciences, as knights of industry who are only occupied in hiding their penury. If we only knew why the parameter is a constant line, and why vegetables draw from the ground the potash that we discover in their substance!

"For although what the crocodile told us about the formation of the world is, in truth, susceptible of some difficulty, let us agree that we are scarcely more impregnable in that matter; we can, therefore, let it pass. Thus, we hold to this profound truth, that to heat a body to melting point, it requires at least a fifth of the time that it is necessary for it to cool down again; but if that scale is not employed sparingly, it might lead us greatly astray.

"How many times has it happened to those of us who have gone up in aerostats to think that, because their body was being carried all the way to the clouds, their mind was glori-

---

[35] The German quotation is mangled, but the apparent intended meaning is something like: "It is highly unlikely that we can ever achieve our perfection that way."

fied, without there being any need to seek another means of divinization, and that the entire secret of Elijah's adventure is that he was rising up in a balloon?

"We know, it is true, by means of positive experiments, that air makes its dwelling in water, and that a single drop of water contains an indefinite number of living beings; let us make use of that observation; let us see it on a large scale and not be astonished that things obtained their origin by condensation, and that all the living beings that animate nature have arrived at life by that means. I have also read, by the order of Monsieur the chancellor, a work entitled *Origine des origines*, on these causes, wanting to treat favorably the said petitioner in the syndical chamber, signed Sainson."[36]

The President: "Stick to the subject."

"I confess that what appears to me most surprising in the marvels that the crocodile offered us is to have heard it speak, but all the veils with which nature envelops us have perhaps not yet been lifted for us. We can repeat one after another, as Annius of Viterbo made Berosus say,[37] that no religious system or supernatural extravagance exists that is not founded on ignorance of the laws of nature, but, as there is a curve here of double curvature, we ought to agree between ourselves that perhaps there is no scientific theory that we fashion, nor any of our assertions in physics, that is not found on our ignorance

---

[36] The reference might be to one Louis Sainson, who was reported to have worked a miracle in Orléans in September 1786. There is no work of the period entitled *Origine des origines*.

[37] Annius' *Antiquities*, written in the late fifteenth century includes commentaries on the alleged writings of numerous pre-Christian scholars, including Berosus, whom he invented in order to support his revision of ancient history. He also wrote an account of the apocalypse in which Mahomet is the Antichrist and the world is due to end (soon) when the Christians triumph over the Turks and Saracens.

of the principle of religious beliefs and the supernatural order, where the key to all things must be sought.

"For we are a little like rats, which introduce themselves into temples, and drink the oil of the lamps there, and destroy in consequence the light they ought to shed, and the say that one cannot see clearly there.

"Speech, according to our cleverest colleagues, is the play of certain organic strings contained in the throat of animals; some even claim that nothing would be easier than to make Vaucanson's duck talk.

"Others have said that speech is like a hand opening and closing without interruption; that, in consequence, it is impossible to depict, and even more so to compose, since its action cannot be grasped, nor its mechanisms mastered. Let us still say, in accordance with our great physiologists, that nature has probably given the crocodile a few organic strings more than parrots, to enable it to speak on its own, whereas parrots, having those fewer strings, are obliged to wait until we instruct them, to substitute for what nature has refused them; for there has only ever been, to my knowledge, Tasso's parrot that sang songs of its own composition.[38]

"Was it not in order that Couperin could play the *Folies d'espagne* that Ferdinand and Isabella expelled the Moors from the kingdom of Grenada?[39] If we did not have that means of resolving the difficulty, we would perhaps be even more embarrassed to know how the crocodile was able to talk to us about the sciences and history as it did, but is one string more

---

[38] Voltaire famously observed the Tasso's insertion of a parrot that composed its own songs into the garden of Armida in *Gerusalemme Liberata* would seem very strange to a sensible reader, but he was indulging in ironic understatement (the garden is illusory, and calculatedly implausible in its entirety).

[39] Couperin did not compose the original version of the harpsichord piece known as the *Folies d'espagne*, but he did base the music to his own allegorical *Folies française* thereon.

in the organ of speech not sufficient to render that marvel as natural as all the others?

"It is true that an unknown philosopher has told us that it is necessary to combine the emanations of our source with various resistances if we want to discover the origin of languages; that we ought to desire to know the truth, and that we are doing nothing to clean the mirror; that it is as if we were pretending to see clearly through our dirty windows, covered in dust and ordure.

"But you, Messieurs, are not unaware that everything that happens in the universe must have a relationship with and an influence on all the beings who are its witnesses, as inhabitants of that universe; that that influence and those relationships come to strike the organic strings that the throats of various being contain, and produce an analogous effect upon them, either on their structure or the influence they receive.

"It is thus that, as Eusebius of Caesarea informs us, the Imams, who do not have the eyes of Argus, do not want anyone to take precautions against the plague. It is their cupidity that has consolidated among them the impious theory of predestination; it has thus become a source of income for the Turkish clergy, which, in times of plague, is a true tontine.

"You all know that we vary the sounds in a hunting horn either by diminishing or augmenting the volume of air that emerges from our mouth, or by accelerating or retarding its velocity; instead of which, the variety of the sounds of an organ come, on the contrary, from the variety of the pipes, while the air blown into it is always the same.

"But was it necessary for that to introduce into the fundamental principles of music, the theory of arithmetical progressions, whereas, in all the phenomena of nature, there are only geometrical progressions? And instead of measuring the sound as scholars do, ought we not to have informed ourselves of what sound is and shown ourselves that, since it is only forms by fractures, it ought to be possible to reach its dwelling by following the tracks of those fractures? Nevertheless, with the only means that are known to us, we see the various marvels and effects of music operate; we experience gaiety, sadness, love, terror, hatred, an airborne fly, a Dutchman smoking his pipe."

Médicis received that with indifference,[40] for the fuming head of Coligny after having been crowned at the Olympic games.

"I'll return to my subject; do we not see, I say, without emerging from our own example, that all the objects that surround us and which strike us draw from us expressions and words in conformity with the impression we receive? Do we not see that the memory of it is conserved in us, and that we have the faculty of transmitting the memory to others by way of our stories?

"Let us not dissimulate it any longer, Messieurs; in spite of the deterioration in the human mind, which cannot be denied no matter what philosophers babble, there is one thing more incontestable still, which is that the source that formed us can never lose sight of us in our darkness, and cannot separate itself from anything, since everything comes from it; thus, in the few places that we are, we only exist because we aspire its substance.

"Let us therefore leave there the difficulty that the crocodile has been able to live long enough to have been witness to all the events of ancient history; and that in view of the mobility that is proper to it, it has been able to transport itself at will to all the parts of the Earth; as one can see, notwithstanding the aphorisms of Hippocrates and the pathology of Galen, that the cantharid fly is a scarab in which a superior air is con-

---

[40] I have run the text together here, although there is a paragraph break in the original after the comma, followed by a page break, where some text might have been accidentally omitted; the deliberate confusion of the meaning makes it impossible to be sure. Gaspard de Coligny was a Huguenot leader killed during the St, Bartholomew's Day massacre allegedly ordered by Catherine de Médicis.

centrated, and it is there that one will discover why it acts so powerfully on the bladder.

"What is the difficulty, in fact, in the crocodile being by nature equipped with a greater number of organic strings of speech, in the other animals having also been struck by everything that they have seen happening around them—read the scale and you will know, by knowing your income, what you have to eat per day—and that by their natural play they have rendered sounds relative to those events, and that by that means the crocodile has been able, by means of it memory, to transmit once again all that we have just heard?

"I could have had recourse to echoes to explain that phenomenon, as well as the fundamental bass of the famous Rameau, and the research of Monsieur de Pauw on the Americans;[41] I would have been able to prove to the publicists who, in treating human association, have only circled around the principle...I would have been able, as I say, to prove to them that human association did not commence by virtue of corporeal and material necessities, as is taught; that it was after having fallen into the foreign situation in which we are that it was necessary to think about getting out of it; that it is mistaken for the publicists to regard that epoch of association as the first, when it was only the second.

"But we shall know one day that the hydrogen and carbon combined in the fibers of vegetables and containing portions of alkali, acid, and above all oxygen,[42] form bitumens,

---

[41] *Recherches philosophiques sur les Américains* (1771) by Cornelius de Pauw, considered to be a definitive work at the time, although de Pauw never visited America and was not overly choosy in his use of sources to support his theory regarding the innate inferiority of native Americans to Europeans, for climatic and geographical reasons.

[42] The name oxygen was first attributed to an atmospheric gas in 1777 by Antoine Lavoisier, three years after the death of Louis XV, but as the speaker has also been able to anticipate

oils and resins. So, by means of the influence of caloric and oxide, I have no need to suppose an interlocutor hidden in some alveolus of that great crocodile, and taking its name in order better to mystify the assembly.

"Finally, as we only exist insofar as the immortal verity enables us to aspire its substance, we can no longer say that we do not know where to address ourselves in order to seek to discover its light; for if we do not succeed in finding it, we can only attribute it to our sloth and our pride: one day, one day we shall know one planet more; and will depart from that to make fun of heptomania, but we shall only arrive there in that epoch, although we have always lived incognito under its regime. In conscience, the heavenly bodies are fine instruments for us, which we know how to describe but do not know how to play with, because we do not even know if they were made to be played with.

"One article still remains that might trouble you, Messieurs; it is that of the destination of the pyramids. I confess that physics does not tell us anything about how they might have been built in order to nails down a crocodile's tail in Egypt. But without the collection of Fabricius, and the *Histoire de la Ligue de Cambray*, in two duodecimo volumes, by J. B. Dubos, we would still know very little about antiquity.[43] In the same way, without Hesiod's *Works and Days* and the chronography of Georges le Syncelle, augmented by the knowledge of the times, we would scarcely know today that the male fern is a specific against the solitary worm. Would it

---

the discovery of Uranus in 1781 his advance knowledge of the discovery is not entirely surprising.

[43] The references are to the prolific classical scholar Joann Albert Fabricius (1668-1736) and Jean-Baptiste Dubos (1670-1742). The book referenced, praised by Voltaire and first published in 1709, relates to war fought in 1508-16. Georges le Syncelle was a Byzantine chronicler who was alive in 810 A.D.; his chronicle was continued by other hands after his death.

be necessary to admit, as a famous professor will one day allege, that the kings of Egypt had the pyramids built to shield them from the sun and to serve as parasols?

"It would be in vain, also, to want to suppose that the edifices once served as the natural history cabinets of the Pharaohs, and that a few crocodiles escaped from their menagerie had made their nests there from generation to generation, and had even ended up obtaining divine honors, as one can judge from the belief of the Sabians.

"Thus, without settling on an explanation that could not instruct us, I prefer to think that the crocodile was speaking to us there in allegorical terms, in conformity with the taste of all the ancient peoples to whose lands it had traveled, and that we ought not to hasten to fix the meaning of that allegory until we have further clarifications.

"I shall sum up by saying that, all beings reposing on their own root, it is to the fermentation of the same root that they all owe their development, as Baltasar Gracian said in his *Homme universel*;[44] that if the root in question does not operate within us the vegetative action of light, it brings about its own destruction, by devouring itself; that that is the reason why we bar within us our life or our death, and that is why it is written that he who wishes to hoard his life will lose it. I leave Kepler to dispute with Newton the discovery of the laws of attraction; I leave Aeschines to make the case for the velocity of the heavenly bodies against the inverse ratio of the square of the distance; I restrict myself to the idea that I have just explained to you of the task of humankind, and I claim that the most useful truth that has been said to humans is that there is only one thing necessary for them, and that that exclusively necessary thing is that they renew themselves from head to foot."

---

[44] The Spanish Jesuit Baltasar Gracian (1601-1658) published *Ed discreto*—translated into French as *L'Homme universel* and known in English as *The Complete Gentleman*—in 1646.

The President: "Orator, keep you conclusions to your subject."

"In view of all these considerations, my advice is that we can only admire the astonishing properties of this crocodile; and that if it could leave Egypt, and diminish its volume slightly in order to live among us, we could not refuse to give it the first vacant place in each of our academies. There are my reasons

"The crocodile has given us one theory more of the universe and physics; that is an entitlement to belong to the Académie des Sciences. It has explained in a new manner the destination of the pyramids of Egypt; that makes it appropriate to the Académie des Inscriptions et Belles-lettres. Finally, it has made us a speech the like of which we have never heard; is that not sufficient for it to appear with glory in the midst of the Académie Française?

"Remark above all, Messieurs, that it has not once pronounced a certain name that has fallen into desuetude among us, and that it is what we call 'within the principles.' I think, therefore, that in favor of that attention on its part, which adds to its great talents and its great knowledge, we could dispense with the customary visits, and that it is up to us to invite it. On the subject of the name in question, however, philosophers of antiquity, who spoke a language other than ours, had an idea that it's necessary for me to communicate to you, which is that it isn't the name itself that confuses us, as we imagine; that what we really hold against it is the monastic taint (forgive them the expression) with which it has been impregnated and deprived of vigor, and in consequence, if a time comes when there are no longer any monks, we will perhaps be very embarrassed to know what to say and to sustain ourselves.

Let's go, my soul, and since it's necessary to die
Let's at least die without offending Climêne.[45]

---

[45] This couplet doesn't rhyme in the original.

Canto 42
The broth of books also nourishes the Academy.

The members of the audience genuinely thought that the orator had wanted to amuse himself at their expense, and were on the point of giving him a hard time when the maids and nurses who had shown themselves in the various libraries appeared again, carrying ladles full of the same scientific broth, and came to give that pasture to each of the members of the Academy. That deflected their attention momentarily. Then, adopting a more serious tone, they decided to put their colleague's conclusions to the vote.

The opinions being divided in equal numbers, tempers rose and minds became heated; they argued with an unprecedented fury; all the fire of the various scientific compositions they had swallowed was exasperated; the strength they had acquired from the nourishment drew them to excesses previously unknown in that sanctuary of reason.

Finally, at the end of those scandalous scenes, a recommendation for scrutiny was about to be made, when the hall was suddenly filled with a fine dust that obscured the eyes of those present. They did not know where they were; they got up from their seats, wanting to get out of that dark place, but they bumped into one another, stumbled over one another, and did not know how to get out of that frightful situation.

Canto 43
The Academicians tormented by a fine dust.

That accident originated from the same broth with which they were filled. The heat of their dispute had caused all the humid radicals to evaporate and had transformed it in their stomachs to little grains as hard as sand.

The agitation to which they had yielded had served to shift those little hard grains and had expelled them, by way of transpiration, with a violence that had attenuated them further in passage and had launched almost all of them at the same time into the atmosphere. That is why the powder was so fine and why, arriving so suddenly, it put those learned men into such great embarrassment.

If only I had, said one, the secrets of the sphinx
The paws of a mole, or the eyes of a lynx!
But alas, the insensate was caught very well.
Another one said: I believe it's a spell:
Be humble; knowledge, in spite of its weight
Puts mind and body in a pitiful state.
A third said: Can't I find the least respite
In order to enjoy both air and sight?

But lamentations were futile! It was necessary that they sense the power of darkness.

Canto 44
The Academicians rescued, but on one condition.

When the darkness had lasted for twenty-five and a half minutes, a benevolent but just hand, which was acting under the supervision of the Society of Independents, wanted to apply itself to returning sight to the unfortunate Academicians, but to do so in such a manner that their self-respect could not take any glory in the event. It therefore caused all the grains of hard dust that were filling the hall to agglomerate into little quadrangular pyramids, which rose up to the ceiling, the faces of which did not correspond to the four cardinal points of the world, like those of Egypt; and those masses had to remain in that state for a time, to indicate how far the sciences had deviated from their veritable direction by the inadvertence of those who wanted to submit them to their administration, without having penetrated any of the depths of nature.

By contrast, the same benevolent hand left in circulation the subtle fluids, the ingredients of verities that, by means of that same broth of books, had passed through the mouths of the orator and the other Academicians; and it is those ingredients that will one day assist the immortal science to emerge from the slavery that retains them in enmity to all true science, and teach people the real elements of grammar, which are offered to their eyes in nature and in action everywhere in the world.

Clarity then returned in the room; but that did not dissipate the internal irritation that the scientific fibers of the learned men had experienced by virtue of the kind of nourishment that they had taken, and they felt a sort of loquacious titillation, which they could only relieve by giving vent to the flood of words by which they were filled, and the desire they had to make everyone party to the marvelous adventures of which they had been the witnesses and the actors.

They would surely have consigned them to their academic papers if the plague that had fallen on books and paper had left them the means; but, being unable to write, they at least had the resource of going hither and yon to talk about those prodigies to everyone they met.

They did so in the same language that the commission's orator had employed in the presence of the Academic assembly, in such a fashion that the people, who expected from men so eminent in science some clarification and a ray of hope, did not receive either. So, not finding themselves any further forward after their recitation than they had been before, they began to murmur all the more.

Thus, nothing was heard in the streets but groans, lamentations and complaints.

Indigence, misfortune, blindness, dearth
How long will you come with cruel mirth
To afflict our sad citizens with your darts?
Why do you multiply the frightful arts
Of the pleasure you take tormenting our ire?
Why not suddenly light up a fire
Within a pit and hurl us thereon
Combining all your blows into one?

Canto 45
The people's fury against the Contrôleur général.

The people, whom hunger is afflicting more and more, and are unassuaged by the discourse of the scholars, finally seek to discover the author of all those disasters—or, rather, seek to wreak their vengeance on him, for he is not unknown to them. They go in a crowd to his house, and surround it; the door is broken down, and they go in. What do they find?

> In those disastrous times, those times of indigence
> In which everyone unwillingly practices abstinence,
> The minister is at table, surrounded by meats,
> Fresh bread, exquisite wines and sweets;
> And better to forget the woes of the public
> He summons to his feast the god of music.

But his joy is soon troubled by the tumultuous visitors who have arrived; some break the windows and the furniture, others throw themselves on the foodstuffs that are on the table, and go to search the whole house to see whether there are any provisions in reserve. The most furious pursue the master of the abode, who runs away as fast as he can, and escapes through a window that overlooks a little rear courtyard, without their being able to find him.

Terror accompanying him everywhere, however, he thinks he sees at every moment all Paris up in arms against him, and he is obliged to renounce doing anything at all in daylight, so no one ever found out afterwards what became of him.

Seeing themselves thus deprived of their prey, the furious resolved to avenge themselves on the house itself, and after having taken away all the provisions, they set fire to all the floors, and did so regretting that they were not able to throw the minister into the midst of the flames.

The court soon appointed someone in his place, but the evils he had attracted to Paris had made too much progress to be cured by that mediocre remedy; great measures would be necessary to contain the great mechanisms that were manipulating the enemies of public repose.

Canto 46
The union of Sedir and Eleazar against the crocodile.

Honest Sedir, it is time to unveil the sources of these extraordinary events, which, instead of calming the needs and the famine of the fatherland, are only plunging it further into the abyss and tormenting it with the anguish of fear. Your dear and worthy Eleazar arrives; he laments like you over the horrible situation of the capital, and the futility of all the steps taken by the Academicians, although that was only to be expected. He has instructed his daughter Rachel, who has remained in the house, not to neglect anything in her power to assist him in the particular task that he is about to undertake, and above all not to worry on his account; and it is with his usual serenity that he presents himself.

"Be welcome," said Sedir. "You're the only one from whom I can receive consolations and clarifications regarding what has happened, and I hope that the moment has come when you won't refuse me your help."

"I left home with that intention," Eleazar replied, "and knowing of your distress by my ordinary means, I did not await your orders before coming. Recover your confidence and have courage. The impious man will see coming upon him that which he dreads, but the just man will see that which he desires; because the man who only sows the wind can only reap the tempest, while the man who sows justice will reap consolations.

"I did not deceive you, as you see, when I told you that the rumors of the crocodile that were spreading were not so indifferent; all that you have seen for yourself, and all that the voice of the public has told you since you quite the location of the scene ought to have convinced you that there are great secrets beneath all this. They will develop successively. For today, be content to know that this crocodile is a cruel being, but cunning, as the wicked are, and timid, like them; he has a horror of saffron, because that plant is an exalted sulfur like him, and reminds him of his origin.

"But in order not to anticipate things to come, for the moment, dip your little finger in this box, and breathe in a little of the power that will stick to it; afterwards, you'll make another usage of it. I can only life the veil for you by degrees."

Sedir obeyed.

Eleazar collected himself momentarily in a corner of the room, and said to Sedir: "Now, look into the flame of this candle, which I've just lit without your being aware of it. "What do you see?"

"Something very singular: I see several moving figures there, similar to Chinese shadows."

"Focus on them; follow them attentively, and tell me exactly what is presented to your eyes."

Sedir, struck with astonishment and arming himself with all his courage, then rendered him the most faithful account of what he saw.

Canto 47
What Sedir saw in the candle flame.

"First I see on the ground, in the depths of a dark cabinet, a cast iron vase, a handspan wide. At the back of the cabinet, which is only illuminated by the fire in the hearth, I see three people dressed in long black robes. Of the three people, it seems to me that I know one, and that it is the very woman of consequence about whom we have already talked. She is very agitated, always moving, and appears to have anger and rage in her eyes. I believe I also see the tall arid man she has summoned from Egypt. He seems calmer, but he has a very affected and sad attitude. As for the third individual, I have no idea who that might be. He is bronzed, and seems to me to be employed there in the service of the other two, for he's holding a bowl and a water-jug, as if he were giving it to them for washing.

"In fact, there they are, washing their hands. The water is giving off a thick black smoke, in which I can even see a few flames springing forth, and which is spreading a violent odor of sulfur. The domestic pours the dirty water into the cast iron vase in the middle of the room, and the water fills it to two-thirds of its capacity. He leaves the room. Our two individuals remain alone, and they sit down as if to converse."

"Listen carefully to what they say," Eleazar put in, "and write it down. You have the means to do that, because I've preserved your study by my presence from the scourge that has fallen upon the libraries, and you'll find it easy, for they won't speak any faster than I wish, and I'll make them stop expressly, between sentences. It's the tall arid man who is about to speak."

Canto 48
Sedir writes down the discourse of the tall arid man.

Sedir took a piece of paper and a pen. He followed Eleazar's instructions exactly, and wrote down what the tall arid man said to the woman of consequence.

"You see me sad, Madame, and full of very importunate ideas, at the moment when I have such a great need to be by myself, to carry forward successfully the enterprise that brings us together. Something inconceivable has been happening within me for some little time. I have sometimes felt remorse before for the life I've led since my youth, but never as violent as that which is gnawing at me now. How happy and tranquil those people must be who have not, like me, neglected opportunities to advance in verity!

"My mother, who was a Copt, did everything she could to maintain me in useful and salutary paths, and she had advantages in that regard that many other mothers lack. She possessed the most sublime enlightenment, the rarest virtues and the most extraordinary gifts, which rendered her dear and commendable to everyone who knew her. She never ceased to engage me, by all kinds of means, to follow in her tracks; she even admitted that she belonged to a society called the Society of Independents, and that it was by virtue of her fidelity in following its instructions and precepts that she enjoyed such great privileges; and to prove to me that she was not imposing upon me she gave me the most signal proofs every day of her powers, her knowledge and her supernatural gifts, which she obtained without any other means that that of prayer, her entire confidence in the supreme principle and the exercise of all the virtues.

"Thus, she recommended me, above all, not to place my confidence in all the secretive men with which my country is swarming, and not to receive anything, by way of powerful and extraordinary means, except from providence, or from those who, by their conduct or by all the signs that she gave me, were evidently of the number of its faithful servants, and who, as recompense for their virtues and their services, had been put in possession of the key to nature.

"However, more seduced by the lure of all those marvels than devoted to the wisdom that ought to lead to them, I listened to masters other than my respectable mother, inasmuch as those masters promised me the same prodigies without putting the same conditions on them; in order to convince me, they too gave me proofs, which I did not even take the trouble to examine very closely. They had soon drawn me into their career, by means of the hope of disposing in my turn of their means.

"Indeed, from the simple fortune-tellers to the possessors of the most complicated recipes in matters of the occult or dark sciences, there is hardly any door of that genre that has not been opened to me, and where I have not found a partial satisfaction of my penchant.

"My poor mother made continual efforts to bring me back to her, but her efforts did not succeed, because I had allowed myself to be subjugated. Even today I sense that I am forcefully combated, and that it is surely her voice that pursues me, but I do not have the strength to listen and yield to it; I only have enough to tear myself away from the horrible conflicts I experience.

"It is, therefore, very terrible, the empire of the secret ceremonies through which those masters have made me pass, since, as soon as I set foot therein, the yoke was placed upon me, and has not allowed me any respite since. Instead of the peace they had promised me, I only have trouble; and instead of the enlightenment I thought I would be able to acquire by the ways they presented to me as the most comfortable, I only have a universal uncertainty, which is such that if you believe me, Madame, we will put off out work until another time, for I do not feel, at the moment, that I am in a condition to undertake it."

The woman of consequence, furrowing her brow, said to him: "That's not what you promised me. If you don't keep your word, I'll denounce you to the parliament as a disturber of the public peace and even, if necessary, as a magician—for although they don't believe in magic, I have credit enough to have you condemned when I want, as I want, and for whatever I want."

Then a hissing sound came from the direction of the door; a thunderous voice was heard, and, abusing the arid man, it said to him in an angry tone: "Egyptian, Egyptian, have you forgotten the oaths that you have made to our common mother? Have you forgotten the marvelous gifts that have been accorded to you, your numerous successes, and the inexpressible advantages that await you? Have you forgotten, finally, that if you do not keep your engagement immediately, you will not have another minute to live? For although I am your friend, I am also the executor of my master's orders—who, as you know, does not relax any of his rights."

The voice fell silent. The woman of consequence, astonished, tried to discover where the voice could have come from.

Sedir did not know either, but he put on a brave face, and he continued:

"I see the arid man reanimated; pride, ambition and the threats are having an effect on him. His eyes light up. He turns toward the woman of consequence and says to her: 'I beg your pardon, Madame, for my weakness; I was not myself when I lamented as I did; I even forgot all the great things we have already accomplished, and which promise us such a brilliant success. Yes, Madame, yes. I have fulfilled your designs adequately, and you have no reason to regret what it cost you to have me come from Egypt. A minister, your mortal enemy, has been entirely humiliated, and plunged into the greatest embarrassment; there is a revolt of the most determined; a crocodile, one of my compatriots, has come to swallow an entire battlefield. There is also the force with which I constrained an Academic deputation to listen to the lessons of a reptile; the destruction of all books, converted into broth; the academicians themselves lost in their own science and professing in a matter so unfavorable to their own glory; and finally, the most complete dearth, and Paris delivered simultaneously to famine and the horrors of brigandage. It seems that all that is sufficient to pay you for your benefits; but I would consider myself ingrate if I did not take gratitude further. We have a redoubtable adversary to combat. So long as he exists, whatever we do will accomplish nothing in his regard, because it will be possible for him to destroy it, and to repair all the evils that we have poured into Paris.

> That terrible enemy is named Eleazar
> Against that Hebrew, I need the bizarre.
> Once his peers would have lent me aid
> But today, on his own, he makes me afraid;
> Alone he could thwart us; in order to beat him
> We will need all our resources to defeat him.

"Oh, Monsieur," said Sedir, turning to Eleazar, "what do I see appearing close to those to interlocutors? I perceive two writers there who are suspended in the air, and one of them is writing as the arid man speaks; the other is next to the woman of consequence, and the pen in his hand is not writing."

Canto 49
Explanation of the stenographers.
Continuation of the arid man's discourse.

"Monsieur," said Eleazar, "since you can see that prodigy, which I have perhaps not yet mentioned to you, I cannot refuse you the explanation. Each of us has such a stenographer next to him, who writes down faithfully not only everything we say, but also everything that we do, and who keeps the most exact account. Those stenographers follow us everywhere, all the way to the tomb; there, they present our annals to us, which become our only judges and the evidence for our prosecution.

"Among those items of evidence are found especially those that accuse frivolous and imprudent men of having run after prodigies and marvelous deeds without having fathomed their source, and more to nourish their ignorant curiosity that to seek the wisdom that matches by simpler ways. The true science holds the key to eternal and natural marvels; that key is only found in the light of intelligence; and the light of intelligence is only found in the humble and vivifying virtues of the soul, as we see that the light that oil procures for us is only brilliant and pure because that oil is the mildest and most benevolent substance on earth; and it is to that fortunate terminus that we ought to direct ourselves. But while prudent men seek wisdom, others in greater number only seek prodigies; that is what forces the truth to put in usage all the sensible means that you see me employing, and which would otherwise by needless, because the simple way would have sufficed for the primitive and natural labor of humankind. It is, therefore, a consequence of the corruption of imprudent men, and the vigilant surveillance of their principle, that so many extraordinary things have already happened and will still happen in this great city.

"Nevertheless, the stenographers you see are only a sign that the truth has wanted to make in the order of things in which you live, and where one has writers; for the annals in question are also held in a simpler manner, and extend even further than you have been shown, as you will learn in due course. For the present, let's continue our work. The tall arid man who has been interrupted by your question is going to continue; write."

"It isn't just today, Madame, that I have to protect myself from the powers of that Jew, and before commencing the work that ought to give him death, it's necessary for me to tell you how much I have to complain of in his regard. I have collected on these engraved sheets all the bad turns he has done me. They are represented in emblematic characters, which I shall explain to you.

"This one is a head of Medusa petrified itself by the presence of a javelin made from an ash-branch. The Bey of Algiers wanted to employ me some time ago in a secret enterprise against a great lord. An immense fortune was promised to me and I put to work all the resources that my art could furnish, but Eleazar caused the coup to fail, and the discontented Bey of Algiers, thinking that I had deceived him, instead of the fortune I had expected, gave me three hundred strokes of the rod on the soles of the feet.

"I did not know at first that it was the Jew who had combated me so successfully; I was only informed when one of my familiars brought me an arrow of ash-wood that he had received through the body without seeing anyone, while he was on the way to accomplish my designs against the great lord; for on that arrow was written the name Eleazar; in addition, it was half-covered by a vegetal powder unknown to me, which I have never been able to decompose.

"This second picture represents a golden cage in the middle of a prison; an important lord in the estates of the great Mogul had already immolated several victims for the conservation of a considerable treasure buried in a nearby forest; an avid rival had immolated more, and by that means seemed to have assured himself of its possession. The important lord had recourse to me to render him the possessor of the treasure forever by placing reliable guards on it.

"I arrive, I make a tour of the forest; I go in and I acquaint myself with the locale. I summon two of my most faithful servants, in order to place them as sentinels close to the treasure, but just as they are preparing to take up their posts, an immense gulf forms in the place where the treasure was. I also received by the power of my enemy a blow similar to that of a club, and I immediately feel myself plunging with an incredible speed into the gulf, the horror of which is indescribable.

"I immediately find myself imprisoned with the Mogul lord in a golden cage, where I recall that we suffered a great deal from hunger, and where someone said to us incessantly: 'Gold is pure; it should not be obtained by corruption and crime, and above all not by bloodshed. For gold and blood are friends; one ought not to purchase one with the other, as people do every day.'

"I did not understand those words very well; I cannot tell you how long we remained in that gulf; we had no mans of making the calculation. Finally, one day, after a very agitated sleep, I woke up, able to see quite clearly, no longer imprisoned in the gulf, nor in the cage, and no longer having the Mogul lord with me, finding myself in my own country, in my own house, without ever being brought back there.

"The third emblem that you see is a cup of chocolate; it's the one I made a famous sovereign of Italy swallow, which caused the malady of which he died. For once, the science of my enemy was found wanting. But scarcely had I achieved my object than I had certain proof that he was seeking with all his might to avenge himself; and I can say that since that moment, I have not gone a single day without perceiving his stubborn pursuit.

"He has just given me a striking proof in the adventure of the book broth; that was a joke that I had employed on superior orders in order to poke a little fun at the learned academicians, in the shadow of whom I intended to advance my designs. But that terrible Jew had been cleverer than me. He perceived that I was seeking to depict for the learned academicians their illusions and their ignorance, but what I sought as well was to take them further from the truth, because, as I only reign in a zero, I do what I can to retain humans in my realm. He therefore found the means in my joke itself to extract a fruit opposite to the one I intended, since he was able to employ against me the elements of science and wisdom that were also in the liquid residue of the books, and to make the orator say true things that, thanks to my cares, had not until now been very familiar to the academicians and not commonly found in their mouths. It's thus that he never ceases to thwart me.

"All the other emblems are as many items of evidence of his obstinacy in opposing me, and if it were not for the strength of my art I would have succumbed a long time ago. I have comrades in the world who have similar complaints. I have found people in Africa who accuse him of having annihilated the power of their fetishes; our Arabs proclaim loudly that he is the greatest enemy they have ever encountered in all the enterprises of geomancy; it is the Jews above all who resent him, for the majority of those among them who are occupied with the secret sciences are so forcefully opposed that they can hardly succeed in anything any longer.

"I have even seen a famous rabbi in Venice who had been obliged to abandon entirely the occult career that he had followed for a long time with great success. It is to that rabbi that I owe the most for my advancement in the science, but he told me that nothing would be lacking in my knowledge when I had been able to join another rabbi who lives in Goa, and who was in a position to render me so knowledgeable that the crocodile himself and the powerful genius that governs him would be obliged to kiss the lance before me; and destiny, omnipotent as it is, would no longer be able to order anything against me; for I would not only preside over the horoscopes of all men, but even over the horoscope of the universe.

"Oh, if I had already been to see that rabbi of Goa, how much simpler our work today would be! How I would already have molested my enemy, and I would not even have waited until now to cause him to perish. But let us hope that we have lost nothing by waiting.

"You know, in fact, Madame, that there are not enough of the ingredients that we have employed thus far in our precious endeavors to resist that enemy; all those same ingredients will be necessary for me to resist him still, since he can combat my enterprises at every point. But as well as those ingredients, which are only defensive weapons, it is necessary for me to obtain offensive weapons in order to attack his prison directly. This is what I have prepared: a spear-head steeped in the juice of colocynth; three heads of asps infused with a decoction of tytimale;[46] five fox-spurs ripped from the living animal; the soot of a chimney in which holly and thistles have been burned; dirt from the head of a Karaite Jew which had not been combed since two quarters of the last moon; and finally, smoke from the pipe of a renegade Christian.

"Although all these ingredients are indispensable for my enterprise, I cannot obtain any advantage from them myself, and I have been obliged to employ the secrets of my art to procure me the help that I need. I have been able, by that mans, to obtain the assistance of a good friend, who will soon put everything to work for the accomplishment of my desires. That good friend is not yet well known to you, although he has often been in your presence, and it was him whose voice rendered me courage and astonished you slightly a little while ago.

"Know that the good friend in question is a powerful genius, who, like all genii, has the power to take any form he

---

[46] *Tithymalus dendroides*, nowadays more often known as *Euphorbia dendroides*, or tree spurge, used since ancient times to treat excrescences on the skin.

wishes; it was him who distinguished himself in the assembly at Cape Horn under the name of the genius of Ethiopia. Finally, since it's necessary to tell you, that genius is the same man who came to give us water in which to wash, for that preliminary of cleanliness is obligatory in the endeavors that we are undertaking. I sent the genius away for a moment in order to prepare you for his appearance in another form, for it's necessary for you to wait and see him return momentarily."

Canto 50
*Sedir sees a genius clad as a warrior,
and several other prodigies.*

"Here he is arriving," said Sedir to Eleazar. "He's clad as a warrior, holding a large saber in his right hand and two black wands in the left."

"Follow everything that happens, and give me an account of it," Eleazar replied. "This session is designed especially for your instruction. That is why I can dispense with contemplating this work in person. I'm saving myself for moments when I shall have another role to play."

"The warrior," said Sedir, "commences by saluting the tall arid man and the woman of consequence with the saber. He gives each of them one of the black wands. Now he plunges his saber into the iron vase, and comes back without the saber to the back of the cabinet. The other two do the same with their black wands, and come back in the same way. All three of them sit down together.

"Oh, Monsieur, here's a singular prodigy! I see emerging from a corner of the cabinet a multitude of vegetables of every sort, which pass close to the cast-iron vase; they're exceedingly beautiful. But out of the vase comes a swarm of worms, which leap upon the vegetables and attach themselves to them as they pass by; and I see those vegetables wither after they have passed by. I see a multitude of animals emerge in their turn from the corner of the room from which the vegetables emerged and throw themselves upon them to eat them; but then I see a large number of insects of every sort emerge from the vase and hurl themselves on the animals, tormenting them in a frightful manner.

"Finally, I see emerging from the same corner of the cabinet a lion of great beauty, which advances toward the iron vase; the three witnesses seem to have gone to sleep, and not to be seeing everything that's happening. The lion crushes the

165

worms and insects that came out of the vase with his paws; the vegetables resume their beautiful color, and the animals their tranquility. The lion takes the saber and the two wands that were in the vase; it breaks them into a thousand pieces and throws them in the fire. It comes back to the vase, which grows larger before my eyes, almost to the size of a vat, but nevertheless remains two-thirds full.

"Oh! A singular thing! The lion picks up one of the sleeping people and comes to plunge him head down into the vat. He goes to fetch the second and plunges him likewise. He does as much with the third; the three individuals have not woken up, although the lion has transported them; they aren't agitating in the vat, as I would have expected, in view of the fact that they're head down in the water—especially water that must have such a disagreeable taste and qualities."

"I'll suspend these partial prodigies momentarily," said Eleazar. "Since they're for your instruction, it's necessary to give you some clarification right away of the singular things you've just seen.

"You can presume, to begin with, that those animals and vegetables spoiled and ravaged by the insects show you the sad state in which the sciences of every kind are in, by virtue of the power of the enemy we're combating."

"Yes," cried several voices then, all at once, without anything being visible, "we're all captives in its power, awaiting our deliverance by you."

After a moment of collection, in which Eleazar and Sedir were touched to the depths of their heart. Eleazar continued, and said:

"These signs have an even more direct meaning relative to the enemy himself. They depict the number of phalanges that he trails in his retinue, and which are incessantly occupied in eating away the universal and particular bases of nature. He recruits these phalanges everywhere in the gulfs that enclose them by the order and the authority of the supreme power. He is continually searching in the Red Sea, the Asphaltite Lake,[47] and all the places on land and sea where malefactors have been engulfed, in order to withdraw the legions that have been precipitated with them, in order to make them serve for further seductions, and new engulfments for the mortals that they can win over.

"If the urgent moments in which we find ourselves left us the time to go over those great scenes in detail, I could enable to you pass in a veritable review all the phalanges with which the enemy tries to surround himself.

"You would see there not only those who were engulfed with the inhabitants of Sodom, with Pharaoh's army, with Core, Dathan and Abiron; not only those who were imprisoned in the golden calf in the rock of contradiction, in the sepulcher of concupiscence, in Jericho, in Ai and in all the cities of Canaan; but also those who were engulfed with the human race during the deluge. Finally, if it is necessary to tell all, you would see there all those who were engulfed in the entire universe and all the elements when that enemy received the price of his iniquity, which natural history indicates to us by showing us that there is not a single production on the earth that does not have its insect.

"You would see, therefore, passing in review, the phalanges that have been engulfed in water, and those that have been engulfed in fire, earth and air; that is the true meaning of the numerous insects that you have perceived. They are innumerable, the phalanges that the enemy recruits as best he can; but such is his personal weakness that he cannot operate anything very considerable in this world without having assembled them all; that is why he is so strong in movement at this moment. The power that is his opposite, by contrast, is so great that it only needs a single action to dissipate all those phalanges like dist; and that is what was indicated by the lion you saw.

---

[47] Also known as the Dead Sea.

"When we have more leisure, we'll occupy ourselves with studies of those kinds; I shall also enable you to consider and recognize the hidden correspondences of all these facts with the history of my nation; and you will see by that what the plans and designs of providence were. If we have responded so scantly to its designs, that was not an entitlement for the other nations to decry us as they have done. The entire species is degraded; divine wisdom takes humans as it finds them, and if he had manifested his will to some other people, would any more of them have been faithful to it?

"As for the three sleeping individuals who did not wake up when the lion brought them from their place, and did not even react on being plunged into muddy water, they depict for you the degree of blindness of those who deliver themselves to the false sciences; since, in the midst of their most illusory magic, it seems to them that they are in their natural state; and since, in the midst of the dangers most appropriate to give them certain death, they sleep in security. In any case, these scenes, which only have you for an object, have in fact only happened for you, and nothing has changed in the cabinet, of everything that you have previously seen. Look into the flame of the cradle to convince yourself.

"Indeed," said Sedir, "everything appears to me to be in the same condition as before: the animals, the vegetables, the lion, and the insects have all disappeared; the vase is what it was, and the three individuals are sitting on their chairs."

"Listen attentively," said Eleazar. "The warrior is going to speak to the arid man."

Sedir obeyed, and copied what he heard.

Canto 51
The warrior's maneuvers against Eleazar.

"I have thrown into a drain in the Rue Montmartre all the drugs that you made me assemble for our enterprise against Eleazar. That drain passes close to his house, and I have no doubt that, by means of the conjurations I have combined with those ingredients, the house will blow up before long; but to ensure the success of our great project, this is what we need to do, in order to attack the life of our adversary radically. My saber and the two wands are sufficiently infused in the water of that vase to have brought it to the necessary point of corruption. We now need to throw as many fiery coals into it as there are letters in our enemy's name; that is the blow that he will be unable to resist. Take out your wands, as I shall take out my saber, and follow me in all the steps I am going to take."

"I see the warrior," said Sedir, "taking his saber and waking to the fireplace. The other two take their wands and follow him. He picks up a hot coal on the end of his saber and comes to throw it into the water of the vase. He returns to the fireplace for a second time and picks up a second coal on the end of his saber, which he brings again to the water of the vase. He does the same a third time. His two companions always follow him, and do so seven times. Every time an ember is thrown into the water it causes a vigorous tremor in the vase, but at the seventh coal the quivering is so forceful that the three companions appear to enjoy it greatly."

"Now," said the warrior, "we can regard ourselves as being sure of having won the victory, and we can have the crocodile come himself in order to devour Eleazar's remains—and he will make him disappear so completely that no one will ever find his cadaver or trace the source of the cause of his death; for have no doubt that he has just expired."

"Monsieur," said Sedir, "I can see that you are quite well, in spite of the conviction they have that you are dead, and I sense that we shall no longer have to fear the appearance of the crocodile."

"I like to see you devoid of anxiety," replied Eleazar. "In fact, the wisdom that watches over you and over me, is founded on a fixed and unbreakable plan, so it is a thousand times more stable than the regular solids, which cannot lose their aplomb since they rest on one of their faces. That is why no more harm with come to us from this second attempt than came to me from the first."

Canto 52
The failed appearance of the crocodile.

He had no sooner proffered that last remark than Sedir exclaimed: "I hear it, I hear it coming. Finally, we're going to reckon with it."

"Yes," Eleazar replied, "and to prove to you that we have nothing to fear, and that I can dispose of this particular event according to my will, I warn you that the crocodile will not show itself, and that you will only hear it speak. Continue to be attentive, and render me an account of everything you observe, in order that I can direct myself in consequence."

(And I, dear reader, will tell you independently the means that were in Eleazar's power: a benevolent hand linked to the Society of Independents, caused to pass invisibly to that worthy and courageous Israelite an active and supramaterial ingredient that corresponds in the natural order to the spirit of saffron.)

Sedir went on: "The three individuals seem very impatient and very anxious at not seeing the crocodile appear; now they are each swallowing a pinch of ash, and now they are twirling like dervishes, and then they appear to be listening very attentively.

"'I am the croc... croc... croc...crocodile... that you have su... su... summoned. I cannot sh... sh... sh... show myself; there is someone who is pre... pre... pre... preventing me; I am even having diff... diff... diff... difficulty mo... mo... mo... moving my tongue. I have ma... ma... ma... ma... many things to tell you; I cannot re... re... re... reach the end of them. Goo... goo... goo... goodbye.'"

(Dear reader, I have no need to call your attention to the power that is thus opposed to the crocodile giving voice to

171

everything that it has to tell you. I sense, however, that it will sadden you not to know yet what has become of that crocodile, and to be so close to learning it from its own mouth, only to see your hopes immediately dashed. But if the invention of the painter who covered Agamemnon's face with a veil has been praised, why criticize me for also putting a veil over the face of my crocodile? One is as difficult to paint as the other. Nevertheless, in order that you will not accuse me of cutting the Gordian knot instead of untying it, you shall soon be able to learn what you desire, and you will owe me one obligation more, for having had it related to you by a mouth less frightening than the maw of a crocodile.)

The crocodile, in saying goodbye to the three associates, caused a wind to blow that extinguished the fire in the hearth, and Sedir saw nothing more; the crocodile also spread an odor that infected the three associates. It imparted such a shock to the house that it was partly collapsed, and two of the associates, who found themselves buried under the debris, had a great deal of difficulty getting themselves out of that perilous situation. As for the third, which was the genius transformed into a human, it was not formed of a substance that could be retained under material debris, and it disappeared immediately, leaving its two companions in difficulty.

A fount of black and muddy water also sprang from the subterrains of the house, which never dried up thereafter, and which rendered the house uninhabitable by virtue of the insupportable odors that emanated from the water.

When that magical image, which as only a representation of what was really happening in the house in the Rue Montmartre, came to an end, Sedir wanted to fathom the marvels that had just been offered to his eyes, and Eleazar gave him rapidly the instruction that circumstances permitted, on all those objects.

Madame Jof also presented to the Society of Independents at the same time a depiction related to the incommensurable superior power that preserves mortals from the fury of their enemy on a daily basis, while they do not even perceive it, and pay no more attention to it that children do to all the protections of their nurses. She explained that the tender surveillance of that supreme power was so continuous, and the dangers so great, that humans would shiver simultaneously with fear and gratitude if their eyes were opened for an instant to the situation of the human species in this base world.

But that is the whole of the extract what we have of that conference for the present, and we are truly afflicted, for we would much rather nourish humans amply with all these great verities, which ought to be their natural and daily aliment, than accompany them as we do in paths so broken and so thorny. But events too vast summon us out of the enclosure of our three malefactors, in order to devote ourselves to a moment of reflection.

Rise up, then, my Muse, expose to the world's eye
That which your proven science can supply;
Take my spirit all the way to the Inferno's lair;
You can carry it afterwards into the air
To those various lands, with your bravery's aid
And the confident hope of a journey well made.

Canto 53
The unexpected arrival of a traveler via the gutter of the Rue Montmartre.

Near the drain of the Rue Montmartre, not far from Eleazar's house, a subterranean noise was heard, like that of a rolling chariot. The violent shocks of earthquakes were felt, which agitated the entire quarter horribly. The winds blew; the animals bellowed; the sky was even seen to darken over the whole extent of the horizon, and people thought they remarked strange bodies in the air, launched upwards with great force. In sum, everything appeared to be in convulsion, when a muddy stream was suddenly seen to emerge from the drain, and a man in a green coat, who was swimming in the stream to reach solid ground.

All eyes were fixed on that green man. As soon as he had emerged from the water, everyone surrounded him.

"Oh! It's the volunteer Ourdeck!" said someone who recognized him.

They pressed around him even more closely, and asked him where he had come from.

"I've come from the army," he replied, curtly, and they could not get another word out of him.

The unfortunate was so wet, so dirty and so hungry that his silence was perfectly forgivable, having so many pressing needs to satisfy. It is true that a few friends hastened to dry him off, to clean him, and even to lend him clothes—but how were they to assuage his hunger?

That did not prevent curiosity choking all sentiments of compassion in the people; they crowded around him, took possession of him and tried to force him to render an exact account of his journey since the disappearance of the two armies. As there is always, however, in all great tumults, one cool head that recalls the others to common sense and reason, a man advanced into the midst of the people and harangued them.

"Dear fellow citizens, companions of my misery, who render it less harsh to me since I share it with you, I experience, as you do, an urgent desire to know what you are asking of this unfortunate man with so much insistence; but even so, if he were to tell you now all that you desire; it would then be necessary for him to start all over again before the leaders who have your confidence, and are surely at least as interested as you to hear what he has to say. Now, judge from that state in which you see him whether it will be possible for him to fulfill such a task several times. I believe, therefore, unless you have a better idea, that it would be best if we went with him to the house of the respectable Sedir, and that we all listen together to what he has to say."

"He's right," said someone in the troop—and the others repeated after him: "He's right."

They took the new arrival to the house of the Lieutenant de Police—who was surprised by the visit, inasmuch as Eleazar had given him no warning of it. A number of curious people came in haste to hear the voyager, for the news of his arrival had spread.

Even the sensible but curious Rachel, agitated by the explosion of the drain in the Rue Montmartre, attracted by the news that was running around, and anxious for her father, had also set forth to find out what was happening, and to give everyone, to the extent that she could, words of encouragement and felicitation, as the occasion required.

"Let us yield to the desire of these people," said Eleazar to Sedir. "They cherish you; they know that it is impossible for you to procure them subsistence, and the adventure of the moment serves to distract them from their needs. I have contributed more than you think to the arrival of this volunteer, who must inform you of things little known, and I will contribute with all my power to the events that might follow, but I do not want to flatter you in advance; peace and abundance will not be reborn in Paris until three people have been stopped. It is time to make them known. I also warn you that the captive sciences will not recover their liberty until the crocodile himself is entirely deprived of his means to do harm. Don't ask me why these fortunate events are not accelerating faster. The great wisdom leaves all these good and evil powers the time and the liberty each to fulfill their measure, in order to lead matter to repentance even more than to judgment.

"For the moment, have as many people as possible gather in the nearby square, and put the voyager in the middle of them; I will have him take a pinch of my saline powder, which will sustain him during his story. As for me, while he acquits his function thus, I shall withdraw in order to follow mine, which is becoming more urgent with every passing minute. I know all that he has to say, and I need to devote myself entirely to my work. When he stops talking, you and I will come together again."

Sedir did exactly what Eleazar said, and the voyager Ourdeck, after having put a little of the salt on his tongue, spoke to the assembled people, among whom there were a few Academicians, hoping to learn from this new historian a few things more in conformity with their doctrine that those they had learned from the crocodile.

Canto 54
The volunteer Ourdeck's story.

"You see before you, dear fellow citizens, the faithful volunteer Ourdeck, who, naturalized among you, thought it his duty to lend you the assistance of his arm in the combats that are taking place in the various quarters of Paris. Although our first efforts have not had all the success I could have desired, you know that our arms ended up by being more fortunate, and that we were promised a complete victory. I had reason to believe that, after an extraordinary event that had changed my somewhat incredulous ideas. In that hope, I followed the combatants to the Plaine des Sablons, especially having had the good fortune to see Roson's sword fall before me. But there I was swallowed, with the two armies, by a monster the vastness of which I cannot express to you.

"First, we experienced a frightful shock, and we all found ourselves piled up pell-mell, as many people as weapons, and the earth that the monster had swallowed.

"In the first moment, we were plunged into a profound obscurity, but after a while, either because the monster had ventilation shafts at intervals or because an illumination was affected in the darkness that made it possible to habituate oneself even to that frightful abode, we began to perceive a few glimmers, and soon had sufficient light to be able to discern the objects that surrounded us—above all, the various organs and viscera of the monster that had swallowed us without digesting us. I remarked with surprise that the viscera and interior organs of the animal each bore an inscription in which one saw the name of one of the genii that had figured in the narrative of Cape Horn, which caused me to suspect what kind of place and company I found myself in.

"I was even more convinced of that when I felt myself pulled in all directions and in all the aspects of my existence by all the various powers attached to the names that covered

177

the monster's interior. Everything that constitutes that being, and all the ingredients that compose it, must be in a state of continual separation and dissolution, since the frightful sentiment of a similar separation and a similar dissolution was operating on my own elements. Such is the terrible impression that one experiences at first on entering into the monster; it never ceased as long as I remained there, and if I never lost my life there, it must be because a superior power extended a protective hand over our mortal bodies.

"Soon we were stripped of our garments and they were replaced by extremely tight coats of a cloth whose coarseness is unimaginable; and all those coats were marked with the stamp of one of those genii. That done, the two armies received orders to march, one before the other, without their being permitted to approach one another. The army of the good Frenchmen brought up the rear, and seemed to be chasing the other before it, as if in consequence of the victory we had already won on the plain. We even had an extreme ardor to continue the battle and to measure ourselves hand-to-hand, but the animal's power seemed to want to make us suffer by means of our very anger, by compressing it, and not giving it any outlet.

"After nine stations in different viscera of the animal, it was as if I were dragged with the two armies into a great gulf, which I assumed, with reason, to be the lower abdomen of the monster, the capacity of which seemed to extend all the way to the end of its tail. Soon, we were surprised to learn of a tradition that reigned in that abyss, which is that the tail itself was bolted to the subterrain of an Egyptian pyramid, unable to detach itself whatever efforts it made, but that the body of the animal had the power to extend itself at will to any part of the world. Once, I would never have believed everything I had just seen and all that I saw, even if a thousand witnesses had sworn to it, so I do not flatter myself, Messieurs, that you will believe my story, but you wanted to hear it and I am responding to your desire."

At that beginning, there were a thousand handclaps, and a thousand cries; that was, in fact, what it crocodile had said itself.

Canto 54
Continuation of Ourdeck's story.
Entry of the armies into the crocodile's depths.

"On entering that gulf, or into the lower abdomen of the animal, which was illuminated like the rest of its body by a light that you might call gloomy, I found it filled with living beings, men and women of all nations and professions. Although alive, all those beings were not palpable like us; they only had the form of beings, and not the substance. Although we were alive corporeally, however, we did not experience any hunger, because all our digestive faculties were suspended.

"The men and women of various nations were divided into families, or little particular societies, and although we were more material than that new species of humans, we were nevertheless attached to their various societies; in an instant, the individuals of the two armies were distributed between those various impalpable families. That distribution was made, not only in accordance with the various professions or habits that we had previously had on earth, but also in accordance with the signs that the genii had attached to us, because we were only placed in the families that were ruled by the same genius as us.

As a traveler in the North and by the nature of my sign, I fell into a Tartar family that had been attached to the new doctrine of Fo. The goal of the genii, in distributing us thus, was to try to extract from us, by means of those with whom they associated us, all the secrets they could, either in politics, in nature or in the sciences.

"So the members of the Tartar family with which I was linked neglected nothing to make me talk, and the genius who governed them, and me, never ceased to press them in that regard. But in the situation in which I found myself, convinced as I was that that class of beings only had evil designs, I did not open my mouth, and I would not have opened it even if I had had more things to tell them than I really had.

"Our genius, perceiving my resistance, wanted to take charge of questioning me itself, and it began by threatening me with all its rigor if I did not satisfy it. Seeing that I was holding firm, it said to me: 'See how the other genii are treating your companions, who have surely not been as recalcitrant as you.'

"In fact, I saw how they were being maltreated in order to make them talk. It seemed to me that the same torments were being exercised on them that the malefactors of our world sometimes exercise on the unfortunate to make them confess where they have hidden their money.

"'Will you tell me,' said one genius to my sad companions in misfortune, 'how to make gold?'

"'Will you tell me,' said another, 'the present state of the political cabinets of Europe?'

"'Will you tell me,' said a third, 'what the secret is of the astonishing property of the magnet?'

"And then they redoubled the tortures, as my companions were obstinate in maintaining silence, either because they did not want to talk, or because they had nothing to say.

"When the genius who was questioning me had seen that, in spite of that horrible spectacle, I persisted in remaining mute, it got ready to treat me like my companions; it was then that the striking words of a person who is unknown to you returned to my mind. That memory reanimated my confidence, my confidence reanimated my courage, and I directed a gaze at the genius so proud and so imposing that it calmed down, and did not question me any further; I only heard a few words that it muttered covertly, and which seemed to say that if they only encountered people as stubborn as me, they would never learn anything about what was happening in the world, and would not know how to govern it..

"I understood by that how important it is to be on one's guard when one devotes oneself to a career in the sciences, since, by virtue of the envy and exactions to which it exposes us on the part of those malevolent genii, one might become one day, through weakness, a contributor to iniquity, as scholars often are down here through their self-esteem; for, even without talking, scientists, by their pride alone, must open the door within them to those evil genii, and communicate a part of their science to them.

Canto 56
Continuation of Ourdeck's story.
The Tartar woman.

"Finding myself less obsessed, and as free as I could be in such a place, I struck up a conversation with a Tartar woman who appeared to me to be the least wicked in the family to which I was attached. She had taken an interest in me, and, seeing that I had resisted the genius, especially when she knew that I had traveled through her country, on my way to China in the capacity of secretary to the ambassador, she spoke to me in a manner far less abrupt than the others. This is a summary of what I learned from her.

"'I came here, she told me, 'several centuries before the time when Confucius lived; it is from our family that the Tartar dynasty descends that was the first to overthrow the Chinese throne. Destiny punished us in advance, because it knew the spirit of ambition and cupidity that we transmitted to our descendants; it even perceived that for as long as we had existed on the earth, we had been so restless and so inconvenient for our neighbors that we could not live in peace with any of them. So, in the middle of a revolt that we provoked, in order to take possession of a country adjacent to ours, we all perished and were transferred here, to stay here for as long as it pleases the powerful destiny that masters us, and from which we cannot defend ourselves. Not that, as a woman, I was able to act very forcefully in that evolution, but I shared the fate of my family, and find myself condemned with them, for not having held them back as much as I could.

"'All the other families you perceive here are, like ours, under the yoke of the same power that masters us, and makes use of us to torment one another, for it often happens that we have rude combats with one another, in which we do more harm, and strike blows more cruel, than material bodies can inflict on one another.

"'You see in front of you the Chinese family whose throne ours overturned, and since that moment, we have always been in a state of war, all the more frightful because, although we can strike one another and cover one another with wounds, we can never die. Further away you can see the family of Agamemnon and that of the unfortunate Priam. Over there is the family of Caesar, and facing it, that of Pompey, which are likewise continually at odds. In the other direction are the families of Augustus and Antony, and between the two of them the beautiful Cleopatra, to serve them continuously as an apple of discord.

(You will not be surprised, dear reader, that all these historic recitations, and all those of a similar sort that might have followed, bored a large fraction of the audience, who did not understand them, and the assembly thinned out somewhat.)

"'You see in that dip the families of Alexander and Darius, Marius and Sulla, Shapur and Valerian, Ali and Omar, Bajazet and Tamerlane, York and Lancaster, Orléans and Armagnac, and, finally, those of Fiesque and Doria, Stuart and Orange, Pizarro and Atahualpa, Charles XII and Patkul, and a quantity of other illustrious enemies who devoured one another on earth. Here, all the families are always in opposition to one another, as they were in your world, in order that the tableau of their passions should never be effaced.

"'Destiny deposits here, in accordance with the same law, all the other famous adversaries that have disputed on earth for ambitions other than conquests. Scholars, learned men, and zealous fanatics of religions are all in dispute with one another here, and their fury even surpasses that of the former conquerors and usurpers. All those who arrive here are immediately put to the question, in order to extract all the knowledge and enlightenment that they might have, as you have seen your companions questioned, and preparations being made to question you; and my family and I have suffered that like all the rest—but the questioning is even harder for us than for those who still have their material bodies, because the blows that we endure strike us in the quick.

"'Another unfortunate consequence of our destiny, when we have merited coming into these abysms, is that, being more intimately linked to the monster by our death than living people are, we do not have, as you had, the power to resist him for long, and he always ends up extracting all our secrets. Finally, what ensures that he gains more from us is that, by virtue of our deaths, our knowledge develops far more than it did during mortal life, and that is what the monster accumulates carefully and daily, in order to be able to glorify itself on earth thereafter, with those stolen goods, to rule the world, and dazzle and lead astray unfortunate mortals.

"'That is also why, when it no longer finds new enlightenment to extract from us, and the living people on your earth are too recalcitrant or too prudent to lend themselves to its designs, it stirs up troubles, wars and diseases, or even occasions violent catastrophes in nature that take the lives of a number of mortals, and precipitate them down here, where the monster rapidly seeks to exert upon them the thirst and ardor it has to acquire knowledge—all the more so because, its memory beings unreliable, it can make no use of its knowledge, and always has to begin again; which is the true source of the proverb that says that there is never any profit in stolen goods.

"'I cannot tell you how deep these abysms that we inhabit are; no one can travel them because each family is condemned to remain in its enclosure with the adverse family. All that we know is that in the utmost of these depths reside those humans who, on earth, made a profession of iniquitous sciences and perverse magic, by which the rendered themselves ministers of the monster, which holds them now in chains even tighter than ours; and that is the recompense of its disciples, It is said that sometimes, one of those unfortunates escapes that imprisonment and comes to augment the disorder of ours, but during my sojourn here I have not yet seen an example.

"'As for other mortals, all that we know is that as new families arrive here from the earth above, these abysms expand proportionately, so that we have no reason to believe that they can ever be filled and that room would be lacking to imprison malefactors.

"'As the same spirit that governed all the different families that you see still governs those that are on earth, and will govern them until the end of time, all the agitations that it occasions among humans will be felt even by us, all in accordance with the laws of correspondence and similitude; no evil occurs up above to which we are not linked, and from which we do not suffer a thousand times more than humans who are still mortal.

"'It must be the case that the evils that have caused you to descend here are very great, for we have never suffered as much for a long time; all Hell seems to have been unleashed; ardent fires appear to have been lit everywhere, and threaten at every moment to devour us with their heat; we have experienced extraordinary shocks; we are struck by a thousand thrusts; all these abysms have trembled, and in that chaos we thought for a moment that all these caverns were about to split and that we were going to recover our liberty, or that the world was about to end. We heard nothing but howls and imprecations; we heard names uttered that were unknown to us, among which there was one that seemed to have an absolute empire over these sad regions and over the one who directs them.

Canto 57
Continuation of Ourdeck's story.
The Tartar woman's confidences.

"'If I were sure,' she told me, looking at me intently, 'that you would keep my secret, and would not expose me to all the corrections that my indiscretion might provoke, I would tell you by what means, independently of the natural correspondences that your world has with this one, the animal that keeps us imprisoned maintains relations with the whole world, and governs all cabinets, all politics and all the authorities on earth.'

"'Oh, count on me,' I swore, hastily. 'I've never repaid a kindness with a treason.'

"'If you were not as good as you appear to me to be,' she replied, 'I would not have been able, since I have been here, to confide a secret to a corporeally living being, for of all the warriors the monster has swallowed since I have been here, whether those of the army of Cambyses or those of a thousand other troops on land and sea, you are the first ones who, to my knowledge, have descended alive; all the others suffocated here. I am therefore tempted to take advantage of the opportunity; in any case, my indiscretion, if it is one, will be mitigated by the fact that you will only have to look, and I will not have to say anything. Remember, in addition, that the images under which objects will be depicted to you are adapted to be proportionate to your manner of being, and that it is given to us to see things more intimately.'

"Then she made me approach an indentation that was only separated from her by one of the animal's membranes, transparent enough to allow me to see through it what was happening in that redoubt.

"In accordance with comparative anatomy, that redoubt appeared to me to correspond to what is called in humans the bile duct, and it bore for an inscription the name of the genius

187

of sulfur. I perceived several niches therein, on one side, each containing a statue. Those statues were all crippled or mutilated, and were also wrapped in chains. Above each niche was written the name of a science, such as metaphysics, politics, physics, etc., and beneath each of the niches there was one of those poultry cages in which birds are enclosed to fatten them, but instead of birds, I saw in the different cages as many human figures, slightly pale but swollen in the abdomen.

"An intelligence was opened up to me, and I learned that those various figures represented those of the false scholars of the earth, who blindly and proudly nourished themselves on all those mutilated sciences, with which they deceived people; that the sciences, which had long ago lost their principle of life, had remained under the hand of the master of that menagerie, who only employed them for perfidious and destructive ends; that the master retained those partisans of the truncated sciences in his menagerie in that fashion until he had fattened them and judged it appropriate to cut their throats for the service of his table; and that in the meantime, it is by means of the knowledge that he extracts from them that he corresponds with all the scientific societies in the world.

"I then perceived on the opposite side a great harpsichord, each key of which was marked with a different character, one representing a lizard, another a toad, another a flaming thunderbolt, and all kinds of objects such as stars, planets and comets. An invisible hand was incessantly playing those keys and drawing sounds therefrom of such discord and disharmony that my ears were tortured, and I presumed that the world must be suffering by means of parallel correspondences.

"I saw in that same redoubt three individuals seated around a table, playing triumphantly with cards, which, instead of the usual designs, depicted the various kingdoms, sovereignties and other establishments of the entire earth; the hazards of their game were what regulated the fate of the sovereignties of this world, and as the game never ended, and the vagaries of chance were continual, I understood the origin of the perpetual upheavals of the empires of the world.

"Alongside those three individuals I saw several others occupied in receiving letters and sending others in response, so promptly that my eye could scarcely follow the rapid movement. However, I was able to read, surreptitiously, two or three of the addresses while they were being written: one in Tartar, to the High Lama; one in French, in the name, unknown to me, of a woman of consequence in Paris; one in German, to the University of Groningen;[48] and one in Latin, to the diet of Ratisbon.[49]

"Given what the Tartar woman had already revealed to me, I no longer had any doubt that this was the general bureau from which the advice and instructions departed that regulated the world; and I had the proof that the animal that had swallowed us did indeed have relations with the world that could not be counted, and that it must be very well informed of what was happening there.

"However, I would have had difficulty believing that nothing was lacking in its knowledge of that sort, and that the instructions it was sending always infallibly fulfilled its designs. In fact, I saw some of the letters, whether departing or arriving, shrivel in mid-air and disappear in a puff of smoke—which proved to me that there must be lacunae in the commerce of the animal with the world.

"Satisfied with what I had just learned, I drew nearer to the woman who had put me on the track, and renewed the assurances of my discretion.

---

[48] The mathematician Johann Bernouilli (1667-1748), who played a leading role in the development of the infinitesimal calculus was the professor of mathematics at the University of Groningen during the later years of his life.

[49] The Perpetual Diet of Regensburg [Ratisbon in French] was the rather ineffectual parliament of the Holy Roman Empire.

Canto 58
Continuation of Ourdeck's story.
Depiction of correspondence.

"But Messieurs, scarcely had we renewed our conversation than we were deflected by a spectacle that we could not understand, and to which you might perhaps have the key, as well as that of all the enigmas I've just reported to you.

"Know, then, that at that moment, we saw an immense cauldron appear, a short distance away from us. After having considered it for a few moments, we waited to see what usage might be made of it, what was going to be put into it and how firewood was going to be placed underneath it, since it was set on the ground. Soon, we saw and heard falling into it, without our being able to see where they were coming from, books of every size and every species of writing, which piled up pell-mell in the cauldron, until it was full.

"Instead of the fire that we expected to see lit, we saw several pale stars pass over the cauldron, mat white in hue. The atmosphere became colder than before, and laden with dense vapors; and in a short time we saw those books fall into liquefaction; and to hasten the dissolution further, several women appeared around the cauldron with long rods, with which they stirred and swirled the books in all directions, until they were reduced to a soft paste, like that of veritable broth.

"When that was done, the scene changed and offered us a singular picture: the same women who had just worked on the liquefaction of the books suddenly appeared sitting down, each having a large swaddled baby in her lap; then they drew the broth from the cauldron with a spoon, and gave it abundantly to each of their nurslings."

At this point the Academicians that were present could not help frowning, and the people smiling a little—and the reader will recall the reason, although the orator was not party to the secret of the prodigy he had seen.

"When that extraordinary meal was finished, every-thing—the cauldron, the women and the nurslings—disappeared; the air resumed its ordinary temperature, and there were no longer any traces of what had just happened, except that we heard several loud bursts of laughter.

"I asked the Tartar woman if she could explain the meaning of that prodigy to me, but she said that she had never seen anything like it before, that she did not understand it at all, and that it was probably on earth that the explanation would be obtained.

Canto 59
Continuation of Ourdeck's story.
Commotions in the crocodile's depths.

"That unfortunate and obliging woman had spoken only too truly in telling me about the commotions that occurred from time to time in that somber abode, and it was not long before I had proof of it. I saw various troops of people arriving, who had just died in various parts of the world. As they descended, they were placed among the different groups that filled the various distributions of the subterrains, and they were immediately put to the question in order to extract from them everything they might know relative to the world they had just quit. I cannot describe to you the frightful contortions that I saw them make, which informed me of the excess of the tortures inflicted upon them. For although the majority of them recounted everything they knew, and even what they didn't know, in order to obtain relief, they were tormented nonetheless, because, in the place where lies alone are dominant, they were still suspected either of lying or of not telling everything that they knew.

"In the midst of those scenes of horror, I saw an old man advancing who had arrived from your world, where he had just died. He said loudly to those who were getting ready to put him to the question; 'There is no need for you to use violence to make me speak; I shall tell you willingly something that will surprise you, which is that I learned on earth, shortly before quitting it, that all the people worthy of mercy who are here will soon be liberated; and that, shortly thereafter, the sciences will also recover their liberty, because the mold of time will be broken, and the empire of the evil genii will be abolished.'

"At those words, all the evil genii were inflamed; not only did they martyrize the unfortunate old man, but they spread the word to exercise new furies on all the shades and the other beings that were in their power, and instantly, everything was in combustion in the abysms, because a quantity of shades filled with hope defended themselves all the more ardently against their torturers, and the other shades only sought to take the side of their masters. So I shall not attempt to depict for you the frightful commotions that I witnessed.

"They were further augmented by the desire that gripped the evil genii, in such an urgent matter, to consult the iniquitous magicians who were detained in the utmost depths of the abysms and, at the same time, to summon them as reinforcements, in order to contain the rebel shades more easily.

"In fact, those utmost depths that the Tartar woman had mentioned to me must have opened up at that moment, and some of the iniquitous magicians that she had told me were detained within emerged, for I saw emerging into the chaos by which we were surrounded individuals even more frightening than the others, and a thousand times more redoubtable, since it was a real fire that emerged from the hands of one, the feet of another and the whole surface of another's head. They crossed the entire battlefield with an inconceivable rapidity and fury; they shouted barbaric names unknown to me, and everything they touched burned immediately with the real fire with which they were burning themselves without being consumed.

"All those horrible scenes soon became so confused that I could no longer distinguish either forms or faces in everything that surrounded me. My eyes sought in vain the excellent Tartar woman to whose family I belonged, and in the fortune of whom I was intensely interested. Everything seemed to me to be a single mass of fire, extending entirely from one side of the abysms to the other, almost at the same moment, and everything caused me to dread that a conflagration might at any moment reduce to ashes the enclosure formed by those abysms, along with the poor mortals who were imprisoned there, and who were not as impalpable as the shades. I tried to recall the good advice given to me by the same person that you do not know, but whose memory had been so useful to me

193

in that horrible abode, and who had even announced the voyage that I was going to make.

"So, fate protected me in a signal manner in the midst of those fatal catastrophes. It determined that, by the effect of those powerful commotions, I found myself placed at the orifice of a capillary vessel of the monster that had swallowed us all; I took advantage of the opportunity; I entered into the capillary vessel, and moved therein at my ease for a time that appeared to me to be very long, although it was impossible in that dark place to measure its duration because, in spite of the gloomy light that reigned there, there was no daybreak or sunset there.

"I found a mild and refreshing temperature there, by comparison with the place I had just quit; I even felt that I was being naturally stripped of the new and inconvenient clothes that we had all been given, and that my own garments were extended over me. As for the two armies, I know absolutely nothing about the fate to which they were subjected in that shock, and it is very painful for me to have nothing to tell you about them.

"Finally, I arrived at the external extremity of the capillary vessel that had been so salutary for me, and it opened into opened into a great subterrain where I had occasion to make observations worthy of attention, which concluded with an earthquake to which I owe my salvation."

At this point Ourdeck fell silent; but then a voice was heard above the assembly, and said: "It is not from his mouth that you will hear the things worthy of attention that he has announced to you. You will learn them from the psychograph."

Canto 60
Temporary subsistence procured by Eleazar.

No one knew what the psychograph was, but Ourdeck's nearest neighbors, all talking at the same time, hastened to tell him briefly what had happened in Paris while he was absent, and it was not without surprise that he heard mention of the crocodile's scientific lesson, the broth of books, the report to the Academy, and above all, the particular gifts with which Eleazar was provided, and which had already been so useful to him.

What he heard only augmented the desire he had to go and throw his arms around that good Israelite; he also wanted to fly to Rachel, whom he recognized, by virtue of having addressed a few words to her in passing in the Rue Montmartre, and who was pointed out to him as being a worthy support of her father Eleazar in all his enterprises, and who was, in fact, occupied in giving various people a few good ideas on the subject of what they had just heard.

But the assembly did not give him the time to follow the penchant that pressed him. As it had listened to a rather long speech, during which it had had a distraction of sorts from its devouring need, the horrible hunger renewed in that interval, resumed al its assaults. Soon, nothing was heard but cries and wailing. A few of the starving fell to the ground, others wandered hither and yon, in accordance with their strength; nothing was to be seen but groups forming, breaking up, and forming again, offering everywhere the image of dolor and confusion.

Those unfortunates would have succumbed momentarily if the powerful Eleazar, suspending his own labor, had not extended to them the salutary aid of which his hidden means were the source. Alas, he could not do for all the members of the audience what he had done for the orator—which is to say, give each of them a pinch of his saline powder—because, even supposing that it had the property of not diminishing, and of sufficing for that multitude, it would have consumed a considerable time to make a tour of the whole assembly.

He preferred a quicker means, but which, in truth, was inferior in its efficacy; it was to throw a pinch, of the saline powder on the ground, taking the precaution to disperse it as much as possible.

Scarcely had he made that aspersion of sorts than everyone saw emerge at his feet something akin to clumps of verdure, which even seemed, here and there, to form a few ears. In any other circumstances, surprise and admiration would have been the only impressions that the extraordinary event would have occasioned, but in the state of starvation in which the assembly found itself, the avidity of a devouring hunger was the only effect that resulted therefrom in the audience, and they all hurled themselves furiously on those unexpected foodstuffs.

In an instant, all the verdure was grazed, and the need that had surely not yet been calmed by that initial refection continued to make itself felt with more ardor.

It is thus that a penchant far more dangerous
Only at first becomes more clamorous
If a few temptations excite remorse;
A force always attracts another force.

Canto 61
A supernatural event.
The armies emerge from their abysms.

At least an unexpected marvel came to distract them from their suffering momentarily; and for that marvel, valorous Ourdeck, you were surely not prepared—but you were made for surprising adventures. It is therefore necessary to know that a bright star was suddenly seen to appear above the assembly, and a soft and silvery voice emerged from the middle of that star, which spoke these consoling words:

"I am the Tartar woman with whom Ourdeck was occupied as he emerged from the monster; that simple interior impulse on his part has procured my deliverance; I am free, along with all my family, and we want henceforth, to the extent that is permitted to us, to collaborate with all our power in the defense of his adopted fatherland, out of gratitude for him.

"I also know that a number of other families have been drawn forth by our atmosphere, and that in extracting us from our prison, our attraction has also allowed them to recover their liberty; such a benefit and good desire are fecund and engender innumerable fruits! Those families have spread out over various regions, where they will bring about good effects, as my family and I intend to bring about in this country; and it is Ourdeck's desire that will have produced all those good things.

"Only those who were retained in the utmost depths of the monster's body remain within it, having attained the ultimate degree of crime on earth, and being unable to be delivered by human desires. I have still to tell you that the two armies have also emerged from their abysms, and are presently breathing the open air, but I am not permitted to tell you any more about their fate."

The voice fell silent, and the star disappeared.

A spectacle so extraordinary, so new and so unexpected, and such a reassuring, albeit brief, word about the two armies, was sufficient to astonish the listeners and transport them with joy. Alas, it was necessary for them to pay for that joy, since there is no happiness for mortals that is not purchased. It is therefore not surprising that the temporary aid of the light verdure, which had restored the assembly for a few moments, had put the city in motion.

In fact, as soon as the first rumors spread, a crowd was seen flooding from all directions much larger than the one that had run after Ourdeck, and in that number it is necessary to count those who, having gone away because they were bored, came back hurriedly in the hope of finding some nourishment. On the other hand, those who were already occupying the place, and who had tasted the salutary aliment, did not want to be dispossessed.

Here, the same spirit that had occasioned the revolt and all the catastrophes that we have seen, was reanimated in strength, to exact a dear payment for Eleazar's benefit, and although there were no longer any armies in Paris, there were nevertheless on the terrain of the auditorium as many enemies as individuals—which is to say, as many as the square could contain.

There were no longer, it is true, the fully armed warriors who had distinguished themselves so much in the wheat-marker; military forms and methods were set aside, and were replaced by less distinguished but equally imposing means of doing battle. In addition, powers more than human, but blind and malevolent, had no hesitation in joining the combat, for dark clouds were seen in the air from which flaming darts emerged that were launched indiscriminately upon all the combatants on both sides, knocking them down and causing them to suffer greatly, in anticipation of the imminent death that they did not give them.

But who can doubt that the man from Egypt, the woman of consequence who employed him and the crocodile that employed both of them were the principal motive forces and the primary agents of that new disaster, as they were of all those that Paris had suffered since the beginning of the revolt, above all since the failure of their last enterprise against Eleazar.

Canto 62
Eleazar opposes himself manifestly to the Parisians' invisible enemies.

It was then that the great power and the great virtue of the Israelite was mobilized; for in the affliction caused to him by the unfortunate people that he had before his eyes, he felt a vivid indignation ignite against the aerial enemies that occasioned so many ravages. He launched himself into the middle of the square, took out his box again, and took out three pinches of his powder, which he threw into the air one after another, each time proffering menacing words that history has not preserved for us.

What history has conserved for us, however, is that at each of those words, Rachel was lifted into the air, and directed her eyes skywards with the keenest ardor; and also that each of those words and demonstrations of the most ardent faith, calm was reestablished, and the aerial enemies disappeared, not without murmuring further threats; the verdure was reborn, and the people were able to take a light meal without being exposed to the risk of perishing under his adversaries' weapons.

Ourdeck, pressed by the crowd and struck by those prodigies, still trying to get closer to Rachel and Eleazar, and also incessantly remembering Madame Jof, was agitated by a thousand diverse sentiments. How is it that the most splendid marvels exist in such close proximity to human beings and yet remain so profoundly hidden from them?

At the very moment when Eleazar deployed his powers and the brave Ourdeck was thinking about Madame Jof, she was there without him knowing it. The entire Society of Independents also had eyes open upon the great events that were in progress; each of the members of the society burst forth in transports of joy at seeing the reign of a just power accelerate thus, and the triumph of the truth. There were among them holy canticles sung in advance, and new prophecies announced, regarding the even more considerable successes that must follow and crown the good cause. This is one of the triumphant canticles that was sung on that occasion, and which has reached us,

"Soon, soon, the enemies of truth will be overthrown; they will be unable to resist the power that is entitled the Invincible; the captive sciences will be returned to their primitive liberty. A light brighter than the Sun is reserved for this great city, which has purchased it with such great ordeals!

"Glad, glad, those who will be its witnesses and participate in its splendor; they will be as if aflame with a sweet joy that the human heart can only know insofar as, by means of its desires, it becomes similar to that splendor itself. That joy is such that the person who experiences it is always ready to groan over the dolor of those who have the misfortune to be deprived of it."

Those canticles were accompanied by a delightful music, of which our human music can give us no idea. But those canticles and the harmonious sounds that accompanied them were lost on Ourdeck and all those who were around him; the time for them to have knowledge of them had not yet come.

They were even more lost on the aerial enemies who, in drawing away from the battlefield, had declared that they would only renounce their hostile projects for a while, in spite of the benevolent promises of the Tartar woman, and that they were only retiring to prepare even greater misfortunes for the people and the capital; and, indeed, they still had the power had the power to deliver such a forceful blow to the populace that a ship sinking to the bottom of the sea could not have been in greater danger.

The terrible misfortune that menaces the capital will not, however, be a new deluge; it will not be the plague; it will not a new war; but it will be worse than all those evils put together; and that disaster is such that, in order to strive to know it in advance, and to prevent it if possible, or at least to lessen its impact, Eleazar is obliged to make use of the means that he had already employed in the presence of Sedir, and which his will rendered invisible to the multitude

This time, however, he wanted to envelop Sedir with him in the atmosphere he formed, in order to fortify him against the shock that was in preparation.

Canto 63
Explanation of the Psychograph.

The crowd, having nothing more to expect from Ourdeck, and no longer seeing either Eleazar or Sedir, did not take long to ebb away by degrees into the adjacent streets. As for Ourdeck, he discovered, from a distance, Eleazar's daughter occupied in picking up two unfortunate women knocked over by the crowd; and as the important people in whom he was also interested were veiled for him, as for the rest of the crowd, he hastened with all the more urgency toward the virtuous Rachel.

"Finally, Madame," he said, as he reached her, "it is permissible for me to approach you, and to renew the assurances of all the interest that you inspired in me the first time I had the honor of encountering you. That interest has only been increased by all the surprising things that I have been told about you and your respectable father, for whom I am searching in vain with my eyes. My thoughts, my opinions and my entire being have changed so much since the numerous and extraordinary events that have happened to me, that I would regard it as a real felicity to be able to confer about all this with a person as instructed as you are, and who combines with her gifts and knowledge a soul like yours.

"For it is time, Madame, to open mine to you; I cannot explain myself what is happening within it, especially since the moment when I had concluded my speech to the assembled multitude. Although you were not close to me; although you said nothing, I sensed that you were acting within me in a manner as sweet as it was incomprehensible; I dare say that I have acquired by that a veritable idea of celestial liaisons. An extraordinary woman has astonished me by showing herself to me and disappearing as if by magic, but you, Madame, without the help of all those prodigies, have penetrated to the most intimate depths of my heart. It is for you to render me and account of that phenomenon."

"Monsieur," Rachel replied, "I shall begin by reassuring you as to the fate of my father. I know that he is very busy for the moment, and that he will shortly be even more so, but I have every hope in the hand that guides him. As for you, Monsieur, it is because I had the opportunity to know the beauty of your soul that I had the desire to penetrate the depths of your being, and it is, in fact, because it is good that it wanted to open free access to me; I cannot do anything to operate on the wicked. If the extraordinary woman who astonished you has not penetrated so deeply into you, it was because you were not then at the point of development that you have now attained, and she had no other object in approaching you but to alert you.

"Yes, Monsieur, your soul suits mine, I have no hesitation in making that confession. I am charmed that you have experienced the impression of what was happening in me, and that you have given me by that evident proof of the relationship that exists between us. I want in my turn to give you evidence that will augment your attachment to the truth and your belief in the power of the desires of the human heart.

"It is not our tongues and our pens, it is our souls that speak and write; the celestial beings know that even better than we do. Take this piece of paper that has just been brought to me by a domestic in Sedir's house, and which was written in his study; it will give you the key to the word *psychograph*, which you have heard pronounced, and which, as you are not unaware, means: the writing of the soul."

Ourdeck took the piece of paper and scanned it rapidly. How surprised he was when he saw on the paper all the astonishing things that he had announced, and even a prophetic and provisional response that he had not indicated and did not know himself. He was stupefied by astonishment.

"Monsieur," said Rachel, "cease to be surprised, since you believe. Would humans have been able to discover the art of writing as rapidly as speech if an art of writing as rapidly as thought had not existed previously? I saw that you desired to converse with me; I saw the fatigue that you experienced in speaking; I desired to spare you that, by formulating the desire for everything that you had to say, and even everything that you could not say, to be written down; and my desire was accomplished immediately, as easily as my soul had conceived it. It is a helpful hand that has written everything in Sedir's study, on the little paper that has been conserved there; several copies have been made, and various people have gone to read it in various locations in Paris."

Transported, Ourdeck continued to converse with Rachel.

(As for you, dear reader, while waiting until we occupy ourselves with the great events for which Eleazar is preparing, it is only just not to deprive you of the fruits of the psychograph.)

Canto 64
Description of the city of Atalante.

"The subterrain that I entered led me to a great portal built in marble, on the frontispiece of which there was a Greek inscription that I read, and which signified the city of Atalante. I recalled, on seeing that inscription, that history speaks of an earthquake occurring 425 years before the Christian Era, and that the earthquake destroyed the city of Atalante in Euboea, which, having been a peninsula beforehand, became an island after that accident. I soon realized that the city had been engulfed and not destroyed, for on entering into it, I perceived all the houses standing, and even the streets entirely free, and I remarked that there had formed above the city a kind of vault of brute rocks, which, having doubtless opened up beneath the city during the quake, had come together and sustained its air after having engulfed it, as has sometimes been seen in the collapse of quarries; and that had ensured that, although it was under the sea, it was nevertheless not submerged.

"You are doubtless astonished by what I am telling you about seeing that city standing, since, in such a subterrain, it seems that one ought not to be able to see anything. Your astonishment will increase much further when I tell you that in traversing the streets, the squares and the public edifices of that unfortunate city, I saw still existing all the utensils, all the furniture and everything that can serve for the pleasure and utility of the mind and the body: the monuments and the instruments of métiers, arts and sciences, the weapons, the books, the jewels, the animals, the vehicles, and finally the people of every age, sex, rank and profession, and that each of them although deprived of life, and motionless, had nevertheless conserved all the attitudes of the various occupations that they had at the fatal moment that surprised them; and there were interesting things there of which I cannot refuse an account to your curiosity.

206

"I would first like to extract you from embarrassment regarding the two difficulties that give you pause, firstly regarding the phenomenon of the conservation of everything that was contained in Atalante at the moment of its disaster. That phenomenon is, in fact, more surprising than that of Herculaneum and Pompeii, where time has only conserved what it could not corrode. But how can you be content for that with the simple ordinary physics of our various professors? However, I cannot offer you another. Now, it tells us that the action of air is what corrodes and destroys everything; that in consequence, bodies that are preserved from the action of air ought to be conserved, and since the city of Atalante was hermetically sealed by the vault of rocks that had formed above it. It is therefore not astonishing that all that it contained had conserved its form and its external appearance. That advantage was not found in Herculaneum or Pompeii, and will not be found in any of the other towns that perished during the famous eruption of Vesuvius, because the lava and the ash have been in contact with everything there as in those towns, and must have dissolved everything that was not of a nature to oppose resistance to it.

"As for the light that I enjoyed while walking through the city of Atalante, I cannot explain that other than by reminding you that I still had eyes full of the somber light that I had brought from my sojourn in the body of the animal that had devoured us; in any case, the physicists would perhaps be even bolder than me in removing that difficulty; they tell us that light is a substance; that as I found everyone occupied in their functions in the city of Atalante, it is obvious that the earthquake that engulfed it happened during the day and not at night, and thus it is natural to think that a portion of the light that illuminated it then was engulfed with the city, and was conserved there like all the other substances and bodies, having been similarly preserved from contact with the air.

"'Have lamps not been found,' they would say, "still alight in the tombs of a few Vestals who, like their lamps, have been buried hermetically for hundreds of years?' They would tell you that even air, since it is so charged with humid parties, cannot be enclosed without falling into dissolution; thus, they would conclude, the animals and humans could not be conserved, like the light; they had to perish, although they kept their forms.

"But you will perhaps also ask me how I was able to avoid dying of suffocation in a place where there was no air, since that lack of air had caused everything animate to perish. That difficulty is more pressing, and yet there is only me who can respond to it, since the scholars do not have the same information about it as I have. I will tell you, therefore, that the animal that had swallowed us all had a free communication with the atmospheric air, since it had come up to the surface of the earth in order to swallow us; that that air extended from the surface, all the way to the inferior regions of the animal, which held us imprisoned; that the same air was introduced into the capillary vessel that had served me as a conduit, and from there had passed into the subterrain where the city was buried. In addition, that air was so prepared, in passing through those different filters, that it could suffice for my respiration in the subterrain but was not sufficiently active to make everything in the city of Atalante fall into dust; which could not have failed to happen if all those objects had been exposed to the open air.

Canto 65
Continuation of the description of Atalante.
Conserved speech.

"The most astonishing marvel among all those I have announced to you is that not only had all the objects that I have mentioned been conserved there in all their forms and external appearances, but that I also perceived there everything that could give me cognizance of the character, mores, intelligence, passions, vices and virtues of the inhabitants. For the same law of physics that had enabled all the substances and bodies hermetically sealed in that city not to suffer externally had extended its preservative power over the very speech of the citizens of Atalante, and had enabled its traces to be corporized and sensible, like all the other objects in that unfortunate enclosure.

"It is necessary not to accuse the curé of Meudon[50] of plagiarism for having shown in his novel speech unfrozen on a battlefield, expressing the cries and sufferings of champions and the dying a long time after the combat had taken place. Firstly, he had not been to Atalante like me and could not have been acquainted with the phenomenon that I witnessed. Secondly, the phenomenon that struck his ingenious ears could not have taken place in the hermetically sealed gulf of Atalante since it requires free air to hear speech; for the same reason, he could not see like me the sensible traces of the warriors of which he speaks, since he was in a free atmosphere, and those traces can only be found in a hermetically sealed atmosphere.

"I shall not pause to give you a description of the various objects, utensils and other inanimate things that I encountered in that exceedingly curious city. There would be little to gain for the increase of your knowledge, since all those things are

---

[50] François Rabelais.

the same everywhere, but I will tell you about more useful things, and newer for you.

"The first edifice at which I paused was the dwelling of a professor of morality; I knew that because his title was inscribed on the frontispiece of the entrance door, a custom that was common to all the houses in the city. I found at the door a crowd of people who were crippled, one-eyed or lame, who were going into the house, and a crowd of sound people who were coming out, enjoying all their limbs and healthy in body. That piqued my curiosity. I therefore went into the courtyard right away, where I saw the door-keeper's dog, its mouth open, as if desirous of stopping a malefactor, who had probably introduced himself with evil designs; and I could not doubt it when saw in the air the menacing words that the door-keeper was saying to that malefactor, as if he knew him perfectly.

"I searched in vain around the mouth of the guard-dog for the characteristic traces of its barking; I could not perceive any, and that made me understand how our philosophers have abused us when they told us that animals have a language like us; for if they had a language like us they would have words, and I would have seen them congealed in the air like the words of humans, and I did not see any. I saw nothing around the muzzle of the dog but formless masses.

"On going through the various rooms of the interior, I saw on all the faces of the people I encountered the marks of a serenity that was astonishing, in the catastrophe in which those people found themselves; and that spectacle gave me an excellent idea of the house. I went all the way to the professor's study; his physiognomy announced the same serenity. I found him standing up, his head slightly inclined, his right hand on his heart and the left on his forehead.

"I was quite astonished, on looking everywhere in his study, not to find any books or papers; that, combined with his attitude, caused me to suspect that he drew his morality in ways more active than those in which our ordinary professors draw theirs. I also had reason to believe that the fruits that he obtained therefrom were much more powerful, for I perceived several framed pictures attached to the walls of the apartment and at the bottom of those various pictures I read the inscriptions: Such-and-such cured of incredulity; such-and-such cured of superstition; such-and-such cured of anger; such-and-such cured of avarice, such-and-such cured of marital infidelity, such-and-such cured of his liking for magic spells.

"I even had reason to think that he did not limit himself to moral cures, and that he also occupied himself with corporeal cures, for I read under some of the pictures: such-and-such cured of blindness; such-and-such of deafness; such-and-such of mutism; such-and-such of gout, such-and-such of gallstones, and so on for various maladies that afflict the human body, which provided an explanation of the two crowds that I had seen on entering. I saw several speeches that had congealed around the professor's mouth, but as they were not traced in a language that was known to me it is impossible for me to report them to you. I can at least report the extreme veneration that I conceived for him, and I have no doubt that you share it.

Oh worthy professor, marvel of Atalante,
Your virtue sublime, your science adamantine
Would impress the vastest intelligence;
In Paris you would earn great recompense.

Canto 66
Continuation of the description of Atalante.
A few malefactors.

"Near his house was that of the governor of the city, which did not inspire me, at close range, with the same veneration. I went into it, and I found him surrounded by several individuals with haggard eyes and menacing attitudes, all of them armed from head to toe. I could see in their speech, traced in the air, that they were planning some sinister projects; I could not understand exactly what they were, because I could only see clipped sentences, which interrupted one another, but I saw a piece of paper on his writing-desk on which the plan of a conspiracy was written, which involved nothing less than delivering the city and all of Euboea to the king of Persia. The man that had engaged him in this treason announced himself as an emissary of the great Odin, and had promised him as recompense the means of evoking the dead at will, especially when they had lived in opulence and in high political offices, in order to obtain state secrets from them, and to discover whether they might have left any hidden treasures. He had even told the governor that in all these matters he could obtain more advantage from the dead than the living; and that thus, when he was pressed, and he found difficulties....

"But I want to keep silent about that article.

"I cannot doubt that the governor had already made use of the means that had been promised to him, because I saw several names written in the air, including those of Croesus, Periander, and even that of the famous Pythoness of Endor, and a few phrases that indicated to me that those shades had been evoked by the governor, and had spoken to him. But I did not see them in person, because the governor, no longer being alive, had been unable to retain them in his power, or, because, having died themselves in free air, concentrated air

212

had no purchase on their larvae, although their speech had remained visible, having been surprised by the concentrated air.

"The governor was not the only malefactor that I found thus, *in flagrante delicto*. I encountered all species in various places, including thieves, murderers, poisoners and people occupied in secret endeavors that would make you shiver if I reported them. The catastrophe of their city had conserved all their sins, which they believed could never be known, as long as they committed them out of the sight of humans. But if I had not obtained that new evidence against the abusive security of culpable mortals, what I had learned during my sojourn inside the crocodile would have sufficed to enable me to conceive that criminals who let themselves be surprised by death remain in the same state in which they found it, in order that one day their abominations will be known to all the eyes from which they had sought to hide it, and that by that means, hypocrisy, which is devouring the earth, is covered in confusion and cannot have any triumph.

"I could also understand that the same thing happens in the inverse order for those who did in humble virtue, in order that they too will receive compensation for their sacrifices, and the neglect in which society had left them, or the scorn that it had heaped upon them.

Canto 67
Continuation of the description of Atalante.
The philosopher.

"When I had quit the malefactors, I entered a house in which a philosopher lived, an intimate friend of the professor of morality, who, as you know had received my first visit. I knew that they were friends because I saw a scroll on the philosopher's table bearing the heading: *Summary of my conference with my friend the professor of morality*.

"I recognized in that writing on what the professor and he founded their union. It was a conformity of taste for the high sciences that had linked them together. The philosopher knew, as well as the professor, all the extraordinary events that the famine had occasioned in Paris. He also knew all the predictions that we have all seen in the narrative of Cape Horn; and they were exposed in several passages reported under the name of Pherecydes—who, as is well-known, had been the master of Pythagoras.

"In spite of the knowledge that our philosopher had extracted from the writings, and even, it seemed to me, from the letters of Pherecydes, it seems that his master believed that he was far from having attained the necessary degree of development to fulfill the human mind, and he admitted himself in one of those passages that his enlightenment indicated to him, in several centuries, an important and sacred epoch, which he would have liked to see in realty, but which he could only see in speculation.

"He announced to him that those who would come after that epoch would have the advantage of seeing pathways open before them much vaster than those previously accessible, because, during their lifetime, the mold of time would begin to break; and among those privileged people, he designated, without naming him, a man of good who, several centuries after the epoch in question, would play in Paris one of the most considerable roles in the crisis that capital would be undergoing at the time, by virtue of the rapacity of a culpable minister and the wickedness of a woman of consequence.

"I have no need to indicate to you more clearly the man of good announced in those predictions; what we have just seen him operate in the scene of the verdure designates him to you clearly enough; and the saline powder that he made me take is for me the most positive of the privileges that have been predicted for him for so many centuries.

"Nevertheless, what gave the knowledge of the philosopher a great degree of importance and great weight is that it was supported by the most exact and the most definite political calculations.

"I found, among other things, in the writings of the philosopher, a natural demonstration that there can only be ten bases of numeration in calculation, and that those who increase or diminish them can, with the number of characters they choose, operate exactly on the exterior results of things, but not deviate by doing so from the principle of those same things, which is denary; because, whatever system of numeration they adopt, they cannot prevent indicating by that means one of the ten bases, either in the multiple form or the fractional form.

"Occupied with that discovery, I went out mechanically, and soon perceived in the nearby square the house of a physician, which appeared to me to be that of a man in credit, to judge by its extent and its beauty, and I allowed myself to yield to the desire to go into it.

Canto 68
Continuation of the description of Atalante.
The dying physician.

"I did not take long to reach the physician's bedroom. I found him in bed, ill, and disfigured as I had never seen any human creature. With him were several of his colleagues, who were striving to care for him. But I understood, on reading their words, that they did not expect their services to succeed, and that even the things he said to them astonished them slightly.

"'No, my dear colleagues," he said to them, 'you won't get me out of the condition I'm in by means of the medicinal sciences that are taught in our schools. My illness is due to hidden causes, which you can do nothing to oppose, since our entire doctorate leads us to believe that those causes do not have any reality. However, if the confession of a colleague who is ready to terminate his days, and no longer has any interest to propose in this world, can appear to you to have any weight, listen to me.

"'We have been very wrong to believe, as we have, with such a tenacious and general obstinacy, that our being is nothing but an assemblage and the result of simple physical and passive causes. By lowering our gaze on a daily basis to the mechanism of the body we have accustomed ourselves not to perceiving any other source of life within us, or any other active components that muscles, sinews and fluids, neural, sanguine and others. Independently of those mechanisms, however, which are the basis of all animal economy, I must attest to you loudly that there are also, in respect of our thought, secret mechanisms analogous to it, similarly living, whose operation is entirely unknown to the sensible and material order.

"'The attentive and prudent usage of those mechanisms is what makes the difference between human minds. We only judge the results, while the causes of those results act in silence, as if apart from what strikes us externally, remaining null to our persuasion, and we even believe ourselves wise in eliminating them from the list of entities. We believe ourselves even wiser when we deny that those pretended causes can result in effect other than those that affect out material senses, and that, in consequence, occult forces exist that it is dangerous to approach.

"'I believed that, like you, my dear colleagues, until the moment when I made the acquaintance of the hierophant who lives in the Rue des Singes. I would perhaps believe it still if I had not, by virtue of a prideful curiosity, witnessed secret ceremonies in his home, in which, by his criminal audacity, he activated those same occult forces, the existence of which I had not even suspected. I have been punished for my imprudence; it was from the moment that I yielded to those prestigious suggestions that I was gripped throughout my body by the malady that is taking me to the tomb, and which, as you have determined, is entirely foreign to the profound knowledge that you have in the art of medicine.

"'Change opinions on these objects if you do not want to distance yourselves from the truth; but above all, stay away from the ceremonies of the hierophant.'

"I did not see any more words after those. The physician had greatly piqued my curiosity in speaking about the hierophant, and he had given me the hope of finding his house by saying that it was situated in the Rue des Singes, because the names of the streets could be seen inscribed on every corner, as in the majority of our great cities. I went out with the intention of reading the names of all the streets until I had found the one that I wanted.

Canto 69
Continuation of the description of Atalante.
The pulpit of silence.

"Still seeking my Rue des Singes and the house of the hierophant, I arrived at an isolated circular square in the middle of which I perceived a rectangular edifice having as an inscription: *Court of Silence*. That title excited my curiosity, and I went in. I found a number of seated people, of both sexes, and a professor standing in the middle. I did not see any words in the air. Then I looked everywhere for some paper or a few books, in order to inform me as to the subject matter that the professor was treating in his circle. I did not find any, but I soon discovered the reason.

Like Harpocrates, the professor had the forefinger of his right hand applied to his mouth, which indicated to me that he was, in fact professing silence, and that he was not speaking any more than his disciples, and thus offering an example as a precept.

"After having reflected for a few minutes on that singularity, I was getting ready to leave, since I could not read anything there, either on paper or in the air, but just as I was about to retire, I began to perceive very extraordinary things in effective nature, which focused my attention. The harder I looked the more they developed, and came to life before me, in such a fashion that I soon saw the room filled with prodigies unusual to me until then, and on which the eyes of the audience seemed to be so fixed that drowsiness surely had no access to that sublime school, as often happens in auditoria where someone is speaking.

"Those prodigies opened my mind anew to knowledge of which the discourses of scholars and the lessons of all the professors I had ever heard had never allowed me to suspect the slightest trace; for they taught me in reality principles and active verities that those discourses and scientific lessons seemed, on the contrary, to have banished from understanding. I also learned at the same time to evaluate the price of those abusive and deceptive instructions.

"I shall not report to you here what those marvels were, and what that knowledge was, because to report it to you it would be necessary to speak, and as I only learned them by means of silence, I believe that it is also only by silence that you can learn them.

"I believe that if humans, instead of yielding to the profusion of their words, as they do every day, surrendered themselves carefully to the silence that was so instructive to me, they would be naturally surrounded by the same prodigies; I also believe that if they did not speak, it is then that they would express the most magnificent things in the world; and if the nations wanted to advance the reign of the sciences and enlightenment among them, I believe that instead of all the scientific courses that the accumulate within them, they ought only to establish pulpits of silence everywhere.

"For I am sure now that the harpocrates[51] were not, as so many people have said, a sacerdotal ruse, the object of which was to prevent anyone revealing that the mythological divinities and idols were human; the source from which they derived is infinitely more profound.

"I soon found myself so full of everything that I saw that, still so unfamiliar with those prodigies, I was obliged to bring them to a conclusion. I went out nourished in my entire being by the incomprehensible charms of that new existence, intending soon to return to that school, and I set forth once again in search of my Rue des Singes, without paying much attention to all that I encountered, such as jugglers, burials, carriages and shops of every kind, and other things that one sees in all great cities, with the difference that instead of hearing words, I

---

[51] Harpocrates was the Greek god of silence, derived in Ptolemaic Alexandria from the Egyptian Horus; Saint-Martin's use of the term here as a trivial noun is slightly enigmatic.

was reduced to reading them, the atmosphere being sown with them.

Canto 70
Continuation of the description of Atalante.
A preacher in a temple.

"A rather long way away from the place I had quit, I perceived a vast oblong edifice with the appearance of a temple. I approached it, and saw from the inscription that it was indeed a temple, and that it was dedicated to Truth. I went in; I found a large crowd of people assembled, apparently listening to a man who was doubtless in a pulpit and who was speaking to them. I could read all the words of his speech at my ease, because he alone was speaking and they were conserve in a very distinct manner; and I can say that the discourse contained all that the wisest philosophy of the Portico and Piraeus[52] has ever instructed of the purest and most important, with regard to the severity of principles and the sanctity of doctrine.

"However, astonishingly, independently of the visible words that had emerged from the mouth of the orator, I perceived some in his interior that were somewhat less marked, but which were sufficiently so for me to be able to read and discern them; they were like the seeds of words, some of which were almost entirely developed, others half developed and others a third. What amazed me and filled me with indignation was to see that the words I perceived inside the body of the orator had a meaning absolutely opposite to those emerging from his mouth; as much as the latter were sensate, sage and edifying, so the others were impious, extravagant and blasphemous, in such a fashion that I could not doubt that the orator was imposing audaciously upon his audience, and that he did not believe a word of what he had told them.

---

[52] Zeno, the founder of Stoicism, allegedly developed it after being shipwrecked in the Athenian port of Piraeus, and named it from the word *stoa* (portico).

(It's the same as here, the audience will cry;
External words that internal thoughts belie
Among preachers are sufficiently common;
Two tongues would suit them better than one.)

"You will perhaps ask me how I was able to discern the orator's internal speech when I had not made the same remark among the other people whose words I had observed. I had a great deal of difficulty rendering an account of it myself, but I eventually explained it, it seems to me, quite clearly.

"As that orator was treating holy and divine matters, and treating them publicly, it was necessary for him to make every effort, not only not to scandalize his audience, but also to edify them; on the other hand, those efforts being contrary to his interior sentiments, he was also redoubling internal efforts to provide a counterweight to what he was obliged to say aloud , and it was his secret efforts that, giving a greater degree of fermentation to his sacrilegious thoughts, simultaneously gave to the internal speech born of them a more determined form and a more marked character.

"Perhaps also those same efforts, either external or internal, that the orator had made, had been violent enough to have acted on his physique and rendered his body thinner, more transparent and more diaphanous than the bodies of the other people I had already seen, who were not so outrageously criminal and him; and, in fact, he only had the skin on his bones.

Canto 71
Continuation of the description of Atalante.
A double current of words.

"My astonishment had reason to increase again in a manner that will surprise you, when I tell you that not only could I see thus, inside the orator, words opposite to those emerged from his mouth, but by dint of examining him attentively, I also remarked that there was something like a current of those same impious and sacrilegious words emerging from his mouth.

"That current was dark and bronzed in color; it was double—which is to say that there was one going in and another coming out—and the heart of the orator was simultaneously the hearth and the terminus of that double current. Those effluvia succeeded one another rapidly, and extended into the temple, and even beyond, for they passed outside through the large entrance door; but as I also saw them entering by that same door, I presumed there must be a second hearth at the other extremity of the current, and I resolved to search for it right away, following the evident traces of that extraordinary phenomenon.

"I therefore followed, not without suffering, that long chain of impious words emerging from the heart of the orator; I did not look at any other object, so desirous was I of satisfying my curiosity. In truth, hunger was beginning to afflict me somewhat, because my corporeal faculties had been returned to me, but the desire to reach my goal was even more powerful, and the promises of the extraordinary woman that I had seen before being swallowed sustained my courage with the hope that we would not be separated forever.

"As I emerged from the main door of the temple I saw that noxious current turn left into a wide street, at the end of which there was a rather vast elliptical square; it went straight through the middle of it and from there entered a narrow, dark, dirty and poorly-aligned street, long enough to become tedious.

"At the end of that street it entered another, which appeared to me to be even more disagreeable, dirtier and more tortuous—but those disgusts were partly tempered by the joy and hope I had of finding what I desired with so much ardor, for, on looking at the inscription of that vile street, I saw that it was called the Rue des Singes.

"I had not reached the twentieth house of that street when the double current of speech that had led me there went through a doorway above which I saw inscribed: *Hierophant.*

"Imagine my satisfaction. I did not doubt that the hierophant was the same person of whom the words of the dying physician had given me some indications, and that he was the same one that I had just seen preaching in the temple.

Canto 72
Continuation of the description of Atalante.
The hierophant's dwelling.

"I went through the doorway precipitately; I traversed a dark alleyway, still by the dim light of the double current, at the end of which was a staircase, part of which rose up to the upper apartments, while the other, only covered by a trap-door, descended into a cellar; the current led to that trap-door. I lifted it up and followed it down to the cellar, where I arrived after having gone down fifty steps.

"There I found a large area, pentagonal in form. Fourteen people were arranged around it on iron seats, each having a name inscribed above their head, which indicated their function and employment in the assembly. At the back of the cellar on a platform elevated by two steps was another iron seat more ample than the rest and better wrought, but empty, and above that seat was inscribed: *The Hierophant.* I was then fully convinced that I had found the object of my search.

"Independently of the current of speech that had brought me to the cellar, and which had the armchair of the hierophant as the second center, there were similar currents going from the hierophant's armchair to the mouths of each of the fourteen members of the audience, which were turned toward that chair, in such a fashion that I inferred that the hierophant was, as it were, the soul of their speech, and they were only his organs and instruments.

In the middle of the area there was a large iron table, pentagonal in form like the cellar, and on that table was a kind of transparent paper lantern, similarly pentagonal, the sides of which were aligned with the sides of the table and the sides of the cellar; in the center of that lantern there was a brown shiny stone, which continually rendered visible words and entire phrases written on the paper faces corresponding to it; and those phrases responded to the words that I had read inside the hierophant.

"In front of his armchair there was another table, oblong, also made of iron, and on the table there were two iron monkeys, which each had an iron chain on each foot and the neck, riveted to the table; which made ten chains in all. In front of the two iron monkeys there was a large book, all of whose pages were also iron, which I could turn and read at will.

I read there clearly the treaties of various emissaries of the occult doctors with several conquerors of the earth, and the horrible conditions under which they delivered the nations of this world. I read the one that one of the emissaries had made with the hierophant himself, the abominable means that he had confided to the emissary in question, and the promises that had been made to him if he conformed to his plans. But I read forceful imprecations against Pherecydes, who had greatly impeded the enterprises of the hierophant and had prevented several people from taking part in them.

"I read that those enterprises had the goal of annihilating the order of everything and establishing in its place a fictitious order that was only a false image of the truth. They had to overturn all the calculations known since as the calculations of Pythagoras, and confuse them so much that the simplest and best conserved mind would never be able to recover their traces.

"They had to reduce by that same law all the rules of nature and the mind to a single rule; all substances, whether elementary or spiritual, to a single substance; all the visible or occult actions of beings to a single action; all qualities, good or bad, living or dead, to a single quality; and that single rule, that single substance, that single action and that single property must reside in the chief of the assembly, or in the hierophant, who would soon launch that doctrine authoritatively into the world, and demand as recompense, for as long as he lived, the honors of apotheosis and his divinization, to the exclusion of any other God. I cannot think without shuddering about the horror that that reading occasioned me.

226

"I then read in the same book the story of our present famine; but I also read there the description of a holy and respectable man who would overturn all the projects of our enemies, and who would appear to be for the hierophant himself one of the most redoubtable adversaries. Then I ardently desired to know the name of that respectable man, who is now known to us, not only out of curiosity, but also in the interests of France, and the need I had to fill my mind with hope for the salvation of my country; although, to tell the truth, finding myself in a place that was filled with nothing but death, and offered me no issue, I would never have been able, without the promised I retained in my heart, to flatter myself that I might share in the future fate of my fatherland, fortunate or unfortunate.

Canto 73
Continuation of the description of Atalante.
The tragic end of the hierophant.

"That desire took such possession of me that it was like a fire burning in my bosom; but soon, that fire could no longer be contained in me, and a light emerged therefrom of dazzling whiteness, in the midst of which I clearly saw the name *Eleazar*, three consecutive times.

"My joy was equal to my surprise on seeing such a phenomenon; but that phenomenon produced another so frightening and so extraordinary that I would not have been able to sustain the spectacle if it had lasted any longer.

"Know, then, that at the instant when the name of Eleazar was manifest thus in that enormous subterrain, the fourteen men who were sitting on the iron seats came back to life, making grimaces and frightful contortions; know that the particular currents that linked them to the hierophant's armchair were detached from that chair and reentered into the fourteen men, which seemed to render their condition more violent; know that the two iron monkeys chained to the small table were instantly released, that they came to life, and that each immediately engendered six more monkeys, alive like them, and that each of those fourteen monkeys hurled itself like a hawk upon one of the fourteen men, and devoured them all.

"Know that the hierophant himself, by virtue of a violent attraction, was brought in the blink of an eye from the temple to his armchair, where he appeared to me to be more tormented than the other fourteen; know that the fourteen monkeys immediately pounced upon him, and devoured him, after having plucked out his eyes; know that the fourteen monkeys, after having eaten everyone, ended up eating one another, without any vestige remaining before my eyes and without my being able to tell what had become of them.

"Know that all of these events happened with a rapidity as prompt as that of thought.

"Know, finally, that there was an earthquake so violent that everything trembled, ready to collapse on top of me. But in the midst of those frightening scenes, an invisible hand took possession of me, and without my making any use of my faculties, it transported me I know not where, or by what means, into a drain in the Rue Montmartre, where you know that I ran aground."

Canto 74
Hostile preparations against the capital
and against Eleazar.

The conversation that Rachel and Ourdeck had together, after they had received the writing of the psychograph, was not long. Soon, they perceived Eleazar and Sedir, whose surrounding atmosphere had dissipated, and immediately wanted to go to them. But the moment of the great catastrophe was approaching, and the secret enemies of truth would have had too much to lose from such a reunion not to oppose it with all their might, as they had previously done.

Those secret enemies, who had already played so many cruel tricks on the audience, were preparing to pour the entire cup of their poisons over the capital, in order to take the most resounding vengeance for the blows that Eleazar had inflicted on them. They did not come in the quality of deliberating genii, as in the assembly at Cape Horn, but they gathered as furious warriors from all parts of the world, and set forth like the swarms of locusts that ravage entire regions in certain countries.

They wanted to take away any species of hope from the starving inhabitants. They wanted to render their torture frightful, by drying up at a stroke the source from which those good Parisians had just drawn some temporary relief; in sum, it was at Eleazar's very life that all their efforts were about to be directed, not doubting that if they could cause him to perish, the capital would then be lost forever.

But in order that their blows would be surer, they did not want to try to blow up and burn his house, as the tall arid man had already tried and failed to do; they wanted to attack him bodily, by means of their most determined agents.

It is thus, dear reader, that Clement once
Came to end the days of the last Valois prince;

The Guises flattered themselves in their impatience,
They would instantly become the masters of France.

Canto 75
The gathering of the airborne genii.
Three of them are transformed into soldiers.

Enormous masses of gray clouds are therefore seen forming in the air, which do not seem to be driven by a single wind, or traveling in the same direction, as happens in ordinary times, but are seen coming from all points of the horizon, all traveling toward Paris with an incredible speed. The east, the west, the north and the south open their nebulous caverns, and immediately send their airborne armies toward the capital.

In an instant, the sky is covered by a thick dark veil. The storm forms, lightning flashes, thunder rumbles; torrents of hail and rain fall on the Parisians, and force them to seek shelter in their houses. This is the moment that the airborne armies have chosen, to bring their enterprise to a conclusion.

Three of them are transformed into soldiers of the watch, and under the pretext of soliciting orders from the Lieutenant de Police, who is standing close to Eleazar, they approach and come between the two of them, in order to be better able to act against Eleazar when he is isolated.

One of the three presents himself to Sedir. Taking his hat off, in order to speak into his ear; the other two attack Eleazar and try to knock him down—but it is him, on the contrary, by means of a simple glance, who commences by filling them with fear and causes them to fall to the ground. Feigning then to be submissive, they crawl toward him, while he turns his head away, and wind themselves so well around his legs that in an instant, they have tipped him over and come to their feet again.

Alerted by the noise, Sedir turns round, and seeing the condition of his friend, runs to help him, calling the two soldiers to him, whom he is far from suspecting, so much does a man fall back on ordinary ways of seeing when wisdom leaves him to himself; now, as the two soldiers are among the number of the conspirators, what could he hope for from them?

Indeed, the two men make use against him of the powers that they have in the quality of supermaterial beings, and the first thing they do is to trouble poor Sedir's vision to such an extent that he sees nothing at all; they even take away his powers of hearing and speech, only leaving him the use of his legs; but, not knowing which way to go, he leaves his friend Eleazar exposed to the greatest dangers, without having any means of being useful to him.

Even the good Rachel, who has tried to approach her father, finds herself so confused by the event that she is devoid of strength, and cannot bring him any assistance.

The volunteer Ourdeck, who is with her and would be no less desirous of acting in the circumstances, is as if paralyzed by the afflicting state in which her sees Rachel, and also to some extent by the malign influence that the three corporized champions take care to pour upon him, and he cannot move any of his limbs.

The three conspirators, finding themselves at liberty, combine all their forces against Eleazar; they strike him with the rudest blows, and there is nothing they do not employ to massacre that redoubtable adversary of the wicked. But those tenebrous beings, although they are supermaterial beings, are too blind themselves to know who it is that they are addressing; otherwise they would surely not have that foolish audacity.

In fact, although, in a moment of surprise, they have been able to trip Eleazar, who, then occupied with avoiding the rain and the bad weather, could not have been entirely on his guard, it does not take him long to recover his self-possession, and it is now that he is going to give unequivocal evidence of his power.

Canto 76
Eleazar, knocked down, gets up again.

It is not unprecedented to see villagers who have attempted to pull upon a flexible tree, and after having caused it to bend over, attach themselves precipitately to its branches, believing that they have entirely felled or uprooted it; but nor is it unprecedented to see that tree, which was only curbed, spring upright again by virtue of the laws of elasticity, and lift those same villagers into the air, at risk of making them pay dearly for their imprudence.

(Dear reader, that is the most accurate comparison I can find to help you understand what happened between Eleazar and the three assassins.)

Eleazar had a sash knotted around his body in the form of a belt. The three assassins, who had no doubt that they had taken his life by means of their redoubtable blows, seized him by the knot of his sash, and were getting ready to carry him away, in order to show him to their leaders and give them evidence of the success with which they had carried out their enterprise.

By the aid of the power that watched over him, however, and did not want him to be subjected to any sort of proof, the three assassins all found themselves seized by both hands in the knot of the sash, which tightened by virtue of their own efforts. Then Eleazar, like the most sinewy of trees, immediately recovered all his vigor. He came to his feet and, seizing the knot of his sash with his left hand, he pulled it so tight that the three adversaries could not disengage themselves, and he dragged them forcibly after him with the greatest facility.

An astonishing phenomenon, easy to comprehend
When one reflects, and hear me recommend

That although six exceeds one in human estimation
One just hand is more than six in moral calculation.

With the other hand, Eleazar seized his miraculous box. As it was not a matter here of causing nature to produce anything, but merely of containing malefactors and repelling the evil that they operated, it was sufficient for him to hold the box in his hand; that contact alone prevented the three champions from quitting the form they had taken and from flying through the air toward their companions. It also had the property of tempering the rain that was then falling, as well as rendering Sedir the use of all his senses.

As for Rachel and the volunteer, who were further away from Eleazar and were affected in two ways, they were only able to experience a fraction of the remedial effect of that contact; and they would have needed the powerful powder to approach them itself to procure them a more efficacious help, so, to their great regret, they found themselves in almost the same condition.

That did not prevent the triumphant Eleazar, dragging his three prisoners after him, from reappearing next to his friend Sedir, and thus presenting to the eye of the people who were beginning to come back into the streets those marvelous signs of his victory, as glorious for him as it was humiliating for his adversaries.

Alas, brief victory and temporary glory
The peace you offer the victor is transitory;
And we shall see his arrogant adversaries
Bring mourning by revenge to all of Paris.

Canto 77
The deliberations and decisions of the airborne enemies.

The airborne enemies remaining in the clouds did not lose sight of their companions; they were inflamed by a new fury on seeing their disaster and their shame, and a thousand oaths were proffered at once, of not to fall idle until they had exercised in their favor the most striking vengeance.

Immediately, one of them, named Haridelle, advanced and said: "Powerful companions, there is none of you who is not filled with indignation at the sight of the sad fate of those of our brothers who devoted themselves to our common glory. I beg you to believe that I share those just sentiments with you, and if I could die, and in dying save the honor of my colleagues, death would be absolutely nothing to me, and I would make the sacrifice of my life with a veritable transport of joy; but since that sacrifice is impossible on our part, and since, being spirits, our principal weapon is intelligence, I want to make you party to the observations with which my intelligence furnishes me, and I submit them to your judgment.

"That makes two futile attempts that we and the crocodile have made against Eleazar's life, and we ought to shiver with dread in recalling the marvelous predictions made in his regard in Atalante more than two thousand years ago, and which announce him to us as our most redoubtable adversary. Until the moment when he deployed the powers of his saline powder, to force the earth to furnish subsistence to an entire audience, we did not know of what his redoubtable gifts consisted, but since then, and especially since he has merely taken his fatal box in his hand, treating our three companions as puppets that he moves at his whim, we can no longer doubt that all the magic of his powers resides in that talisman.

"We no longer have any need to seek a new Delilah in order to discover by her means where the strength of his new Samson resides. We know where that strength resides, and we know, in consequence, where our blows ought to be directed in order to destroy it. My opinion, therefore, it that we should put to work all the intelligence and cunning that we have to steal that treasure, which is for him like an arsenal, a citadel, or rather an entire world, being sure that when that talisman is in our power, we shall have nothing more to fear, and that we can do whatever we wish with Eleazar.

"And you, my dear companions, if zeal can determine your confidence, if the honor that I have had of being the genius who presided over the assembly of Cape Horn engages you to believe that that confidence will not be misplaced, and finally, if the extreme desire I have to be useful to you appears to you to be a sufficient entitlement for your choice to fall on me in their perilous enterprise, pronounce; you will not find anyone among you who is devoted with more ardor to your glory and your utility."

Haridelle having finished his speech, all his companions congratulate him on his zeal and his courage; they adopt the proposals he has made, and appoint him their delegate by a unanimous vote. More than that, all his companions give him *carte noire* to acquit his commission, and only recommend him not to waste an instant, since the danger is so urgent.

Perhaps, dear reader, you have the suspicion
That there, unwittingly, I'm offending reason
In putting *carte noire* instead of *carte blanche*
But I say no, in a fashion staunch.
To the airborne enemy, cruel by preference
Whose only power is that of malevolence
One only ever gives *carte noire*;
If you doubt me, consult the Grimoire.

Canto 78
The disaster at its peak.

Haridelle has no sooner received is commission than he sets about fulfilling it. He commences by agitating all the thrones of his colleagues; he makes them collide with one another to such an extent that those thrones, which are only clouds, soon begin to warm up and resume their fulminating quality, all the more so as his brothers and friends assist him ardently in that endeavor, in order to accelerate the effects.

When Haridelle sees that the clouds have reached the appropriate degree of inflammation, he transforms himself instantly into lightning, breaks the envelope that the clouds form, and precipitates in fire toward the place where his three companions are being led in triumph by Eleazar.

The lightning approaches the breast of the Israelite, but cannot attain it, so irresistible is the force that opposes it; suddenly, the lightning ricochets, and goes to strike the tail of Sedir's coat, who is standing beside his friend, listening to a brief account of the combat sustained against the three champions he could not see. The lightning only strikes his coat because it does not have the power to strike his person. The coat catches fire; Sedir tries to put out the fire, but by agitating it, only increases the blaze. Eleazar, drawn by the desire to be useful to Sedir, leaps toward him, and, with a single sweep of the hand that holds the box, he extinguishes the fire in his coat and restores him to tranquility.

But Haridelle soon returns to the charge. A second lightning-bolt, twenty times more terrible than the first, sets fire to the entire atmosphere. The three champions tied to Eleazar's sash, excited by the sulfur exhaled in all directions, agitate with all their strength, and by means of that agitation they shift the knot of the sash in Eleazar's hand that they might perhaps have escaped if he had not made prompt use of his right hand to tighten it.

Alas, the fatal hour was approaching when Paris was about to be precipitated into the abyss. It was with the hand that was holding the precious box that Eleazar hastened to secure the vacillating knot; unfortunately, he puts so much haste into that movement that the box bumps into his left hand, escapes, and falls!

Suddenly, Haridelle presents his hands to the genius of Saturn, who lines them instantly with a layer of lead, of which he is the genius, in order to serve them as protection. With the same promptitude, Haridelle covers that layer of lead with a layer of mercury, which is comprised especially in his department, all to be better able to seize the precious box. He seizes it, in fact, like a vulture; he flies away with it into the clouds and announces his triumph with further claps of thunder.

On arriving among his airborne brethren, he is received with a thousand times more honor than has ever been rendered to any warrior of this world after the most brilliant conquests. Everyone heaps him with praise, everyone hastens to get closer to him, and above all to see the redoubtable talisman that has operated such marvelous prodigies. It is decided that in future, Haridelle will have the most honorable rank among his own kind; then, with a common voice, it is pronounced that the glorious spoils captured from Eleazar will be paraded in pomp throughout the empire, and will afterwards by placed to dwell in the heavens as a new constellation.

But it is necessary not to believe that the proud Haridelle, in spite of the precautions he has taken, can hold that box in his hands so easily. It has in itself such a great activity and such a great fire that it would soon have volatilized the mercury and melted the lead with which he was armored, and would finally have burned him if he had held it any longer in the same hand. So he is obliged to transport it continually from one hand to the other, and even to agitate it, and juggle it while he holds it, as one sees people do who try to carry hot coals in their hands.

It is for the same reason that he was never be able open it, although he tries with all his might, in order to take possession of the powder that was inside it and cast it to the wind, which would have protected him and his kin forever, so they believed, from any defeat and any danger.

Canto 79
Eleazar's triumph.

While these things are happening in the Empyrean, Eleazar, who no longer has his strength, is doing everything he can to avoid collapse. The volunteer and Rachel find themselves even weaker.

The volunteer is thinking about Madame Jof and all the prodigies he has previously seen operated by Eleazar, but he cannot pronounce a word. Rachel is paralyzed, and at the most, can only raise her eyes to the heavens. As for Sedir, he is still totally bewildered, struggling against the fire that has again taken hold of his coat.

The three champions, no longer being contained, detach themselves from the knot of Eleazar's sash and stand up firmly on their feet. A veil more somber than the first extends over the entire capital; instead of the bread of which the sad inhabitants have such great need, it is stones that fall from the sky on them and crush them.

They try to take refuge in their houses, but they find in each of them, in the form of crocodiles, some of the airborne enemies composing Haridelle's army, who are demolishing the houses rapidly, burying the unfortunate Parisians under their ruins. Plague, fire and all the evils threaten them at once, and despair becomes their unique affection, as if it were their unique existence.

Although the situation of the virtuous and sensible Eleazar becomes more frightful in consequence, he nevertheless maintains the serenity appropriate to the dignity of his character. He has certainly been seen to be pierced by a secret dolor, but that was his compassion for the unfortunates and his zeal for the glory of the truth rather than the shame of seeing himself humiliated by his redoubtable enemies.

In fact, his heart was lacerated on seeing how the truth was about be lost in the spirit of the impious, by virtue of the disastrous triumph of his airborne adversaries; and that dolor affected him so much that no idea or clarity came to his mind, and his genius did not suggest to him any means or resource to aid him and reanimate his strength, so certain is the verity that neither thought nor light are ours, and that the moment when the source that communicates them to us is withdrawn from us, blindness and impotence are our lot.

But that state of darkness and anguish could only have a limited duration, because a just man can never be abandoned permanently, and if wisdom permits that he sometimes has the sad experience of his poverty, and the dangers by which he is surrounded, it also desires even more ardently to compensate him a hundredfold and render him all the charms of its divine mercy and its virtuous consolations.

In fact, Eleazar's desires were so pure that he soon felt the seed of hope reborn within him. That fortunate change was announced in him by the star in which the Tartar woman showed herself in the air in order to sustain him and make him see that she was faithful to her promise.

That sensible testimony and the seed of hope that he felt reborn within him reanimated his courage and gave a new strength to his desires. He concentrated himself then in his most intimate depths and, reassembling all is faculties, he represented to the invisible wisdom, by the gentle movements of his soul, how much interest the glory of the truth had in enabling him to triumph over his enemies, and rendering him the powerful talisman that had preserved him from so many dangers until now.

That violent concentration filled with energy the faculties that were within him and were the true model of the three substances for which the savant Arab had given him the recipe. That virtuous ardor, sustained by the most touching desires, was crowned by a fortunate success, very similar to what had happened to the volunteer in the subterrain of Atalante when he discovered the name Eleazar in such an unexpected manner.

A kind of effluvium of his desires, which he had fortified by concentrating them, emerged from Eleazar. That effluvium, even more active than the saline powder contained in the box, had an effect so sudden and prodigious that his airborne enemies, having had a moment of triumph, paid dearly for it in the humiliation with which that triumph was followed.

For that effluvium emerged from within Eleazar soon attracted, by virtue of the laws of affinity, the box of which they had taken possession, and which they had flattered themselves that they would make a into a glorious monument among the stars, forever. It returned, as if of its own accord, to replace itself in Eleazar's hand, and even did so in so subtle a manner that the airborne enemies did not perceive it at first, believing for a few more moments that they were still in possession of the treasure they no longer had, because they only knew abrupt and noisy movements, which meant that there was no illusion to which they were not susceptible.

Canto 80
Eleazar moves on to other labors.

Eleazar could not recover that powerful treasure without immediately recovering his mastery over his adversaries. He took a pinch of his precious salt himself, in order to procure relief for his own body, which, exhausted by the great efforts he had made, would not have been able to resist fatigue any longer. Then he threw three pinches of his powder into the air. Rachel and the volunteer recovered by virtue of that the use of their faculties, and united their wishes with Eleazar's works. They raised their eyes and their hands toward the celestial domain. Sedir, who found himself liberated by the same means, did the same.

By means of the collaboration of those virtuous souls, aided by Eleazar's great powers, the clouds suddenly dissipated; daylight reappeared, and the airborne enemies fled to other regions, cursing those who had thus overturned all their projects.

Only Haridelle, the audacious Haridelle, dares to make one last attempt; he launches himself from high in the air toward the three champions who had disengaged themselves from Eleazar's belt when the box had been captured; he comes to join forces with them in order to recover the box that was the object of such ardent ambition.

But just as a double-barreled shotgun dissipates in the blink of an eye a small number of pusillanimous assailants, so Eleazar's powerful means annihilate all the efforts of those malefactors; he only has to threaten them, simply by opening the redoubtable box before them, and in an instant, the three champions, all quitting the human form they had taken, are dispersed in the air like dust, with Haridelle; and from that moment on, it is impossible for them even to reenter the clouds from which they descended and to rejoin their companions.

As he concludes these glorious enterprises Eleazar finds himself surrounded by Sedir, Rachel and the volunteer, who congratulate him warmly on his success. As for him, whom other tasks await, he promptly renders the most sincere homage to the one who guides everything and then addresses Rachel.

"Don't follow me for the moment. What remains for me to do demands strength that I ought not to demand of you; in any case, your presence will be even more useful in Paris during the moments that I'm absent from it. It's during those moments that it will have the most need of a preservative, and it's your prayers that provide it. You'll harm it greatly if you leave."

To Ourdeck, he said: "Similarly, interesting voyager, I cannot permit myself to expose you to the great tasks that await me, but I have no other limits to prescribe for you or particular orders to give you; I only engage you to support me as you have done with all your internal means."

To Sedir, he said: "As for you. Monsieur, whom I have already admitted into the career, come and continue it: it will inform you itself if it will permit you to go on to the end, or whether it is necessary for you to stop."

Immediately he separates from Rachel and the volunteer, who quit him with keen and tender gazes, and he takes the virtuous Sedir with him.

Rachel and the volunteer, who submit with a sigh to that separation, are nevertheless satisfied to find themselves together, having all reciprocal motives to be interested in one another: motives that have increased so much by the event of the psychograph and the scant conversation that they had already had regarding what had happened before their eyes, and the subterranean history of Atalante.

Ourdeck, still full of the memory of Madame Jof, cannot help asking Rachel what she thinks, all the more so has he had heard no further mention of her since her extraordinary apparition.

Rachel formed a little smile and said: "Fortunate mortal, you have fled what you sought, now search for what has escaped you. That person has gone to hide in your heart, and you would have difficulty seeing her in any case." And, immediately taking a pencil, she replaced the letters of the name in their natural order,[53] which opened the eyes of the volunteer Ourdeck and filled him with an inexpressible joy.

Then she added: "It's necessary that you search very carefully for that interesting person in your heart, if you desire me to be there too, for I can only dwell with her.

"You are offering me there, Madame," he replied, "a powerful means of encouragement. What are, then, these impenetrable ways of wisdom, in which nothing is ordered or promised that is not delightful, and in which joy is itself the price of joy?"

"Monsieur," she told him, "there is nothing as delightful as the discoveries to which sage reflection can conduct us. But in spite of the pleasure that I would have in delving into that profound knowledge with you, the idea of my father occupies me too much, and my mind is not sufficiently free for us to deliver ourselves to similar speculations. I would even like you, I shall not hide it from you, in order to avoid going against the will of that good father, to do everything you can to follow him at a distance and at least watch over his safety, in case the opportunity presents itself for you to be of some assistance to him."

O Divine Rachel, it is your filial tenderness that makes you forget, for the moment, the confidence that, after so many prodigies, you ought to have in Eleazar's gifts.

Ourdeck draws away without replying; that separation appears to him nevertheless to be exceedingly painful, so much does he sense his solid attachment to that interesting

---

[53] Obviously, she does not rearrange the letters as if they were an anagram, but presumably replaces the vowels and sibilants diplomatically dropped from the abbreviated and softened name, previously indicated as unpronounced: Jehovah.

woman increase. But he is paid in return; that is what sustains him; he leaves with the intention of doing is best to respond to Rachel's tender solicitations; and Rachel remains constantly in Paris to fulfill the desires of her respectable father.

Canto 81
Eleazar's instruction to Sedir.

Already, Eleazar has gone with Sedir to the Plaine des Sablons, to the very place where the crocodile had swallowed the two armies. There, Eleazar, who has eyes *ad hoc*, blows twice on the ground, forcefully and then throws down, in the same place where he had blown, two pinches of his saline powder. Immediately, a subterranean tremor becomes audible, with a frightful racket.

"That's only a beginning," he says to Sedir, "and we must expect more violent shocks, if my desires are fortunate enough to be accomplished. Let's move away a few paces, in order to give the means I've employed the time to destroy entirely the nucleus that was the primary source of all our woes."

As they draw away, they do not cease to penetrate increasingly the great projects that occupy them.

Virtuous Sedir, it is here that you will receive the effect of the promises that Eleazar has made you, on the subject of his marvelous powder. Touched by the zeal that you have testified for him, touched above all by the evils and dangers that you suffered beside him during the lightning, he could not have chosen more favorable circumstances to satisfy your desires.

"You see," he said to him, "what the astonishing advantages are of the secret that my Arab confided to me; I no longer want to make a mystery of them for you. That secret is in you because it is in me and in all humans; and if, following the example of the master who has instructed me, I had not employed all my efforts in fructifying within me the seeds that is given to humans to be the base of all their wisdom and powers, that powder would never have served me in any way; for in the same way that it is the sovereign principle of which we receive all the properties, it is from me that the powder receives its virtues; and after having been penetrated by them, it relieves me in my work and becomes a support for me. If it were not thus, our airborne enemies would not have held it so uselessly in their hands, and they would have been able, at their whim, to plunge us into irremediable evils.

"I have, therefore, no need to extend myself further to enable you to comprehend the true source of my secret; and yet I am only waiting for the moment when I shall be dispensed from making use of it, and I can act directly myself by means of the natural gift that is in all humans—for I would not be able, without that, to complete the enormous labors that remain for us to carry out in order to save the capital.

"I have been able, by means of my accessory gifts, to combat in your presence the sinister and occult projects of the tall arid man and his companions; I have been able to extract the volunteer Ourdeck from the bosom of the crocodile and bring him back safe and sound from Atalante at the very moment when he experienced such a great shock in the hierophant's cellar; I have been able to force the crocodile to vomit up the two armies, although neither you nor the volunteer know as yet what has become of them, and I have not been able to return them to their fatherland immediately, since the crocodile has still had a retreat to furnish them in spite of me; I have been able to destroy the traps set by our airborne enemies several times, and snatch away from them what they had so much desire to conserve.

"But all these things are only feeble enterprises by comparison with what remains for us to do, for all the obstacles that we have surmounted have only been secondary and inferior obstacles. So long as we have not vanquished and subjugated not only the crocodile itself but also the maleficent men who have made themselves its organs, we shall not have completed our work.

"Now, we can only succeed in that by separating them from it, and separating it from them. By virtue of their wickedness, that have made themselves its organs, and by virtue of its avidity to pierce their intelligence, it has become their organ in its turn, by leading itself to all their perverse desires and favoring them with all its power. Thus, a double alliance has been formed between it and them, in which they have become both its tongue and thought, and it has become their thought and tongue.

"That forms something like two cauteries that are continually emptying into one another and filling one another mutually with their respective pus; and even without being wicked, men who talk too much undoubtedly establish similar cauteries between themselves and the universal enemy of the human species, who spies incessantly on our words in order to pump out the fruit they contain to put it to his profit, and to transmit his infection to us in return. That is what Ourdeck saw inside the crocodile; that is why the sciences are in his slavery, and that is why silence is so highly commended by sages. Know, then, that I can only break that double alliance by opposing to it a force of the same genre as the means that formed it, and it's to that fortunate goal that I aspire."

"Oh, my dear Eleazar," replied Sedir, "how eager I am for you to accomplish your sage desires, and subjugate this furious monster that is sowing so much alarm in my homeland! For the power with which its criminal adherents are equipped is a very surprising thing. Even when I did not have the knowledge that you have given me of their secrets, I could not dispense with believing that they were surely directed and protected by an extraordinary power. Since the commencement of the revolt, all my spies have set out on campaign against them; they have seen them, they have talked to them, but they have never succeeded in arresting them.

"Tell me how I can help you in your great enterprise; speak, dear Eleazar. Is it necessary to cross the seas? Is it necessary to travel the entire globe? Is it necessary, as our two armies have done, to penetrate again into the center of the earth? I'm ready for anything; there is nothing I would not undertake to be useful to my country and overturn the iniquitous projects of the wicked. In any case, it's the sole means that remains to me of rendering some service to the capital, the care of which has been confided to me; my presence is useless to it, since I have no aliments to procure it to alleviate its hunger, nor soldiers to send forth to prevent its disorders.

"Must we see our poor fellow citizens perish thus without being able to relieve them? No, no, that cruel condition cannot last any longer without debasing us. And if I have to perish in the enterprise, I'd rather go in search of death than wait for it; you have awoken in me principles whose seeds were sown in my soul in infancy. I loved the truth before knowing it; in giving me knowledge of it, you have only augmented my love for it, and I would be unworthy of your favors and your enlightenment if I did not seek to employ them in a circumstance that is surely the most important of all those that I have encountered in my life."

"You want it, then," said Eleazar, "for the good itself, and not for a vain curiosity! Well, you shall be satisfied. One cannot feign the impulses of the heart. I need a faithful companion like you, but I had to wait for providence to send me one, and I could not permit myself to ask for him. My daughter Rachel has been useful to me until this moment, and will never cease to be, but what remains for us to do requires strength that one does not have the right to ask of her sex. That is why I was waiting for a man. As for the volunteer Ourdeck, I have not had the time to prepare and graduate his instruction as I have done for yours. I cannot know, it is true, whether he might have been the one who was sent to me, but he doubted once, and you have had the good fortune to believe; that is what has made your advancement more rapid than his.

"Yes, you can work with me for the deliverance of our fatherland; but I warn you that the task will be rude and that you will have great obstacles to overcome. If confidence does not abandon you, we cannot fail to crown our endeavor with the most glorious success; for, since your last words, I have felt all the indications born within me. It is not necessary for you to travel the globe or pass over the seas; from the place where we are we can accelerate our enterprise, and perhaps even begin to collect its fruits."

Canto 82
Sedir is separated from Eleazar by a hurricane.

With those words, Eleazar stopped, took the precious box in his right hand and touched it gently three times to his breast, three times to his forehead, and three times to Sedir's mouth.

"Go now," he said to him, "and blow twice on the hearth of iniquity as you saw me do just now."

Sedir obeyed.

(Dear reader, remember that words are only good when they are engendered by our heart and by our mind. I would like to be able to tell you more, but the details of everything that happened in that ceremony have not been confided to me sufficiently fully for me to be able to deliver them to your curiosity. I only have the ability to depict the results for you.)

As soon as the ceremony is finished, a terrible tempest blows up; a furious wind suddenly descends from the sky and falls like an impetuous torrent on Eleazar and Sedir, and knocks both of them over. They get up, and are bowled over again. They get up again, and for the third time they are swept off their feet.

Eleazar alone gets up for the third time, but he is carried off by the turbulence, far enough away from his friend not to be able to join him as immediately as he would have desired for the wellbeing of both of them, and he takes at least an hour trying to find him again.

Poor Sedir is lying at the foot of a tree, so stunned by his three falls that he is absolutely unaware of where he is, bruised in several parts of his body, and not having at his disposal Eleazar's efficacious and marvelous remedy.

In that extraordinary state, which some call stupor and others torpor, and which we do not dare to name at all for fear of being mistaken, Sedir is accosted by a man who tells him tales beyond all belief, such that when he reported them subsequently to Eleazar he could not even say whether or not it was in a dream that he had heard the tales, or whether or not it was a real person who told them to him, for he found himself alone when he emerged from that indefinable state.

Canto 83
An observation.

(For myself, dear reader, I cannot assure you either whether it was in a dream or reality that he was told those tales, as you shall see in the following cantos

    For I am too submissive, faithful to my Muse
To say in her name what might be an abuse.
Because on this matter she agreed in a whisper
With all sincerity, that she did not know either.

Listen, then, quite simply, to what that human figure, real or not, came to say to Sedir while he was either asleep or awake, or while he was neither one nor the other.)

Canto 84
Instructive discourse of an unknown.
Announcement of the two armies.

"The two armies will soon be returned to the Plaine des Sablons; I have come as an advance guard to inform you of that, for I speak to you as one of the combatants, although I belong to a very pacific profession. Know only, for the moment, that I can see everything without changing location, and whether in the stars or on earth, nothing is hidden from my gaze.

"After the long sojourn that the two armies first made in the body of the crocodile, it was forced by Eleazar to vomit them forth from its bosom; although there were very culpable men among them, there were also very deserving men, and in great catastrophes wisdom permits that things are thus disposed, in order that those purifying and preservative salts can conserve the mass from an entire dissolution and an absolute ruination; but as the crocodile did not want the two armies to return immediately to Paris, where it has such a terrible adversary, it still had the power to vomit them forth with so much violence that it launched them all the way to the region of the planets and stars. At the same time, it conserved in the various champions of the two armies all the ardor that had animated them even before they were swallowed, and had only become more impetuous as a result of their sojourn in its entrails.

"Those various champions, launched with so much force, clung on wherever they could to the various planets, comets and stars that they encountered within their reach; from there they menaced one another with eyes inflamed with anger, and prepared to deliver themselves to further combats. The same power that had vomited them up on to those globes gave them the means to make those immense bodies floating in the plains of air move as they wished; suddenly, the two armies were seen ranged in battle order in front of one another, deploying the most savant maneuvers. Soon, they determined to get to grips; at that moment enormous spheres were seen to came together and collide with a frightful noise.

"But that means was incompetent to fulfill the object and vengeance of the combatants, for, those heavenly bodies being elastic and filled with air, like all floating bodies, their impact produced a result entirely contrary to the one that the two armies expected. In fact, on coming together thus with violence, they developed their elasticity mutually, and sent one another rebounding to inconceivable distances. It is doubtless that elasticity, which your scholars have never be able to penetrate, that conserves the form of all the bodies in the universe, since without it they would destroy one another; and that is what, in this instance, set a limit to the fury of mortals. Thus, it has given Eleazar the time to suspend once again, momentarily, the murderous designs of the two armies.

Canto 85
Continuation of the unknown's instructive discourse.
The spheres.

"During these various impacts, I took care, with your intention, to observe very attentively all those spheres that have appeared sufficiently beautiful to a few writers to make them say what they were, notably the Sun, which had emerged from all the cults and religious dogmas in the world. Those writers, so quick to judge, ought at least to have excepted from their decisions the cults and dogmas that condemned those astronomical cults and dogmas as being reproofs on the part of wisdom, and you can quote them the fourth chapter of Deuteronomy in favor of the cults and dogmas that it is necessary to except from their decisions, and which prove what liars they are. The time has not come for those who can tell you more.

"I made a summary of all that I saw traced on the surface of all those vast spheres; there was an innumerable quantity of various imprinted figures on which my gaze was fixed; and I had the leisure to observe them, not only on my own heavenly body, during the long movement caused to it by the violent impacts of all those celestial legions, but also on the other bodies, planets or stars, when we were in their vicinity.

"I saw traced on those spheres various characters and hieroglyphs, such as animals, planets, alphabetical letters, musical instruments, thrones, arms, natural phenomena, fires, floods, battlefields, slain cadavers, diamond-studded crowns, triumphal chariots, books, diplomas, sashes, instruments for the arts and métiers: in sum, signs taken from all of nature and human inventions.

"I saw there not only all those emblems, but humans occupied in the various employments and labors that those emblems indicated. I saw warriors, artists of every kind, doctors of secret sciences whom the curious came to consult, hoping to learn the fate of their material life, while humans of true desire have within them the power to know and determine the life of their spirit.

"I saw somnambulists, and also individuals whose minds had been alienated, and I saw that their condition could stem from two causes: one was a physical derangement of their organs, which occasioned in their thinking either a privation or a contraction; the other was the predominance that those people allowed to take in them of a deregulated affection. For if there are involuntary dementias, there are even more that are the fruit of the false usage of human liberty. That is why, proportionally, fewer lunatics are seen in the humble and laborious class of people than in the elevated or idle class.

"I saw mathematicians continually tracing figures and numbers, in order to pierce scientific verities by themselves, into which they will never be able to penetrate without the hidden guide that is within them. I saw them abusing the most beautiful laws of that beautiful science, in order to extend it into regions that were forbidden to them, and waning to substitute their own means for those they ought to have been content to observe and wait. I saw them spending their lives in being nothing but the surveyors of nature; I saw them measuring the external part of that vast edifice, and the external dimensions of the various stones of which its walls are composed, but never entering into the edifice, and even cluttering it up to such an extent with their innumerable pieces of scaffolding that they hid it from the sight of all eyes, including their own.

"I saw them launched by their discoveries all the way to the vicinity of sublime clarities, and then plunge those torches into the mud, as if they were only good for casting momentary glimmers on heaps of earth. The mathematical sciences are made to conduct humans in the median path and between two the extremes; that is why, on the one hand, they do not know the positive base of mathematical science, and on the other, why they go astray when they want, without the true light that is within them, to exceed the range of that science. If they observed prudently and carefully how that base governs itself the fundamental verities that they abuse so much, perhaps the verities in question would develop before them, including the positive results thy seek, which would be more exact and accurate than all those they can procure by the manipulations they employ.

"I saw people there represented next to an alchemical furnace very busy around their vessel. I saw all the instruments that enter into a laboratory; but alongside the crude alchemists who were reckoned ignorant by their colleagues, I saw some who qualified as alchemists of the most learned class and the only true one, because they do not make use of coal. I saw avid men surrounding those savant alchemists and devouring with their eyes the treasures promised to them; whereas the only alchemy and the only treasures that are veritably useful to us are the transmutation and renewal of our being.

"I saw hosts of authors there who were not writing for the glory of truth, having ceased to take it for a guide, no longer having left their mind open to anything but personal glory, and to all the mingled and confused images that could present themselves to fill it. So I saw all those sources secondary or foreign to the truth entering their minds like a flood.

I saw all the notions there that are scattered and subdivided in a thousand fashions in the regions of the stars and throughout the universe enter into them at the same time and transform themselves into a formless mass, from which the same notions them emerged from their mind devoid of order and passed from there into their books; that was what was represented physically to the Academicians in the scene of the broth of books, in order to make them understand that things always have a terminus analogous to their commencement; it is also what was represented non-physically to the volunteer Ourdeck during his sojourn in the crocodile, to instruct him in correspondences, and to show him what the agents are who are responsible for passing all these universal mixtures from the stars into the minds of human beings, and, in consequence, to show him the services that the host of thinkers and writers of books renders to the world, and how they are duped by their pride when they represent them to you as the fruit of their invention.

"I saw fanatical men there imperiously professing their sanguinary doctrine, inhumanely massacring their fellows in the name of a God of peace, and carrying the emblems of piety for a sign of murder and battle. In sum, I saw all human passions there, each represented with features that one could not misinterpret.

Canto 86
Continuation of the instructive discourse of an unknown. Correspondences.

"That would be nothing if I had been reduced to considering all those objects without having the intelligence of them. You know that I can see everything; I can also understand everything. I have come, therefore, not only as the advance guard of the two armies, but also to communicate to you the intelligence of what I have seen in the stars; they are the first of the benefits that you will receive in future, in recompense for the zeal for the truth, and for the salvation of your fatherland, that you have testified to Eleazar.

"Know, then, that in fact, everything that happens down here among humans in the order of external things is figured on the surface of all the spheres that circulate in the heavens, and that everything that humans operate with so much care, so much importance and so much pride has been represented since the beginning of time on the envelope of those same spheres, which are veritably covered in all those signs, as your skin is covered with little wrinkles and little stars whose arrangement and symmetry is infinitely variable.

"Those spheres rolling continuously in the heavens press the human brain and engrave there the kind of impression of which the figure traced on the heavenly body happens to be directed toward them for the moment; then, in continuing their courses, they engrave another impression there, because another figure is presented in consequence of the rotation of the heavenly body.

"By virtue of that same law of the rotation of the heavenly bodies, it comes about that the same points of pressure return at fixed periods and operate the same impressions among humans; so they are habitually in an ebb and flow of the same ideas and the same movements, as constantly and with periods almost as marked as that of the ebb and flow of your Ocean.

261

"All the marvels of which humans boast on earth, therefore, ought no longer o flatter their self-esteem, since they are not their inventors, and they are only repeating in a servile and mechanical manner what the surfaces of the heavenly bodies imprint on them as they pass over them.

"Nor ought they to glorify themselves on the predictions they can make of the interior and particular events of their globe, since those events are traced like grand plans on the heavenly bodies circling overhead, and which simply imprint the result on them.

"They ought not to extract so much vanity from their scientific discoveries, from all their secrets, from all their sciences and al their arts, since all those things are written before they know them on the celestial spheres, and they are only repeating lessons that the spheres inculcate on a daily basis, but adding to them the influences that a power more malign and tenebrous than the stars never ceases to extend up there in that vast atmosphere, and down here in the minds of human beings; verities that the crocodile has allowed to penetrate involuntarily into all the allegories that it related to you.

"Even if one does not recognize those influences for what they are, one ought perhaps to have more indulgence than one has for human vices and passions, since those same vices and passions are also similarly written on the surfaces of celestial bodies, and it is by virtue of those same imprints that the revolutions of empires and the disorders of individuals are directed; which means that simply by casting a glance at the spheres, one can read, as in very detailed annals, the entire history of peoples, from the commencement of the world to the end, the wars, the massacres, the upheavals of nations, the hidden work that magicians, astrologers and alchemists have operated and operate every day in secret among the kings and the emperors, even among those who are bound to abjure those kinds of sciences by their religious law: all things that are only, as it were, the natural paroxysms of the moral fever to which all human beings are prey.

"But if humans made a little more use of their intelligence, and they listened a little more attentively to what is happening within them, they would no longer be entitled to claim that indulgence, for not only could one no longer excuse their vices and their passions, but one could no longer excuse their mistakes and their errors. I'll tell you why.

Canto 87
Continuation of the instructive discourse of an unknown. Oppositions.

"Those heavenly bodies are so great in number, and each of them has such an ardor to carry out its own plans, that they interfere with one another and combat one another even more than they support one another mutually to collaborate in the great harmony. The consequence of that is that the plans of some are routinely contradicted by the plans of others, and unless humans unite themselves with another light by means of a total transmutation of the self, it is almost impossible to count with certainty on the success of what is announced, since another point of contact might disrupt it.

"That is what introduces so much obscurity into the various oracles that have appeared on earth, and which only march by those troubled paths.

"That is what has so often frustrated the projects of conquerors and the ambitious; and that is what ought to maintain a wariness against those prodigies and revolutions announced by mixed or simply astronomical ways, since all those announcements might be combated a moment later by contrary announcements and plans, and one cannot know before the event which of all those announcements will have the advantage.

"One can no longer excuse humans for their vices and their disorders, although those same vices and those same disorders are also traces on the surface of celestial spheres, because measures, perfections and virtues are also represented in part on those same surfaces, and humans thus have the scope to make a just discernment. Thus, they are inexcusable when they do not profit from that advantage, and are even more culpable when, after having made that discernment, they do not behave in a manner that is in conformity with it.

"That verity is all the more certain because humans have within them the repetition of all the astral spheres that ornament the heavens, and they also have a repetition of all the figures and all the characters that are traced on the celestial surfaces; so, if they only paid a little attention to them, they would always be able to make all the observations that are necessary to them for their surety and instruction within themselves.

"For in the quality of human beings, they have in addition a power superior to that of the heavenly bodies themselves, in that they are born and they reside in the fixed region, whereas the heavenly bodies have been born in the inferior and mixed region full of uncertainty. Thus humans have, above the spheres, the privilege of being able to transpose all the signs that are written within them, to efface those that are false or might be prejudicial to them, and to extend the action of those that are true so much that they make them powerful preservatives; with the result that they would have nothing more to fear on the part of those plans and celestial imprints that no longer have the character of truth, and which might lead them astray, either in matters pertaining to the heart and virtue, or matters pertaining to the mind and intelligence.

"I ought to add for your personal instruction that it is in the rectification of all those signs in human being that true transmutation consists; that is what characterizes the true victory that human ought to win on earth, and it is only that narrow path by which they can achieve the conquest of the domains of peace, enlightenment and truth.

"Work there constantly for the rest of your days. If you devote yourself to that task with courage you will soon harvest its fruits; and the principal of those fruits will be liberating yourself from all the shackles of the region of destinies, which are the astral regions, and of rising so far above them that you renter in spirit into the region devoid of time and destiny from which you emerged, and the only one in which you can find the repose, the life and the science that are your primitive elements and your original nature.

"That point is sufficient for your particular instruction, if you are able to take advantage of what I have just told you. But I ought to add further knowledge to it, by completing the story of what happened in regard to the two armies in the astral regions from which I am supposed to have descended.

Canto 88
Continuation of the instructive discourse of an unknown. Commotions. The two armies en route.

"At the moment when the commotion was at its height and the entire Empyrean seemed to be on the brink of shattering into smithereens, a secret force unknown to the combatants came to change the march of the two armies and purge the stars of the two bodies so foreign to them. The ceremony that Eleazar carried out before you on the Plaine des Sablons had prepared the work; but it is the one that you and he have just carried out together that has consummated it.

"It is those ceremonies that have forced the crocodile to breathe in forcefully. As it was its breath that transported the two armies all the way to the heavens, it is the same breath that has just withdrawn the two armies involuntarily from the heavenly bodies where they took refuge.

"Nothing is comparable to the agitation to which the region of the heavens was subjected at the moment when that unknown force made itself felt, because the crocodile, seeing that only a few moments of triumph remained to it, employed all its power to prolong them.

"So the violent turbulence that you felt on earth was the result of its fury; judge by the law of correspondences that I have explained to you what trouble and disorder there must have been in the superior regions; now that calm is reestablished there, however, the two armies are *en route* through the air, returning down here to decide their destinies.

Canto 89
Continuation of the instructive discourse of an unknown.
The effects of the astral sojourn of the two armies.

"But the power of that unknown force has not been limited to extracting the two armies from the heavens; it has operated an effect no less extraordinary on the individuals of which they are composed.

"Their previous sojourn in the bosom of the crocodile offered you very important verities relative to human beings, both while they dwell on the terrestrial surface and before they make their habitation there. Those truths are that humans cannot be too careful in watching over the maintenance of their essential being and the culture and development of their superior and regular faculties, since the negligence they might allow themselves in that regard has so much influence on those who inhabit the same circle as them that it is possible to draw themselves into the fatal consequences of their blindness.

"That is what you have been shown by the astonishing prodigy in which the crocodile has not only swallowed the army of those in revolt, but has also swallowed the army that sought to defend the good cause; and that is what you see repeated on earth every day.

"But it is in that same law that the remedy is also found or so many evils, since it is also brings out all the good qualities of virtuous men who are avid for justice.

"Thus, if the most culpable of humans is engulfed in an abyss with their vices, they are also engulfed with their virtues, and the eternal reason of things finds a means to filter a universal regulator through to them, which puts them back on the temporary paths of rectification, or the astral paths, until they can rise higher.

"Eleazar has retraced that primitive deliverance of humans by extracting the two armies from the bosom of the crocodile, and in allowing them to be launched all the way to

268

the heavens, which, since the residence of humans on earth, has indeed been a kind of provisional regulator for them, when they follow the law with patient resignation, and are wary of the countless dangers with which those preparatory paths of rectification are perennially accompanied.

"In allowing the crocodile to launch the two armies all the way to the heavens, Eleazar was able by that means to extract the good from the evil, while the crocodile, on the contrary, was only able to extract the evil from the good; in fact, if in the bosom of the crocodile the innocent were tormented with the guilty, it might be that in the astral regions, when they were supervised by a good guide, even the culpable were included in the deliverance and the rectification of the innocent, and that is the deliverance that humans can achieve within themselves at every moment of their lives, since their true thoughts, like the false, are at odds within them on a daily basis in that same astral region, which presently constitutes their envelope.

"That fortunate effect was more common in ancient and primitive times than it has become in the course of the centuries, because the virtues of the heavenly bodies were freer than they are at present, and in their turn, humans did not have as much time to be infected by the poison of their enemy as in the advanced epochs of the age of the world, for the mass of those accumulated poisons is now so enormous that it is a prodigy today when, out of millions of human beings, there is one who escapes the disastrous hand that extends over all the astral powers by which nature is governed.

"So you can see on earth how small the number has been reduced of those who conserve themselves intact, and how immense, on the contrary is the number of those who, instead of turning to their advantage and their renewal those same astral and regulatory powers of your globe, only employ them to their own detriment, or in allowing themselves to be dominated like blind and insensate slaves, or even rendering themselves despicable and shameful playthings of the avid and cruel enemy who seeks incessantly to neutralize those powers, in order to substitute his own, and who succeeds all too often and only too well.

"Although the fortunate effects of those astral and restorative powers were more common once than they have since become, I will not hide it from you that Eleazar's powers have rendered to them in the present circumstance a part of their primitive efficacy, the favorable results of which have been felt in the two armies.

"By a consequence of the ineradicable right that the liberty of humans gives them, the individuals of the two armies have not all made an equal usage of the advantages that Eleazar's powers have procured them; nevertheless, their fruits have been abundant enough for there to be reason to congratulate him in his enterprise. That Tartar woman has not neglected to be of some utility to him in that vast project. He has also been especially seconded by the powerful assistance of a secret society of humans that is not unknown to him, even though he is not yet numbered among its members

"That society I announce to you as being the only one on earth that is a real image of the divine society, and of which I tell you now that I am the founder. It has for its principal guide a woman whose real name Rachel has made known to Ourdeck, and whom he had mistaken until then for the wife of a jeweler. It is true that her husband is a jeweler, but he only shapes the diamonds that the elementary fire cannot dissolve, and that jeweler is the same person who is speaking to you, and whose help will soon be indispensable to Eleazar and to you. I shall say no more, Adieu, Sedir, and get up."

Canto 90
Sedir finds himself with Eleazar again.
The effects of Eleazar's power.

Sedir gets up and finds himself, to his great contentment, beside his friend Eleazar, to whom he reports with an unusual haste everything that has just happened to him, by which he is so surprised himself. Eleazar, delighted to see his friend again and delighted by everything that he hears, says to him: "Sedir, you and I have just experienced a rude assault; however, the moment is approaching when we are going to have even greater evils to endure—but we also ought to expect to collect the fruit of all these endeavors, if we do not cease to put our confidence in the one who has already delivered us from so many dangers."

As soon as Eleazar had pronounced those final words, a globe, red and brown in color, was seen descending rapidly through the layers of the air, spitting fire and flame and heading for the Plaine des Sablons. Above and close behind that globe others could be seen, not quite as large, speckled gray in color, descending with the same rapidity and following the same course; finally, descending from higher still, others were visible in greater number, and darker in color.

That phenomenon transported Eleazar and Sedir with joy, without nevertheless surprising them infinitely, after all the advertisements they had received; but it greatly astonished all the other people who were able to perceive it, and doubtless all those who had remained in the city, and who could not know either what the source of the phenomenon might be, or what its result would be. They could not even know that the Plane des Sablons was the rendezvous of the cortege.

Rachel admired the spectacle like everyone else, and although she did not know its veritable object, that only made her redouble her zeal and her desire for the safety of her father, ardently wishing that he could bring his great enterprises

271

to a fortunate conclusion, and would soon return bringing good news.

She was also far from indifferent regarding the fate of the volunteer Ourdeck, whom she had charged with coming to his defense if circumstances required it, and those various agitations affected her soul forcefully enough for her to desire to see an end to them. Faithful to her father's positive orders, however, she remained in Paris in order to bring, by means of her presence and her prayers, all the consolations and preservatives that were in her power, in spite of all the curiosity she had to know what the globes or balloons were. She did not know, any more than anyone else, where they were headed or where they had come from.

As for the tall arid man and his associates, they were not unaware of the location of the scene, or the great prodigies that were in preparation there; the crocodile had given them that information, in passing on the little that it knew itself. For it had a great need to know all the consequences clearly in advance.

Canto 91
Sedir is filled with joy by an unexpected sign.

At the sight of those globes, Eleazar shook Sedir's hand and said: "You see the commencement of the confirmation of all that you have been told a little while ago while your extraordinary state lasted. Soon you shall have authentic evidence that what was said to you was neither an illusion nor a lie. Yes, our forces and our power would be nothing if a hand more powerful than mine and everything that is known to you had not come to support and assist us; it is the hand in question that will enable us to fight—or, rather, it is the hand in question that will be able to fight and vanquish for us.

"There he is!" cried Sedir, suddenly, as if beside himself, and pointing at someone with his finger. "There's he is! That's the person who spoke to me just now; or rather, judging by the fire I experience, I presume that it's the power itself of which he was only the organ and the envoy. Eleazar, Eleazar, what have I done to merit such favors?"

Eleazar has seen the individual as well as Sedir, and knows better than him what the object of his coming was.

In fact, that individual, a thousand times more radiant than the stars advances majestically to a distance of three or four paces, then stops and says in a loud voice: "Eleazar, Eleazar, come closer to me."

Sedir, simultaneously penetrated by respect and admiration, dare not budge, and is content to look intently. But Eleazar immediately marches toward the one who has summoned him, and tells him, with a surge of delight and humility, that he is ready to obey his commands.

"Eleazar, Eleazar," replies the individual, "you are admitted to the Society of Independents. The tasks that remain for you to accomplish, in which you will act as leader, require that rank to be accorded to you, and those you have undertaken previously are the titles that have obtained it for you; for in

273

that society, it is deeds that occasion all solicitation, in the same way that it is wisdom that makes it sensible internally, and announcing that these endeavors are recompensed comprises all the ceremonial of admission. I have no other instruction to give you. Your new dignity brings all clarity with it, and the knowledge of everything you have to do at any moment."

With those words, the individual disappears.

The first usage that Eleazar makes of his new estate is to return promptly to Sedir, saying to him: "Sedir, I have been summoned to march henceforth by the true motive and the primitive path of humankind. All the other means that have been so useful to me thus far can no longer serve me as a support, and it is no longer appropriate for me to employ them. But since you and I are united to work, each according to his means, for the most glorious of enterprises, I cannot receive advancement without enabling you to share in it, in the measure that is appropriate to you.

"Receive from my hands, therefore, this precious box. You have seen the numerous prodigies that are operated by the even more precious powder that it contains. You know its composition. You know, to a great extent, the manner in which to make use of it. The more you exert yourself, the more you will perfect that knowledge. Although I have to act secretly as leader in the task that is in preparation, you have to act more ostensibly than me by virtue of your place, and the present I am giving you is both the recompense for your zeal and a powerful support for you in the battle."

Sedir, at the peak of joy, is moved to tears in receiving that incomparable treasure, in regard to which he was far from having formed the slightest project. Touched by gratitude, still filled with the vision of the majestic individual who has just disappeared, but burning with ardor to pursue the task that summons them, he embraces Eleazar; then both of them make haste, and soon arrive at the location already so famous by virtue of the great feats the crocodile has performed there.

Canto 92
The two armies appear in the air.

It was indeed the two armies that were descending from the heavens by means of those globes. The army of revolt came down first, its general at its head. As each of the globes reached the ground, it deposited a warrior on the terrain, and then, turning into water, it was lost in the sand. The rebel army landed in the very place on the Plaine des Sablons where the crocodile had appeared for the first time. The faithful army came down a few moments later, some distance away, and followed the same means of landing, except that although the globes that had carried them did, in truth, turn to water, it was water that, instead of flowing into the sand rose up in light vapors so shiny that they could be compared to a silvery dew.

Canto 93
The crocodile sends its army into battle.

The woman of consequence, still dressed as a man, and the tall arid man had already arrived at that important and celebrated location, on the advice that they had received from the Crocodile. They witnessed the arrival of the army of the insurgents, which they supported, and they saw all the individuals composing it touch down.

But none of the latter, or either of the two individuals, had perceived the arrival of the patriotic army, so great and powerful was the hand supervising the good cause. The individual who emerged from the red and brown globe was the famous Roson, the rebel general, whose name signifies "chief of iniquity," and who had perhaps done more evil in the capital than the entire army.

The two evil individuals and he tightened their union more narrowly than ever, and they immediately told him about all the marvels that had occurred during his absence. In any case, they found themselves linked by the same functions and by the same spirit that stimulated all those disasters, for scarcely had Roson set foot on the ground, along with his troop, than the Crocodile appeared on the terrain in person, in the figure of an army general with a superb uniform and a hat ornamented by a huge plume, with a commander's baton in his hand, mounted on a magnificent charger.

He called his three agents to him and attached them to him as aides-de-camp, and made them swear an oath never to abandon him. He left them on foot and did not furnish them with any mount, even though he had a beautiful horse himself. In order that they would easily be able to follow all his movements, however, he transmitted an astonishing agility to them, and the property of advancing, retreating, rising up and pouncing in such a fashion that, although they were distinct from him, one could say that they were really only one with him.

When he had thus prepared his three aides-de-camp he said to them: "Worthy cooperators in my glorious endeavors, the moment has come to win the most splendid victory. Although a redoubtable enemy has prevented me from consummating my hostile projects on his person, and putting a powerful barrier even on my speech, he will not have the same success here, for that speech has been returned to me in spite of him, thanks to the triumph, albeit temporary, of Haridelle. I know that my redoubtable adversary is not far away. As soon as he appears, do not fail to exterminate him; that is the sole means we have of recovering our empire. Let us take advantage of the favorable moment that is offered to us, since the army of the patriots has not yet descended."

Having concluded that brief harangue, he arranged his entire army in battle order, augmented by all the malevolent individuals who were in the vicinity, with whom the rebels had already conversed sufficiently for their projects to be reciprocally concerted, and their reciprocal curiosity to be very nearly satisfied; he remained in the center, awaiting he moment to act.

He had reason to think that his enemy Eleazar was not far away, but he did not suspect that he was in fact right in front of him, at his horse's nose, and that he was about to experience the power of his redoubtable adversary, for his eyes were struck by the blindness that would lead him to his doom.

In fact, while the new general had been preparing his rebel army, the army of the god Frenchmen had immediately been joined by Sedir and Eleazar. As soon as the patriotic army had seen Sedir in the distance, its members had uttered cries of joy and hurled their hats into the air. When Sedir drew closer the cries of joy increased, and he was unable to prevent himself from allowing all his satisfaction to show, and also a great deal of affection, on seeing brave citizens who, in consequence of their devotion to the fatherland, had experienced so much fatigue, and all the extraordinary adventures that each of them had the urgent desire to recount to him.

"You can dispense with that," he said, showing them Eleazar. "This is a precious friend, who, by means of his intermediary, has informed me of everything that has happened to you, since the moment when you were swallowed here by a Crocodile, to the one when you were aspired by that monster all the way to the stars, from which you have just descended. This friend to longer leaves me, and he has come in person to aid me in crowning all your endeavors; you cannot have a more solid support on the earth, or a more essential friend. I shall not add anything more for the moment; time is pressing; you have none to lose in order to arrange your battalions and prepare for combat. You can see that the enemy is present and commanded by a terrible general. Eleazar and I shall go to mount the first attack, and you will move off when we give you the signal."

With those final words, the volunteer Ourdeck arrived, who had been guided by the spectacle of the balloons descending from the clouds. Further embraces followed, even more ardent, so delighted were the warriors to see him again after the perils they had shared, and after the interval of time during which they had been separated. He would certainly have liked to return to Rachel to tell her the good news, and to reassure her on Eleazar's account, but honor and the salvation of the fatherland retained him, and he immediately took his place among his comrades, not wanting to lose his part in the laurels that awaited them. How many things they had to say to one another—and how many they said, in fact, in spite of the brevity of the moments that circumstances left them!

Canto 94
The transformation of the crocodile.

It is in the course of those confidential effusions that Eleazar goes with Sedir, invisibly, to the vicinity of the rebel army, unknown to its arrogant general, and not long after the latter had boasted of having recovered the power of speech. Without allowing himself to be seen as yet, Eleazar says to him: "If you have recovered speech, you won't conserve it for long; and it's as true that you're going to lose it as it is that this hand is going to close before you."

As soon as the arrogant general recovers his sight, Eleazar and Sedir each advance an open hand, and close it before his eyes. Immediately, the general's lips are closed, without him being able to open them. Rage is painted on his face, and fury takes possession of all his movements. His aides-de-camp participate in his rage and his fury as well as his shame, and are all as mute as him, because he has linked them to his person. In his transport, he wants to launch himself forward with his horse at his two adversaries. He makes gestures to his army to give the order to surround them; in fact, the general does make a forward movement, and the army's wings break away in order to advance in a semicircle.

But Eleazar and Sedir say at the same time, and without speaking: "You're mistaken if you think you can prevail over us and the vigilant eye that serves as our guide. You haven't yet reached the end of your humiliations. It isn't enough that we've taken away your power of speech; it's also necessary that we take away your disguise; for don't think that you can impose on us by means of your human form and your pompous adornment. We know what is hidden beneath that appearance; we have the power to lay it bare—and to prove it to you, it's as true that your false and deceptive form is about to be removed as it is that our closed hands are going to open before you."

Immediately, they open their hands before him, and by the effect of that act alone, the audacious and imprudent general changes form in the blink of an eye, and no one can any longer see, in the place of the man and the horse, anything but a vile and disgusting crocodile of unusual length, opening its maw unimaginably wide.

The aides-de-camp do not change form, but still remain attached to the movement of the animal, as they had been to those of the general.

The army, alarmed by that sudden transmutation, begins to recoil. The crocodile runs from one wing to the other to engage its members to hold firm, and its aides-de-camp run with it; but that hideous form frightens the warriors even more. The more efforts it makes to excite the ardor of its army, the more it fills its members with terror, and the army falls back so far as to pass over the remarkable spot that had received such important preparations by means of the mysterious ceremonies of Eleazar and Sedir, in such a fashion that the location is then on the near side of the rebel army, whereas it had previously been beyond it. The crocodile finds itself much closer to the spot, inasmuch as it has followed the movements of its army.

The patriotic army admires all those prodigies and is burning with the desire to advance, but, faithful to Sedir's orders, its members are waiting for him to give the sign; and the moment has not yet come for the sign to be given, inasmuch as the principal enemy that it is a matter of defeating, is not fighting with the simple weapons of warriors.

In fact, by dint of agitating, the crocodile is oozing a thick foam from all its pores, which emits a noxious odor. In addition, torrents of fire emerge from its mouth, which would have intimidated the most intrepid of men. That foam and that fire amalgamate together and are transformed into an innumerable multitude of maleficent animals of every species, which circulate *en masse* in the atmosphere, obscuring it to such an extent that nothing at all can any longer be discerned, and not the slightest particle remains that is breathable.

At that moment, instead of being discouraged, Sedir feels impelled to make use of the treasure that Eleazar has given him; he takes the precious box and throws a few pinches of the powder toward the various points of the horizon, over the masses of maleficent animals—but it is only after repeating that ceremony four times that he succeeds in making them disappear and clarifying the atmosphere. Still he cannot prevent the crocodile from emitting fire from its maw and foam from its pores; he only has the power to exterminate the results of their horrible amalgam and render them sterile.

But what does he see after having thus clarified the atmosphere?

He sees Eleazar himself standing in the open and blazing maw of the crocodile, and walking there as serenely and calmly as if he were far away from any kind of danger, and not in the midst of the moist frightful infection.

In setting foot in that flaming maw, large enough to contain an upright man, Eleazar, by that act alone, had rendered the monster immobile, as if paralyzed. When he entered it, he took fifteen steps, in order to reach the tongue, which is known to be very short. And scarcely had he taken the fifteenth step than the monster no longer emitted flames or foam.

Then Eleazar withdraws with the same composure; and, on emerging from the monster's maw, he allows it to resume the movement by which it is bound to be conducting itself to its doom.

Canto 95
The convulsive movements of the crocodile.

The crocodile, beginning to see the danger that is menacing it, and feeling the effect of what Eleazar and Sedir have just done, makes frightful commotions. Soon it is giving itself spasms from head to tail capable of terrifying bravery itself; and yet, the three aides-de-camp hold firm, and do not abandon it. Sometimes it makes leaps of twenty feet into the air, and falling back to earth with a horrible noise; and still, the three aides-de-camp rise up with it and do not abandon it. Sometimes it runs as if it no longer has its senses round the spot so redoubtable for it, and to which it has deferred its approach for so long, and yet, in the midst of those rotations, its three aides-de-camp follow it everywhere and do not abandon it. One can say that no combatants ever took such constancy so far, and serenity in the face of ill fortune and such a menacing fate.

But finally, the fatal moment arrives. Eleazar, Sedir and the distant invisible man all direct a violent blast of air toward the prepared spot.

Ourdeck, burning with impatience, but full of docility for the respectable individuals he saw at work, made ardent wishes internally for their success. Rachel, who was still in Paris to collaborate with its preservation, felt an internal stir occasioned by that powerful blast; her courage and zeal were further increased by it. The Tartar woman showed herself in the figure of a star, as she had twice before, and there could be no doubt that the Society of Independents, with the famous Madame Jof at its head, was also active. How could the good cause, aided by all those means, fail to take on an increasingly favorable aspect?

In fact, instantly, at the place prepared for the work, the atmospheric air precipitated into it with an impetuous force and noise. The frightened crocodile gave one last leap, but so violent, so sudden and with such a shock that the secret bond linking it with the three aides-de-camp was severed; they were hurled rudely to the ground a long way from their chief, and remained extended, broken and unconscious. Immediately, they were put under the guard of a detachment, with orders not to do them any harm until the laws had decided their fate. The monster's convulsions were only increased by that disaster.

Canto 96
The extraordinary vomit of the crocodile.

It was not enough that the crocodile had previously vomited up the two armies, as well as all the forgivable humans that had been detained in its bosom. It was also necessary that it vomit up the kind of poison with which it had poured so much evil over the earth, and that it only retained the venom that constituted its own existence, and from which it could not be separated.

It therefore vomited, by the effect of its violent spasms, two huge letters of the alphabet, the names of which have not been left to us. We can only say that those two letters were really one, for they were twins; that they had commenced with a kind of perpendicular, and that they had afterwards added to that perpendicular the form of an open mouth with a tongue; but soon afterwards, they had taken the form of a closed mouth without a tongue, and instantly, the closed mouth without a tongue that they had assumed became double.

Those two letters, on emerging from the monster, emitted a strong arsenical odor, and immediately produced a living being that firstly had two human heads, one of which was motionless while the other was returning perpetually; secondly a very hairy body, each hair of which was an insect or a worm; and thirdly, a tail composed of a confused mixture of all the metals, which created the belief that the two letters were simultaneously the grinder and the coagulant of human thought, the born enemy of all regular corporization and the universal metallic mineralizer. The living being they had produced, which was only formed of vapors, passed rapidly over the open gulf, and evaporated in the atmosphere.

Canto 97
The crocodile's punishment.

The monster, deprived of all its correspondences with its aides-de-camp, with nature and with human thoughts, tries to make one last effort, and rises up to a height of fifty feet; but as it descends, it cannot resist the current of air, which drags it into the open gulf, and precipitates it into that opening, all the way to the depths of Egypt, in order to be bolted to the pyramid forever. Henceforth, it will be unable to circulate in the world, for our three operatives blow again, so powerfully that they seal the gulf into which their cruel enemy has just been plunged, and all the other gulfs of the earth that could provide it with the slightest issue.

Then these words are heard above the gulf: "Our reign is over; all our hopes have vanished."

Canto 98
The fruits of victory.

At that moment, either by a natural effect of the disappearance of the monster or as a consequence of salutary influences that the two armies had brought back from their sojourn in the heavens, both armies simultaneously, as if by virtue of a spontaneous impulse, throw down their arms, and as rapid as lighting, run toward one another in order to see which can give the most abundant signs of amity. Everyone embraces an adversary; there are no more enemies among them; there is only a family of brothers. After having given free rein to those two impulses of their heart, everyone picks up his weapons again, and the two armies are no longer but one, for the previous rebel army no longer wishes to be distinguished from the other, and only picks up its weapons in order to take them to the designated depots.

The three aides-de-camp wake up simultaneously; they are filled with fear on no longer seeing the crocodile, and covered with shame on seeing themselves abandoned by their own partisans and surrendered to the power of their enemies.

Those scenes, combined with the monster's defeat, penetrate Eleazar and Sedir with a sincere gratitude for the powerful being that has assisted them so well in the work they have just done, and by a tacit accord of their fate, they satisfy what the piety of their hearts demands. The invisible man gives them both new signs of his presence, and insinuates to Sedir internally that, since he has shown so much confidence and his devotion to the good cause, he will not cease to multiply his favors for him, as he had done for Eleazar for a long time.

The volunteer Ourdeck does not take long to join them, and to depict to them s best he can all the satisfaction he feels at having seen them triumph so gloriously; he has only one regret, which is that his dear and respectable Rachel is not a witness to the touching scenes which are so well made for her beautiful soul. He even disposes himself to go on ahead in order to give her an account of the marvelous victory that has just been won and the fortunate state of things, when he is retained by a spectacle he did not expect, and in which everyone shares except the three aides-de-camp, who were unworthy and for whom it remained veiled.

This is what the spectacle was.

All the sciences that, a short time after the origin of things, had been in deputation to the crocodile and had receives such troublesome conditions were revealed in the air above the battlefield, in the form of young maidens, radiant with beauty, clad in robes as white as alabaster, each having a golden key passed through her belt, all holding hands, with the signs of the most enthusiastic delight.

"Finally," they said, in silvery voices, "the mold of time is broken; we are liberated from the shackles that have retained us for so many centuries, in chains and, as it were, deprived of the principle of our life; henceforth we shall all live with him in an eternal alliance. Thanks be rendered to the respectable mortal who has been our liberator."

Canto 99
Ourdeck's desires accomplished.

As soon as that astonishing spectacle had commenced to appear, the first impression it had upon Ourdeck, after that of surprise, had been to augment even further the desire he had that Rachel might be here. He also sought among those shining faces for that of Madame Jof, but he did not find it. He heard once again, however, in the depths of his heart, the soft words that Rachel had spoken to him: "I can only dwell there with her."

That reminiscence reacted on him to such an extent, and his desires with regard to Rachel became so ardent and efficacious, that to everyone's great astonishment, that worthy friend suddenly found herself beside him, before the canticle had even finished, so that she had the pleasure of hearing the final words pronounced. She had been transported in an instant by the magical power of Ourdeck's desire; she brought the news that the plague of books had ceased, that peace and abundance had been reborn in Paris, and that for a few moments, joy had been universal there.

It would be difficult to depict Ourdeck's transports, and the delight of Eleazar and Sedir at the unexpected arrival of Rachel among them.

But we are assured that the joy she had in hearing the final words of the canticle, so flattering for Eleazar, was not the only satisfaction that she experienced on the subject of her virtuous father. It is said that she, and all the audience, had the pleasure of seeing, if not the respectable Israelite himself, at least his representation, appear in the air in the midst of the young maidens, and receive from them as the recompense for his glorious endeavors, a palm so brilliant that the eyes had difficult in sustaining its glare.

We are also assured that adjacent to that interesting tableau, a temple suddenly appeared, bearing or its inscription:

The Temple of Memory; and that one of the maidens said, aloud: "This is the temple to which all the scholars of the world aspire."

The doors of that temple opened, and allowed the perception of a huge and exceedingly untidy room; and the young maiden said: "Learn by this how, after their death, scholars have to rid themselves of the idea that they all have of their temple of memory."

It was visible that the roofs of the temple were in a very poor state, and the young maiden said: "It is the astronomers who have degraded them thus, in establishing their observatory without precaution; and the astronomers can no longer even continue their observations. Furthermore, that loss would be even greater if those men distinguished by their talents had not limited themselves to tracing for you the regular march of celestial couriers, and had informed you of the dispatches with which those couriers were charged; for you know that humans are even more curious for news than the itinerary of those who carry it."

At the summits of the chimneys a few heads could be seen, stained with soot, singing the songs customary among chimney-sweeps in such circumstances, and the young maiden said: "They are a few poets who, having not found a place in the temple of memory, have preferred serving there as chimney-sweeps and being heard in that capacity than to remain unknown, and in silence."

In the cellars, via the ventilation shafts, four individuals in long robes could be seen teaching caged birds to pronounce famous names, and the young maiden said: "They are philosophers who did not have the means by themselves of obtaining places in the temple of immortality, and who have preferred to make themselves celebrated by beings devoid of intelligence that to remain unknown and unmentioned."

It was evident that the walls of the temple were replete with cracks, by virtue of the water that the degradation of the roofs had let in, and men were also visible carrying mortar on their shoulders and climbing long ladders in order to go and fill those cracks; but they were going up so slowly that the mortar was dry before they arrived, and it fell back to the ground when they tried to employ it; and the young maiden said: "They are learned men who, having spent their lives in the vain sciences of human beings, still think they might be useful in that humble employment, rather than opening their eyes to their abusive occupations; they were convinced that they would have an important place in the temple of immortality, but they are reduced to only working on its surface, and even of only working there in the capacity of manual laborers, and only making continually fruitless separations."

And with those final words, everything disappeared

After all those scenes, some of which had excited delight and others surprise, had passed, Sedir, Eleazar, Rachel and Ourdeck, as well as the entire army, returned to Paris to the acclamations of all the inhabitants, who hastened to give those worthy individuals and the brave warriors who accompanied them the most flattering welcome.

History says that when Eleazar had returned to his peaceful life, he no longer hid his devotion to the faith of veritable Christians—a devotion that he had made sufficiently known to Sedir during their first interview, and the profession of which he could not defer any longer.

History also says that he did not take long to make the volunteer Ourdeck party to his most sublime knowledge, having recognized that he could not place it better.

It says, too, that Eleazar, seeing the attachment of Ourdeck for Rachel, and that of Rachel for the volunteer, increasing, permitted them to unite themselves by the conjugal bond; that the union in question, founded on the purest virtue and the most enlightened piety, was for him as it was for them an inexhaustible source of felicities unknown to vulgar alliances; that the virtuous Sedir, in cultivating assiduously the knowledge of his delightful friends, was able both to augment and share the happiness they enjoyed, and that eventually, he, Rachel and Ourdeck were also admitted into the Society of

Independents; that they were one of its principal ornaments, and that they lived in an intimate and habitual liaison with Madame Jof, and even with the jeweler or invisible man who was her husband.

Canto 100
The condemnation of the three malefactors.
Their punishment commuted.

(So, dear reader, all that it remains for me to tell you is that Sedir, by virtue of his responsibility, was obliged to pursue the judgment of the three malefactors; that in accordance with the laws of the State, they were condemned to capital punishment; but that the same Sedir who had solicited their judgment from the tribunals then solicited clemency for them from the government,

> Who, wanting to moderate their cruel sentence.
> But to make sure of those felons
> Selected the Plaine de Sablons
> For their perpetual detention
> And to make sure of their retention
> Constructed there three dungeons.

SF & FANTASY

Adolphe Alhaiza. *Cybele*
Alphonse Allais. *The Adventures of Captain Cap*
Henri Allorge. *The Great Cataclysm*
Guy d'Armen. *Doc Ardan: The City of Gold and Lepers; The Troglodytes of Mount Everest/The Giants of Black Lake*
G.-J. Arnaud. *The Ice Company*
André Arnyvelde. *The Ark; The Mutilated Bacchus*
Charles Asselineau. *The Double Life*
Henri Austruy. *The Eupantophone; The Olotelepan; The Petitpaon Era*
Honoré de Balzac. *The Last Fay*
Barillet-Lagargousse. *The Final War*
Cyprien Bérard. *The Vampire Lord Ruthwen*
S. Henry Berthoud. *Martyrs of Science*
Aloysius Bertrand. *Gaspard de la Nuit*
Richard Bessière. *The Gardens of the Apocalypse; The Masters of Silence*
Chevalier de Béthune. *The World of Mercury*
Albert Bleunard. *Ever Smaller*
Félix Bodin. *The Novel of the Future*
Pierre Boitard. *Journey to the Sun*
Louis Boussenard. *Monsieur Synthesis*
Alphonse Brown. *City of Glass; The Conquest of the Air*
Émile Calvet. *In a Thousand Years*
André Caroff. *The Terror of Madame Atomos; Miss Atomos; The Return of Madame Atomos; The Mistake of Madame Atomos; The Monsters of Madame Atomos; The Revenge of Madame Atomos; The Resurrection of Madame Atomos; The Mark of Madame Atomos; The Spheres of Madame Atomos; The Wrath of Madame Atomos* (w/M. & Sylvie Stéphan)
Félicien Champsaur. *Homo-Deus; The Human Arrow; Nora, The Ape-Woman; Ouha, King of the Apes; Pharaoh's Wife*
Didier de Chousy. *Ignis*
Jules Clarétie. *Obsession*

Jacques Collin de Plancy. *Voyage to the Center of the Earth*

Michel Corday. *The Eternal Flame*

André Couvreur. *Caresco, Superman; The Exploits of Professor Tornada* (3 vols.); *The Necessary Evil*

Camille Debans. *The Misfortunes of John Bull*

Captain Danrit. *Undersea Odyssey*

C. I. Defontenay. *Star (Psi Cassiopeia)*

Charles Derennes. *The People of the Pole*

Georges Dodds (anthologist). *The Missing Link*

Charles Dodeman. *The Silent Bomb*

Harry Dickson. *The Heir of Dracula; Harry Dickson vs. The Spider*

Jules Dornay. *Lord Ruthven Begins*

Alfred Driou. *The Adventures of a Parisian Aeronaut*

Odette Dulac. *The War of the Sexes*

Alexandre Dumas. *The Return of Lord Ruthven*

Renée Dunan. *Baal; The Ultimate Pleasure*

J.-C. Dunyach. *The Night Orchid; The Thieves of Silence*

Henri Duvernois. *The Man Who Found Himself*

Achille Eyraud. *Voyage to Venus*

Henri Falk. *The Age of Lead*

Paul Féval. *Anne of the Isles; Knightshade; Revenants; Vampire City; The Vampire Countess; The Wandering Jew's Daughter*

Paul Féval, *fils. Felifax, the Tiger-Man*

Charles de Fieux. *Lamékis*

Fernand Fleuret. *Jim Click*

Louis Forest. *Someone is Stealing Children in Paris*

Arnould Galopin. *Doctor Omega; Doctor Omega and the Shadowmen* (anthology); *Harry Dickson: The Man in Grey; Harry Dickson: Tenebras*

Judith Gautier. *Isoline and the Serpent-Flower*

H. Gayar. *The Marvelous Adventures of Serge Myrandhal on Mars*

G.L. Gick. *Harry Dickson and the Werewolf of Rutherford Grange*

Raoul Gineste. *The Second Life of Doctor Albin*

Delphine de Girardin. *Balzac's Cane*

Léon Gozlan. *The Vampire of the Val-de-Grâce*

Jules Gros. *The Fossil Man*

Jimmy Guieu. *The Polarian-Denebian War* (2 vols.)

Edmond Haraucourt. *Daah, the First Human; Illusions of Immortality*

Nathalie Henneberg. *The Green Gods*

Eugène Hennebert. *The Enchanted City*

Jules Hoche. *The Maker of Men and His Formula*

V. Hugo, P. Foucher & P. Meurice. *The Hunchback of Notre-Dame*

Romain d'Huissier. *Hexagon: Dark Matter*

Jules Janin. *The Magnetized Corpse*

Michel Jeury. *Chronolysis*

Gustave Kahn. *The Tale of Gold and Silence*

Gérard Klein. *The Mote in Time's Eye*

Fernand Kolney. *Love in 5000 Years*

Paul Lacroix. *Danse Macabre*

Louis-Guillaume de La Follie. *The Unpretentious Philosopher*

Jean de La Hire. *The Fiery Wheel; Enter the Nyctalope; The Nyctalope on Mars; The Nyctalope vs. Lucifer; The Nyctalope Steps In; Night of the Nyctalope; Return of the Nyctalope*

Etienne-Léon de Lamothe-Langon. *The Virgin Vampire*

André Laurie. *Spiridon*

Gabriel de Lautrec. *The Vengeance of the Oval Portrait*

Alain le Drimeur. *The Future City*

Georges Le Faure & Henri de Graffigny. *The Extraordinary Adventures of a Russian Scientist Across the Solar System* (2 vols.)

Gustave Le Rouge. *The Dominion of the World* (w/Gustave Guitton) (4 vols.); *The Mysterious Doctor Cornelius* (3 vols.); *The Vampires of Mars*

Jules Lermina. *The Battle of Strasbourg; Mysteryville; Panic in Paris; The Secret of Zippelius; To-Ho and the Gold Destroyers*

André Lichtenberger. *The Centaurs; The Children of the Crab*

Maurice Limat. *Mephista*

Listonai. *The Philosophical Voyager*
Jean-Marc & Randy Lofficier. *Edgar Allan Poe on Mars; The Katrina Protocol; Pacifica 1, 2; Robonocchio; Return of the Nyctalope;* (anthologists) *Tales of the Shadowmen 1-12; The Vampire Almanac* (2 vols.); *The French Fantasy Treasury* (3 vols.)
Ch. Lomon & P.-B. Gheuzi. *The Last Days of Atlantis*
Camille Mauclair. *The Virgin Orient*
Xavier Mauméjean. *The League of Heroes*
Joseph Méry. *The Tower of Destiny*
Hippolyte Mettais. *Paris Before the Deluge; The Year 5865*
Louise Michel. *The Human Microbes; The New World*
Tony Moilin. *Paris in the Year 2000*
José Moselli. *Illa's End*
John-Antoine Nau. *Enemy Force*
Marie Nizet. *Captain Vampire*
Charles Nodier. *Trilby and The Crumb Fairy*
C. Nodier, A. Beraud & Toussaint-Merle. *Frankenstein*
Henri de Parville. *An Inhabitant of the Planet Mars*
Gaston de Pawlowski. *Journey to the Land of the 4th Dimension*
Georges Pellerin. *The World in 2000 Years*
Ernest Pérochon. *The Frenetic People*
Pierre Pelot. *The Child Who Walked on the Sky*
Jean Petithuguenin. *An International Mission to the Moon*
J. Polidori, C. Nodier, E. Scribe. *Lord Ruthven the Vampire*
P.-A. Ponson du Terrail. *The Immortal Woman; The Vampire and the Devil's Son*
Georges Price. *The Missing Men of the* Sirius
René Pujol. *The Chimerical Quest*
Edgar Quinet. *Ahasuerus; The Enchanter Merlin*
Henri de Régnier. *A Surfeit of Mirrors*
Maurice Renard. *The Blue Peril; Doctor Lerne; The Doctored Man; A Man Among the Microbes; The Master of Light*
Restif de la Bretonne. *The Discovery of the Austral Continent by a Flying Man; Posthumous Correspondence* (3 vols.)
Jean Richepin. *The Crazy Corner; The Wing*

Albert Robida. *The Adventures of Saturnin Farandoul; Chalet in the Sky; The Clock of the Centuries; The Electric Life; The Engineer Von Satanas*

J.-H. Rosny Aîné. *Helgvor of the Blue River; The Givreuse Enigma; The Mysterious Force; The Navigators of Space; Vamireh; The World of the Variants; The Young Vampire*

Marcel Rouff. *Journey to the Inverted World*

Marie-Anne de Roumier-Robert. *The Voyage of Lord Seaton to the Seven Planets*

Léonie Rouzade. *The World Turned Upside Down*

Han Ryner. *The Human Ant; The Superhumans; The Son of Silence*

Frank Schildiner. *The Quest of Frankenstein*

Pierre de Selenes: *An Unknown World*

Norbert Sevestre. *Sâr Dubnotal: Vs. Jack the Ripper; The Astral Trail*

Angelo de Sorr. *The Vampires of London*

Brian Stableford. *The Empire of the Necromancers (1. The Shadow of Frankenstein; 2. Frankenstein and the Vampire Countess; 3. Frankenstein in London); Eurydice's Lament; The New Faust at the Tragicomique; Sherlock Holmes and The Vampires of Eternity; The Stones of Camelot; The Wayward Muse.* (anthologist) *News from the Moon; The Germans on Venus; The Supreme Progress; The World Above the World; Nemoville; Investigations of the Future; The Conqueror of Death; The Revolt of the Machines; The Man With the Blue Face; The Aerial Valley; The New Moon; The Nickel Man; On the Brink of the World's End; The Mirror of Present Events; The Humanishere*

Jacques Spitz. *The Eye of Purgatory*

Kurt Steiner. *Ortog*

Eugène Thébault. *Radio-Terror*

C.-F. Tiphaigne de La Roche. *Amilec*

Simon Tyssot de Patot. *The Strange Voyages of Jacques Massé and Pierre de Mésange*

Louis Ulbach. *Prince Bonifacio*

Théo Varlet. *The Castaways of Eros; The Golden Rock.; The Martian Epic* (w/Octave Joncquel); *Timeslip Troopers* (w/André Blandin); *The Xenobiotic Invasion*
Pierre Véron. *The Merchants of Health*
Paul Vibert. *The Mysterious Fluid*
Villiers de l'Isle-Adam. *The Scaffold; The Vampire Soul*
Gaston de Wailly. *The Murderer of the World*
Philippe Ward. *Artahe; Manhattan Ghost* (w/Mickael Laguerre); *The Song of Montségur* (w/Sylvie Miller)
Willy. *Astral Amour*

Victor Margueritte. *The Bacheloress; The Companion; The Couple*

NON-FICTION

Stephen R. Bissette. *Blur 1-5. Green Mountain Cinema 1; Teen Angels*
Win Scott Eckert. *Crossovers* (2 vols.)
Georges Grison. *The Heads that Fell in Paris*
Jean-Marc & Randy Lofficier. *Shadowmen* (2 vols.)
Randy Lofficier. *Over Here*
Brian Stableford. *The Plurality of Imaginary Worlds*